M000310265

Legally Wed

"Another excellent book by Rick R. Reed. The story is very entertaining and I got a kick out of the animals and secondary characters."
—On Top Down Under Book Reviews

"If you have read Reed before, you will enjoy this and if you have not read him yet, this is a great place to start."
—Reviews by Amos Lassen

"It's a superbly crafted, emotional tale of one man's journey from hope to hopelessness, onward to compromise, and finally, to finding the courage to go for the gold."
—Hearts on Fire

Hungry for Love

"I loved his writing style, I loved the flow of the book, I didn't feel like there was anything missing by the time the end of the story came around and I was really able to love Brandon & Nate very easily."
—Live Your Life, Buy the Book

"I've gotten distracted reading a book before but never because I stopped to marvel at the genius of the author…. There are some rocky times to get through, but the journey is truly enjoyable, and Rick ends it with a sigh-worthy epilogue."
—Happy Ever After (*USA Today*)

"Characters finding their truths, and realizing the people they are meant to be, and who they are meant to be with, all written beautifully with humor, and love, and intelligence. Rick Reed has done a wonderful, wonderful job with this story!!"
—Mrs. Condit & Friends Read Books

By RICK R. REED

Caregiver
Chaser
Dignity Takes a Holiday
Dinner at Home
Homecoming*
Hungry for Love
Legally Wed
Raining Men

*Only available in eBook

Published by DREAMSPINNER PRESS
http://www.dreamspinnerpress.com

What's your recipe for romance?

DINNER *at* HOME

RICK R. REED

Dreamspinner Press

Published by
Dreamspinner Press
5032 Capital Circle SW
Suite 2, PMB# 279
Tallahassee, FL 32305-7886
USA
http://www.dreamspinnerpress.com/

This is a work of fiction. Names, characters, places, and incidents either are the product of author imagination or are used fictitiously, and any resemblance to actual persons, living or dead, business establishments, events, or locales is entirely coincidental.

Dinner at Home
© 2014 Rick R. Reed.

Cover Art
© 2014 Reese Dante.
http://www.reesedante.com
Cover content is for illustrative purposes only and
any person depicted on the cover is a model.

All rights reserved. This book is licensed to the original purchaser only. Duplication or distribution via any means is illegal and a violation of international copyright law, subject to criminal prosecution and upon conviction, fines, and/or imprisonment. Any eBook format cannot be legally loaned or given to others. No part of this book may be reproduced or transmitted in any form or by any means, electronic or mechanical, including photocopying, recording, or by any information storage and retrieval system, without the written permission of the Publisher, except where permitted by law. To request permission and all other inquiries, contact Dreamspinner Press, 5032 Capital Circle SW, Suite 2, PMB# 279, Tallahassee, FL 32305-7886, USA, or http://www.dreamspinnerpress.com/.

ISBN: 978-1-62798-835-3
Digital ISBN: 978-1-62798-836-0

Printed in the United States of America
First Edition
May 2014

For Bruce, again, for always sampling what I have to offer.

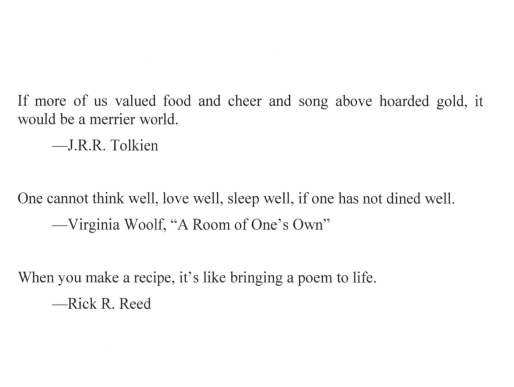

If more of us valued food and cheer and song above hoarded gold, it would be a merrier world.

    —J.R.R. Tolkien

One cannot think well, love well, sleep well, if one has not dined well.

    —Virginia Woolf, "A Room of One's Own"

When you make a recipe, it's like bringing a poem to life.

    —Rick R. Reed

Amuse-Bouche

n. A small complimentary appetizer offered at some restaurants, from the French meaning literally, "entertains the mouth"

HE WANTS the meal to be special, tantalizing, a prelude to the satisfaction of other appetites. He hopes it will symbolize his passion, his devotion, and his desire to nourish and care for—for all the rest of their days.

He keeps it simple, knowing that's how his beloved prefers it. No complicated French cuisine for his man! No tortured soufflés or sauces that must be timed perfectly lest they seize up, their texture and taste ruined.

No, for his beloved, simplicity is key. In the kitchen as well as the bedroom. He knows that appealing to the basic appetites is the way to his heart and the most fulfilling.

So what does he make? He builds their dinner around a classic: a roast chicken. Perhaps there is nothing in the world, save for the feel of his man's arms around him as the two of them drift off to a weary and blissful sleep, more sublime than the simple roast chicken. He knows exactly how to enhance its flavors, to make the moist bird dance on the tongue of his beloved. First, he will salt and pepper the cavity, then stuff it with gently crushed cloves of garlic and a quartered lemon. He will loosen the skin covering the breast, and underneath this he will lay more garlic, fresh thyme, and rosemary, a little extra-virgin olive oil to hold it all together. He will take that same oil and rub the chicken lovingly all over with it, the flesh supple beneath his fingers. Salt, pepper, more rosemary and thyme, and finely minced garlic will be the final touches to this gift. After that, a hot oven, and enough time for the juices to run clear and the flesh to just lose its pinkness.

He imagines his beloved's lips as he takes the first bite of the chicken, moist with its juices. He pictures his man closing his eyes in pleasure, able to utter only the most eloquent of praises: mmmm.

The rest of the meal will be a mix of the easy and the sublime. After all, the meal is a beginning, not an end. A full stomach leads to sleep, and sleep is not what he has in mind, at least not right away.

So he will make a salad of arugula, oranges, and red onion, dressed with the juice of the orange, olive oil, and salt and pepper. Maybe, if he's feeling the need for a flourish, he will top the salad with a few shavings of Parmigiano-Reggiano. Or he will save his flourishes for the bedroom....

He grins as he assembles the rest of the meal: the tiny, multicolored fingerling potatoes he will boil until just tender, then toss with sweet cream butter, sea salt, and a few grinds of the pepper mill; two heirloom tomatoes, one pink and the other yellow, cut into quarters, with only a little salt to make their juices rise, so their flavor is enhanced.

Dessert? Fresh strawberries. These he has not given much thought to. But what he really wants to do with them is this: He will lift his beloved up on the kitchen counter, naked, spread his legs, and crush the berries into his man's sex. He will make sure that not one morsel of pulp and not one drop of juice lands anywhere else other than his mouth. He will continue to devour the berries until the flesh of his lover's cock is clean, shining only with his spit.

And then... and then... well, what would berries be without a little cream?

He smiles.

He cannot wait for his lover to come....

Appetizer:
WINTER

ONE

SINFULLY SOFT SCRAMBLED EGGS

(Serves 2)

- 1 tablespoon of olive oil and 1 tablespoon of butter
- 6 eggs
- Splash of half-and-half or, if you're feeling really decadent, cream
- 4 scallions, sliced thin, very top of the green reserved for garnish
- 1/2 to 3/4 cup shredded Beecher's Flagship or other mild, flavorful cheese
- 1/4 pound pancetta, cubed

Melt butter with olive oil in a skillet over medium heat. Whisk eggs and half-and-half together. When the butter's froth just begins to dissipate, add the pancetta and cook until lightly browned. Pour off some of the fat, return pan to stove and lower heat. Add scallions and sauté until just fragrant. Add beaten eggs and give a quick stir to distribute scallions. Add about half of the shredded cheese. Now, let the eggs cook on low heat. It may seem like nothing is happening, but after ten minutes or so, gently push the eggs with a spoon. Soft curds should begin to form. This is what you want—gentle curds. Continue to gently push the eggs, forming more and more curds. When the eggs are still a bit wet, but mostly curds, add the rest of the cheese, turn off the heat, and cover. Let sit for 2-3 minutes. Serve.

OLLIE D'ANGELO woke up thinking about breakfast. He was pondering the day's earliest, and most important, meal for two reasons. One, it was morning, and often the first question on Ollie's mind in any given situation was "what shall we eat?" Two, today was his anniversary with Walker. The pair of them would celebrate their first blissful year together.

He looked over at Walker, still asleep. Even though Walker was, in every sense of the word, a man, right now he looked like a child. Turned on his side, his mouth was open and a thin line of drool dribbled down to the pale blue pillowcase below, forming a dark stain. The fact that Ollie could see this as charming rather than repugnant was evidence of his love. Never mind that beneath the navy blue duvet lay one of the hottest, most muscular, and hairiest bodies Ollie had ever had the pleasure of lying next to; Ollie was simply happy that this winter morning, with rain tapping softly on the window outside, he was home with Walker.

They were a family.

Ollie reached out, letting his hand hover above Walker's porcelain skin and blond hair, feeling the heat radiating off of them. He wanted so much to touch him, to wake him with a kiss (and maybe more), but the kitchen was calling out to him, and he told himself that after he surprised Walker with breakfast, there would be plenty of time to touch, to kiss, to nibble, to suck, to… well, to do *everything*.

Twice.

Ollie slipped silently from beneath the covers, rubbing the goose pimples that rose immediately on his arms. He reached for his robe, lying at the foot of the bed, and his shearling-lined slippers beneath it and hurried out of the room, not making a sound.

He wanted Walker to wake not to Ollie's tread, but to a symphony of mouth-watering aromas wafting in from the kitchen.

They had been living in Walker's small Craftsman-style bungalow in Seattle's Wallingford neighborhood for the past nine months. Sure, even Ollie had thought moving into Walker's house three months after they had met via the online dating site OpenHeartOpenMind was fast, but love was love. What were you going to do about it?

From the moment Ollie had spied Walker, he had been helpless. They had agreed to meet for the first time, after a week of exchanging e-mails, at a little Korean fusion restaurant called Revel in the Fremont neighborhood. Walker had already been seated when Ollie arrived, and Ollie's first glimpse of the man who would be his soul mate, his one true love, had told him everything he needed to know.

For one, Walker was gorgeous. His pale brown/blond hair, dark eyes, and his strong form immediately put Ollie in mind of a young Brad Pitt. There was something tough about him, a bit of the bad boy, but that was undercut, or maybe the better word was highlighted, by a sense of vulnerability he kept almost, but not quite, hidden.

Ollie had immediately wanted to kiss him and, even more, to take care of him.

When he sat down and saw that Walker had already ordered a carrot and lemon pancake with currants and crème fraiche on top for them, the deal was sealed.

The man knew his food.

Now, as Walker switched the lights on in their farmhouse-like kitchen, with its bright yellow walls and checked curtains at a window over the sink, he smiled at the thought of how much Walker would enjoy this meal.

First, he pulled the bag of coffee beans he had bought just for this morning from the freezer—Godiva chocolate with a hint of hazelnut—and ground them, hoping the whirring noise would not prematurely wake his man. He set the coffee to brewing and turned back to the refrigerator.

He pulled from its stainless confines a dozen eggs, a carton of half-and-half, a wedge of Seattle's own Beecher's Flagship cheese, a bunch of organic scallions, and a thick slice of pancetta, which he would chop into chunks. From a drawer, he pulled a loaf of freshly baked sourdough he had picked up on his way home from work last night.

He set to work whisking eggs and half-and-half together. He shredded an impressive mound of the cheese—to hell with fat and calories this morning! They could burn it off later. He sliced four scallions with hand-blurring speed.

He diced the pancetta and threw it into his All-Clad pan, which he had already preheated on the stove. In the pan were just a touch of olive oil and a pat of butter, which had now turned to foam. He tossed the ham to coat it and let it simmer and render its juices. Normally, he'd pour off some of the grease, but today was all about decadence. Then he threw in the green onions, listening to their sizzle and sniffing the air for the almost immediate aroma they imparted. Finally, he turned the heat to very low, almost off, and added the egg and cream mixture. He added about half the cheese, stirred, and then left the eggs to very slowly, and very perfectly, form gentle curds. The eggs would be soft, silky, and packed with flavor.

The aroma of coffee started to permeate the kitchen. While the eggs were transforming into something magical, Ollie went to the window and looked out; it was another gray, rainy day for Seattle, typical for January. The drops on the windowpane obscured the view, but it was still there: Lake Union, and beyond its steel gray waters, the downtown skyline rising up, the iconic Space Needle to the right. If it had been a summer day, Ollie thought, he would have served breakfast outside on the back deck, with a salad of peaches and blueberries, garnished with a little fresh basil.

The coffee finished brewing, and he grabbed a mug from the cupboard and moved toward the pot, stopping first to give the eggs some gentle nudging with a wooden spoon. They would be ready soon, and he hoped the smells of the pancetta and coffee would rouse Walker from sleep and lure him irresistibly into the kitchen.

Ollie poured a cup of coffee, added some of the half-and-half he had left out for the eggs, and added three teaspoons of sugar to his cup and stirred. He knew he should cut down, but it just tasted so damn good, sweet and creamy. He listened to the rain pattering on the roof and thought that, at age thirty-three, he had finally found his way to a kind of happiness, a sense of fulfillment.

He turned to look at the eggs and saw they were almost done. He threw the rest of the cheese on top, covered the pan with a lid, and removed it from the heat. If Walker didn't get up soon, the eggs would no longer be at their peak.

And Ollie wasn't about to let that moment of perfection pass. He found his phone on the kitchen counter, behind a stack of Cooks Illustrated magazines, and tapped his Pandora app to bring up the Etta James station. He set it in the dock, and in moments, Miss James was warbling her heartrending version of her classic, signature song, "At Last."

Perfect.

Beneath the velvet of Etta James's voice, Ollie paused, coffee mug lifted to his mouth, and closed his eyes almost rapturously at another sound: Walker stirring in the bedroom.

He listened as Walker made his way through the short hallway and the living room. At last, he stood framed in the kitchen doorway, wearing only a pair of boxers. He looked so amazing, mussed hair and all, that Ollie almost wanted to say the hell with the eggs and guide Walker right back from whence he came.

Walker grinned, but Ollie guessed it was his sleepiness that made him also look weary and a little sad.

"What's all this?" he asked.

Ollie continued to smile. "Don't you remember?"

Walker bit his lip and shook his head.

"Today's a special day." Ollie turned to push the bread down in the toaster and then to pour a mug of coffee for Walker, who preferred it black. "What happened one year ago today?"

Walker set his mug down on the counter without taking a sip. He frowned. "Is it our anniversary or something?"

Ollie nodded, neared him, and took him in his arms. He tried to kiss Walker, but Walker pulled away, mumbling, "Morning mouth."

Ollie heard the toaster click, signaling the slices were ready for their butter, and he turned to attend to them. "I thought we should start the day off with a celebration. It was, after all, exactly one year ago when we first laid eyes on each other." Ollie winked. "And I first laid you." He laughed. "I made us your favorite scrambled eggs with a ton of cheese. It will be decadent. And so will what will come later."

He turned back to Walker and was stunned to see Walker wasn't smiling. In fact, the best word to describe his features would be crestfallen.

"What's wrong?"

"I'm not hungry." Walker pulled out a chair and sat at the kitchen table.

Ollie thought that if that was all that was bothering Walker, it was disappointing, but there were other ways to celebrate, especially when the sheets were still warm.

"That's okay."

"No, no, it's not okay. You've gone to all this trouble."

"Walker, they're just scrambled eggs. Really."

Walker laughed. "Nothing is ever *just* anything with you."

Silence fell upon the kitchen. The music had shifted to some other bluesy gal belting out a jazzy, upbeat "You Can't Take that Away from Me." The music suddenly seemed weird and inappropriate, what with the unspoken tension hanging in the air, mingling with the aromas of coffee, onions, and pancetta. Ollie pressed pause on his phone's screen, and now the only sound in the kitchen was the rain pattering on the roof above them.

Walker stared at the table.

This was not going at all as Ollie had expected. He joined Walker at the table, reaching out to cover Walker's hands with his own. "Tell me. What's bothering you?"

"I forgot today was our anniversary."

Ollie laughed, relieved. "Oh, is that all? No big deal. I'm just a sucker for special occasions." It was sweet, Ollie thought, that Walker was so broken up over forgetting. It bode well for their future. He not only had a hot man, he also had a sensitive one.

Walker lifted his head to meet Ollie's gaze. "That's not all," he said softly. Ollie could see Walker's eyes were kind of shiny. Were those tears?

Oh shit….

"Oh?" Ollie said, his heart suddenly beating faster. He found it hard to gather enough saliva to swallow.

"I don't know how to say this." The sentence hung in the air like a sword about to fall. His statement was ominous, ranking right up there with "We need to talk." Ollie wanted to scoot his chair back and run from the room. Maybe what he was anticipating was not it at all. *You're jumping to conclusions. Perhaps he lost his job or something like that.* Yet somehow, he knew the dread he felt deep in his bones was spot on, and something told him he knew precisely what this about. Today—on their anniversary, of all times. He whispered, "Say it."

When Walker said nothing, Ollie prompted, "It's not me, it's you?" He scratched the top of his head. "I think we should see other people?" Ollie shifted in his chair. "You've decided you're straight?"

"What?" Walked asked.

"Standard lines. You're breaking up with me, right?"

Walker shook his head, a glimmer of a smile crossing his features. "No, no, of course not," he said nervously, a hiccup of laughter escaping his lips. Then he swallowed hard, looked right at Ollie, and said, "Yes."

Even though Ollie was braced for it, even though he fully expected it, the words hit him like an anvil being dropped on his chest, knocking the wind out of him. How could this be? He had seen not one sign of dissatisfaction from Walker. Hell, they had even had burn-up-the-sheets sex last night. Two times. If Ollie had been to a psychic the day before and she'd told him he was about to be dumped, he would have laughed—the idea was absurd, inconceivable.

Yet here it was, staring him in the face, an unwelcome presence filling up the kitchen.

Ollie got up from the table and lifted the lid off the eggs. They looked perfect, yellow with a satiny sheen, the bits of scallion and pancetta a mouth-watering contrast. Ollie could have snapped a photo of them and posted them to his Facebook page and gotten a dozen comments, maybe fifty likes. Now they merely turned his stomach and, oddly, made him feel like a fool.

He lifted the pan off the stove and scraped the eggs into the garbage disposal, turned the water on, and set the appliance to whirring. He hoped the disposal enjoyed them. He followed the eggs with his cup of coffee, now gone cold, much like his emotions.

He was numb as he sat back down with Walker. He thought he should shed some tears, holler with rage, something, but all he felt was... *nothing.* Empty. He swallowed, then forced himself to look at Walker who, Ollie had to admit, now appeared scared, nervous. *You should be.* Ollie summoned up some air to force behind the one word that was on his mind. "Why?"

Walker rubbed his arms up and down, shivered. "Chilly." He got up and left the room. Ollie heard the creak of the closet door in their bedroom, followed by a drawer opening and then slamming shut. When he returned, Walker had slid into a long-sleeved T-shirt and a pair of gray sweats. He gnawed at his lower lip, drew in a breath, and then said, "There's someone else."

Ollie guffawed. "What? When would you have time?" He and Walker hardly ever spent an evening apart.

"I work with him."

Walker was a financial planner with a firm in Bellevue.

"Office romance?" Ollie said. "How scandalous. What? Did you hook up in the supplies closet? Xerox your junk for each other? Have naughty lunches at fleabag motels?" Ollie stared down at the table, finding suddenly he could no longer look at Walker. He yipped out a short laugh that contained not one whit of humor.

"I didn't mean for it to happen."

Ollie smiled. He turned in his chair to peer out the window, studying the raindrops as though they were something new and novel. "That's a good one. They never mean for it to happen. Remind me again which soap opera you pulled that line from."

"Don't, Ollie. You're not mean. This isn't you."

Ollie blew out a breath. "What do you want from me, Walker? My best wishes? For me to say I understand?"

"No, no, of course not. But bitter just isn't you."

"Well, maybe you should allow me a bit of bitterness. Maybe I'm entitled." And now, Ollie could feel something: a slow-burning rage that was gradually heating up and threatening to burst into flame.

"I don't understand, Walker. I think it's bullshit." He sneered. "You didn't mean for it to happen. Hah! If you didn't mean for it to happen, it wouldn't have."

"You don't understand—"

"Shut up!" Ollie snapped, surprising even himself. He was always such a nice guy. He looked over at Walker, whose mouth hung open. "I need to say this and you will sit there and listen." Ollie swallowed, feeling a wave of acidic bile rising up from his gut and splashing the back of his throat. With sheer force of will, he held the nausea at bay. He would be damned if he would let Walker see him cry, let alone vomit.

"People who say they didn't mean for something, especially something like this, to happen are deluding only themselves. You just don't want to take responsibility." He shrugged. "Much as it hurts me to say it, there must have been something lacking here. Although God knows what, since *I* couldn't have been happier." And now his emotions shifted, and he wanted to burst into tears. He drew in a great breath, forcing the sadness and despair away—for now.

"You were open to it, Walker. God knows why. If it were just sex, I could understand it. But the fact you're telling me it's over between us tells me this is something more than sex." Ollie couldn't go on for several moments. "And that hurts. Deep." He shut his eyes, stayed mum for a full minute or two. "Guys have sex. I've known lots of guys with wandering hands, wandering cocks, wandering libidos. I can almost accept that. But it's more than that, isn't it?" He forced himself to meet Walker's gaze and was surprised to see the tears standing in his eyes. "You love this guy?"

Walker nodded. A tear slipped down his cheek. "I hate hurting you," he said softly.

And Ollie—damn him—had a sudden urge to comfort Walker. Wasn't *that* ridiculous? He shook it off, cursing his damn need to nurture, even when he was being betrayed. "Sure you do."

"Sure I do. I know it's hard for you to believe, but I was committed to this relationship. I was happy. Then Paul started at the firm last summer and—" Walker's gaze moved to a distance only he could see. Ollie didn't want to imagine just what his former lover might be envisioning.

Paul?

"What do we do?" Ollie wondered, his voice barely above a whisper. He had settled into this little house, had imagined that, in the spring, he would paint the living room a pale blue and maybe the bedroom a similar shade. He had wanted to talk to Walker about pulling up the carpet to see if there was hardwood beneath.

This was home. He had pictured his future here.

How could it just fall apart in a few seconds? He stared at Walker, the man with whom he had planned to spend the rest of his days, and wondered if he had ever really known him. Who was this man? How could Ollie have felt so secure when his very foundation was crumbling beneath him?

"So what happens now?" Ollie wondered. "What are our next steps?" He gazed around the kitchen, its false yellow brightness, and suddenly felt excluded. He had sold most of his belongings when he moved in here a few months ago and had donated the rest. At the time, he wondered why they would need two couches, a bedroom set with no room for it, two desks, a third TV. The list could go on and on.

Walker had it all now. A home. A new love. Stuff.

Walker got up from the table and looked briefly out the window. He turned back to him. "I know you gave up everything when you moved in here."

It was as though Walker was reading his mind. "And why wouldn't I? I thought this was a forever thing."

"I did too," Walker said softly.

"Don't you dare repeat that you didn't mean for it to happen. Is this thing with this Paul person a forever moment too?" Bitterly, he asked, "For how long? Until the next guy comes along?"

"That's not fair."

"It *is* fair, Walker. Why wouldn't it be?" He didn't give Walker a chance to respond. "So, what? You want me out of here?" The prospect was not as daunting as Ollie would have imagined. This *home* was no longer that; it was merely a house now, a shell that wasn't his. No wonder they had never gotten around to putting Ollie's name on the mortgage. Had Walker ever been as committed as he? Or had he simply been doing a "wait and see" kind of thing?

"You can take your time. How about a month? Two? Would that be enough to give you time to find yourself a new place? And I can appreciate you got rid of all your furniture and stuff." Walker drew in a breath. "I could give you some money toward new furniture and whatever you need to set yourself up again. That would be fair."

"I don't want your money." Ollie had plenty of his own. His job as a creative director at an advertising agency in Pioneer Square paid him well. His parents back in Chicago were, as Walker had once said, "loaded," so he also had that safety net. Walker had never allowed him to pay anything toward the monthly mortgage; his savings were healthy.

"Are you sure?" Walker asked. "No. Let me give you a few thousand. It's only fair."

Ollie shook his head. "Keep it. I don't want to complicate things any further. I want you to begin your new life with Mr. Paul unfettered." He smiled, but could imagine how bitter the expression looked on his face. "Footloose and fancy free."

Walker came over to him and began massaging his shoulders. Ollie shrugged his hands away. "Don't," he whispered.

Walker stepped back, and Ollie felt a prickle at the back of his neck with Walker standing behind him. Like Greta Garbo, he wanted to be alone.

Walker said, "Well, if you change your mind about the money, let me know. My offer will always stand. And do take your time looking for a place; you have a home here."

Oh God, that is rich! What Ollie precisely did *not* have was a home. Home was defined not by bricks and mortar, but by the people who lived under a common roof—and that was gone like a wisp of smoke. So easy. Ollie stood and moved toward the kitchen archway. His fight or flight instinct had kicked in, and suddenly all he wanted to do was flee. Being here was like having something hot inserted beneath his skin, burning and painful.

He paused in the doorway to the kitchen and turned back to Walker. "I'll be out by this afternoon or this evening."

"There's no need. Paul and I aren't moving in together or anything."

"No. It'll be better this way."

"I'm really sorry, honey."

"No! No. You no longer have the right to call me honey." He laughed. Ollie moved quickly away, heading toward the bedroom, where he thought the best thing to do right now was to begin emptying his drawers and hiding the gorgeous white-gold ring he'd wanted to give Walker later that day as an anniversary present—and as testimony to their enduring love. To think, he had once thought the ring could one day be converted to a wedding band.

What a fool he was! How blind! Didn't someone once sing some song about being the "Queen of Denial"? That was him. *There had to have been signs*, he thought, opening drawers, *I just didn't want to see them.*

He expected Walker to come into the room, to try again to make amends, but all he heard as he removed his clothes from the drawers and closet was the sound of Walker putting on his running shoes and softly closing the front door as he left Ollie alone.

The fucker's probably relieved. I made it easy for him. Big of me.

Ollie slumped down on the bed, staring at the bottle of lube still on the nightstand from last night, and finally allowed himself to cry.

He stayed curled in a ball on the bed for a long time, thinking Walker would return. He even imagined that he would come back and spy Ollie there on the bed, in a fetal state, with his face puffy, red, and wet from all the tears, and would relent. He would slide next to him on the bed, gather him up in his strong arms, and whisper, "What was I thinking? I could never live without you. I'm sorry. Let's just forget this morning ever happened."

How pathetic was that? After a while, Ollie forced himself to sit up. He went into the bathroom, peed, blew his nose, and splashed cold water on his face.

He peered at himself in the medicine cabinet mirror above the sink. He was surprised to see that, other than the hint of puffiness around his eyes, he looked the same. He almost expected some startling transformation, as though the shock of being dumped would have aged him ten years or his hair would have turned white or something. But the same Ollie looked back at him—the same olive skin, dark brown eyes, beard, and a mien that people almost invariably got around to referring to as "kind."

He went back into the bedroom and thought maybe it was time to stop being so "kind." Look where it had gotten him! Alone and now homeless.

Kindness was overrated.

He began stuffing clothes into the bags he had pulled from beneath the bed, finally stopping when he realized he was flinging in the garments furiously, without regard for how they would look when he took them back out.

He wondered why it was taking Walker so long to go for a simple run. He glanced at the iPhone dock and alarm on Walker's nightstand and saw it was now going on eleven. Walker had been gone for almost two hours.

The realization hit like a powerful punch to the gut. *Of course.* He was with this Paul person; the two of them were probably celebrating. The coast was now clear for their young love.

How fucking sweet.

Ollie decided a break was in order, unless he was going to let the bitterness he felt eat him alive.

He wandered back into the kitchen, where all the ingredients for that morning's "celebratory" breakfast were still aligned on the counter. He got busy making scrambled eggs and toast—for one.

$$Chapter$$
TWO

"YOU REALLY want to feed people this crap?" Hank Mellinger snapped at his new boss. Lined up in the kitchen of Haven, a charity that housed and fed the homeless of Seattle and provided chef training for some of its residents, were several industrial-sized boxes of generic mac and cheese mix. Alongside the boxes were sticks of no-name margarine and boxes of powdered milk.

His boss, E.J. Porter, an African-American woman with her hair braided tightly to her scalp and oval-rimmed frameless glasses, shook her head as she took in her latest charge.

"Hank. We have to face reality here. Now, as much as I would love to serve people mac and cheese with real cheddar, cream, and maybe roasted red peppers, we just can't afford that kind of stuff on the measly funds we get from the state and what donors kick in. Hell, honey, we might as well do a béchamel and throw some lobster in too." She patted his shoulder. "It's a nice dream, sweetie. Now you need to get cookin'. Lunch is only a couple hours away, and I still need you to chop and prep the salad." She pointed to the sorry pile of heads of iceberg lettuce in the sink.

Hank shook his head. "So because people are poor, they have to eat this fucking shit? Why can't we get some fresh vegetables? Is it that pricey? This stuff gives 'em nothin'. Artery-clogging crap that might fill up their bellies, but doesn't do a thing to keep 'em healthy. Fuck."

E.J. moved in close to Hank, so close he could feel her breath and maybe even a bit of her spittle on his face. She spoke softly, but there was an intensity, perhaps even a fury to her words. "Look, Hank, you just got here. I have been trying to run this place for the last nine years. You have no idea what I go through just to get the food we have to work with. You have no idea how grateful some of these people are for this 'shit,' as you call it. It tastes pretty good when the last meal you had came out of a dumpster, if you had anything at all. We work with what we get. Some days it's healthier fare than others, but all of it's food. For hungry people. And you might not think that's something, but it is.

"Now, you are just starting here. We gave you a roof over your head, food to eat, and we're trying to help you find a career path as a chef. Haven may not be Le Cordon Bleu cooking school, but we will get you ready to work in a kitchen. We'll give you knife skills, teach you how to make simple sauces, stocks, and soups. We'll make a real cook out of you. Maybe not a chef, but a cook.

"Now you need to watch your language, watch your attitude, and get to work." E.J. stormed away.

"Fuck you, E.J.! Bitch!" he called after her and then craned his neck to see if the woman had heard him. Fortunately, E.J. was a busy woman, and she was well out of earshot in a flash. The tiny rational part of him he kept so carefully hidden away told him that shouting such an epithet after his new boss was not the best idea. If she had heard him, she would have had every right to turn around, march back into the kitchen, and kick him to the curb.

And then where would he be?

He fingered the "food products" on the counter and wished he had a million bucks, or even a thousand, so he could feed the people who would be lining up outside of Haven something that would not only fill them up, but also nourish them.

He wished a lot of things. He wished he had never started messing around with drugs when he was in his teens, particularly that corrosive bitch crystal meth, who went by the name of "Tina." He wished he hadn't used his body to barter for that same drug. He wished he hadn't stolen from people. Wished, at age twenty-two, he wasn't intimately acquainted with how to get by on the street and the comfort one could take in a large cardboard box on a cold winter's night. He could spend all day wishing for other things. But right now, what he needed to do was chill out so he could stop focusing on the injustices of the world and simply put his head down and work.

Even though he had a ton to do in a very limited time, he knew that taking a short break to center himself would make him more effective in the long run. That was a lesson he had learned both in prison and in rehab. And it hadn't been an easy one, not with the temper with which he was saddled.

He slipped out the kitchen's back door and, even though the day was gray and cold, sat down on the ground in the back, near the dumpsters. He leaned against the red brick of Haven and stretched his legs out. He groped in his jeans pocket for the battered pack of no-name smokes he knew were there and the book of matches. He lip up a cigarette and closed his eyes with pleasure and relief as the oblivion-bringing smoke filled his lungs.

He reminded himself once again that he needed to quit. After all, wasn't it just a little hypocritical to rail against what Haven was feeding its hordes of homeless and then go out and pollute his own lungs? Still, as he drew in on the cigarette, he rationalized the satisfaction he took from it by telling himself he had given up so many other pleasures—illicit sex and drugs and alcohol—that he should be allowed at least one vice.

Right?

Spoken like a true addict, he thought. *Next week. I'll think about quitting next week.* He finished the cigarette and, even though he knew he could scarcely afford it, pulled out a second one and lit it from the butt of the last.

His cell vibrated in his pocket, and he pulled it out, glancing down at the screen. "Shit." The simple word on the flip phone's screen, mocking him as the phone rang, gave him yet another reason to remember the cell was an expense he couldn't afford, even if it was the cheapest pay-as-you-go model.

The simple word that had caused him such consternation was "Mom."

Hank rolled his eyes, debating whether he should simply ignore the call and let it go to voice mail or deal with it now. Later would not be easier because Mom was like an STD: she might go away for a while, but she would always come back, and when she did, it would be worse.

Why can't I just have a couple minutes to smoke in peace? Christ!

He answered the phone. "Mom." He pictured Lula on the other end, clear across the country in the town he had fled when *she* kicked him out four years ago. She still lived in that same run-down duplex on the outskirts of what could laughably be called downtown for a dying steel-mill town in western Pennsylvania called Summitville.

Hank hadn't been back in those four years, but he could imagine that everything in that cramped, airless little space remained the same, right down to the couch where he'd slept every night growing up.

"Hank," Lula responded, with their family's particular brand of eloquence.

"What's up? I'm at work."

"You got a job?"

"Yeah. It's a program I got in through the city. Not really a job, but more like an apprenticeship. I'm at this place called Haven, where they help the homeless with food and shelter. But they also teach people how to cook, professionally."

"You're cooking for people? Lord help them!" his mother said, laughing. The laughter ended in a spasm of dry hacking that reminded Hank once again he needed to quit smoking.

"Did you just call to give me a hard time, Mom?" Hank took his last drag off the cigarette, rubbed out the cherry on the side of the building, and dropped the butt in the dumpster. Briefly, he considered tossing the half-empty pack in after it, along with his matches, but knew he'd be back here in an hour, digging through the garbage to retrieve them. Hank had successfully quit smoking, like, a hundred times.

It was the staying quit that gave him problems.

"Can't I just call to see how my boy is doing?"

"No, you can't. You never call for that. You always have an angle."

"Well, my angle this time is your sister."

Hank closed his eyes. Stacy. He pictured his twin in his mind's eye. Even though they were obviously not identical, she still looked like the female version of him. Same reddish hair and gray eyes. Same slight build. Same button nose the men always found so cute.

Stacy also had the same capacity for getting into trouble.

"What'd she do now?"

Lula made a "tsk" sound on the other end of line. Hank heard her light a cigarette, the quick inhale and exhale that made him long to do the same. *No*.

"Where do I start?" his mom wondered.

"I've heard at the beginning is always a good place."

"Don't be a smartass, mister. Just because you're clear across the country doesn't mean I won't come out there and knock your fucking teeth down your throat."

Hank had to laugh; his mom was such a sweetie pie. "So what's goin' on with Stacy?"

"She's gone."

A little frisson of fear ran through him. "Gone?" he asked, his voice rising with alarm. Like him, his sister was no stranger to hanging out with the wrong people and taking risks that were best described as "ill-advised" and worst described as "fucking dangerous"—or maybe "life-threatening."

"Ah, don't get your panties in a twist. I know where she is: in Pittsburgh, with yet another man. She says this guy's the one. You know, her soul mate. Only thing is, he doesn't like kids. So she left Addison with me. I don't need a four-year-old underfoot! I'm too old to have some rug rat biting at my ankles. I got a life to live too."

"Too old? Ma, you're not even forty yet."

"Don't remind me."

"And with what you're saying, I just can't understand why little Addison isn't the light of your life. Why, you sound to me like grandma of the year."

"You and that smart mouth. You suck dick with that mouth?" Lula barked out a short laugh, and even Hank had to admit his mother's question took his breath away for a second.

He ignored it and posed another one to her. "So what do you want me to do, Ma? Or are you just calling to vent?" Hank had never laid eyes on his niece, although once Stacy had texted him the little girl's preschool portrait. The photograph revealed a very solemn little girl, with café au lait skin, curly red hair, brown eyes, and the same button nose both he and Stacy had.

He recalled thinking that Addison had the wizened face of someone much older, and it made his heart ache. Where was her smile?

"Why son, I'm glad you asked what you can do."

Hank hadn't asked what he could do; he had asked what she wanted him to do. He realized there was little difference between the two. He wondered what was coming.

"I can't take care of her. In spite of your kindness about my age, I am too old for the shit a four-year-old dishes out, especially this one, who is too smart for her own good."

"When's Stacy coming back? She is, after all, her mother."

"She's not."

"What? Not her mother?"

"No. I didn't want to get into the whole thing, but it turns out her soul mate is one of the biggest crack dealers in central Ohio, and she got dragged into a big mess with him."

Hank rolled his eyes and lit another cigarette. "Don't tell me. She's not in Pittsburgh?"

"She's in jail."

"I said don't tell me!" Hank stared hard at the gray, low-hanging clouds above.

"I can't take care of her daughter."

"She's your granddaughter, ma."

"I know! I know! That's just it. Grandkids are supposed to be fun. You kid around with 'em, then hand 'em back when they act up."

Hank looked up as E.J. came to the back door, her features creased with fury. She had a knife in one hand, and Hank seriously worried she had more on her mind than chopping vegetables. He held up a finger to her, signaling she should give him a minute, and she shook her head, her lips compressed into a thin line. She turned away.

"Look, Ma, thanks for letting me know what's going on. I don't know what I can do to help, but I'm here if you need to talk. I need to get going. My boss just gave me a look that would kill and if I don't get back in the kitchen, I'm gonna be out on my ass."

"I need you to help me, Hank!"

"What can I do?"

"You can take her."

Hank felt a tremor go through him. Surely she wasn't asking him to…. No, that couldn't be. "Take her where?"

"Cut the smartass remarks! You can take care of her. She's your niece."

"Mom, I'm across the country. I'm living in a shelter for the homeless. I don't have an apartment. All I got is a room." He sighed. He wanted to say that he was still a kid himself but then realized it wasn't true. Not by a long shot. Not with all he had been through.

"I'll find a way to get her out there. She can sleep on the floor. You'll get a job and get out of there soon. I know my boy. He's smart."

"I can't make a home for a kid. I barely can make one for myself," Hank said, suddenly feeling like the proverbial fly, all wrapped up nice and tight in a spider web.

"Then she goes into the system. Foster care. I'm not becoming a mom again. I don't have time."

Hank bit his tongue to keep from asking when she ever was a "mom." E.J. appeared at the door again.

"Either you get back to work," she said softly, "or just stay out there. But don't bother coming back in."

Hank shut his eyes, feeling as though his world had turned upside down. He wanted badly to light yet another cigarette but knew to do so would jeopardize more than his health—would jeopardize his very future. "Listen, once the lunch shift is over, I'll call you."

Lula started to say something, but Hank hung up on her and hurried back inside.

"Lunch! Coming right up." He pushed E.J., who was chopping up heads of lettuce, out of the way. "You go on about your business. I've got things under control here." He forced himself to smile and thought: *if only, if only....*

Chapter
THREE

COMFORTABLY CURRIED
CARROTS AND LENTILS

(Serves 4)
- 2 cups green lentils
- 2 carrots, peeled and diced
- 3-1/2 cups chicken stock
- 2 tablespoons grated ginger
- 1 small red onion, chopped
- 2 tablespoons curry powder
- 3 tablespoons tomato paste
- 1 cup coconut milk
- 1 teaspoon salt
- 1 teaspoon cumin
- 1/2 teaspoon coriander
- 1/2 teaspoon cinnamon
- 2 cups baby spinach
- Garnishes: Greek yogurt, chopped parsley, sliced jalapeños

Use a 4-quart slow cooker. Rinse lentils and pick through for any stones. Combine all ingredients, except for baby spinach, and set cooker to low for six hours or until lentils are tender. Add baby spinach at the very end, replace cover, and let wilt. Serve with optional garnishes. Can also serve over rice or couscous.

OLLIE HAD thought work would be his refuge and salvation. For the last ten years, his second home had been found among the cubicles and offices found at Strother, Marx, and Henkle, one of Seattle's largest advertising agencies, located in the Pioneer Square area of downtown. Ollie had worked there for the last decade, working his way up from copywriter, to copy chief, and finally, to his current stint as one of the agency's six creative directors.

Now as he parked his car in a nearby lot on Monday morning, he was hungry to sit down at his desk with a cup of Starbucks and immerse himself in the oblivion of work. There would be ad copy to review, clients to appease, meetings to attend. The phone would never stop ringing. Normally, such Mondays, although they would go fast, were a pain in the ass.

But today Ollie welcomed the distractions. He didn't want to think about Walker and how his personal life had gone belly-up over the weekend. He sure as hell didn't want to dwell on the apartment on Tenth Avenue in the Capitol Hill neighborhood he had rented in a hurry over the weekend, nor the attendant quick move-in, which he'd accomplished all by himself.

He hadn't had much to move anyway, since it was only clothes, books, and his computer. And of course, his cooking supplies. He had found a few boxes in the basement in which to pack up his All-Clad pans, his Wusthoff knives, his gadgets—like a melon baller, garlic press, and vegetable peeler. He would need that stuff. For Ollie, cooking and eating had always been his comfort and salvation. Besides, Walker had no cooking tools. He was lucky if he could boil a pan of water. Ordering in and eating out were what he did best.

So in the end, Ollie had looked at the pitiful pile of belongings that represented his life, thinking how it would all fit into the hatch of his

Prius. The bulk of what had made up their house—everything else, really—had belonged to Walker.

The last thing he needed to think about as he headed into his office was how barren his new apartment was. Although the place was only a stone's throw away from the city's gorgeous and tranquil (and sometimes cruisy) Volunteer Park, the unit itself was in need of serious updating. The avocado green carpeting was threadbare and stained. The mini blinds at the windows were yellowed from the previous tenant, who obviously had spent all of his or her time indoors, smoking. Chain smoking. Remnants of the stench still lingered, even if the landlord had managed to slap on a coat of white paint, which must have been called Cheap and Charmless at Sherwin Williams. The kitchen had only a tiny window and hadn't heard of the latest granite and stainless-steel craze. It had the Euro-style veneer cabinets popular in the 1980s, cheap faux-redbrick linoleum, and ancient white appliances, which at least had the saving grace of appearing to be in good working order.

It was all he could find on such short notice. He would have to make it home. But such depressing thoughts were for later. He was at work now, his second home. He never thought he'd be so happy for Monday to arrive.

Before he went upstairs to his office overlooking Elliott bay, he stopped in the Starbucks on the ground floor of his building.

The same pony-tailed, middle-aged, raspy-voiced barista, who seemed not to exist outside of Starbucks, greeted him as she did every morning.

"Hey buddy! How's it goin'?" She was always way too cheerful for the hour, and Ollie suspected her of injecting coffee straight into her veins when she arrived for her shift. Still, it was nice to see a familiar face, even if the woman could not remember Ollie's name, although he had mentioned it a couple times, or what he ordered, which had been the same every day for the past couple of years.

"What can I get you?"

Ollie smiled and did not betray his desire to, just once, have her simply ask, "The usual?" and get it. "I'll have a grande, nonfat, extra-hot, extra-foamy latte with one raw sugar."

"You got it, handsome. You want some breakfast with that?"

Ollie eyed the pastries lined up in their glass case and, for once, did not feel tempted. "Nah."

Ollie took his coffee and went upstairs in the elevator. He was happy to see he was one of the first to arrive. The time in the office nearly alone would allow him to shift gears from his disaster of a weekend and get centered for work.

But that was not to be the case.

The first thing he saw, after he had set down his Starbucks cup, was a bright lime-green Post-it from his boss, Marcia Gordon. With her usual eloquence, she had written only "See me." Ollie wistfully thought it was the plea of an invisible woman.

He peered over his shoulder and saw Marcia's office light was also on. Like the barista at Starbucks, Marcia did not seem to exist outside of her workplace. She was always here. And even when she was at her condo in nearby Belltown, she was checking and sending e-mails to staff.

"Might as well get this over with," Ollie mumbled to himself. She was probably chomping at the bit to do a little micromanaging after a weekend alone with her two cats, Salome and John the Baptist.

He gazed longingly at his coffee and wished he had gotten a coffee cake to go with it as he headed out of his office.

When he saw Marcia at her desk, he imagined she had been there all weekend, like a mannequin, sitting there in her burgundy power suit, white blouse, and Hermes scarf, all of which were way too formal for the agency's very casual dress code. She was looking at something on her computer screen when he entered and, without looking up, said softly, "Close the door and have a seat."

Such statements were seldom the prelude to anything good, and Ollie could feel anxiety, like tiny rows of fangs, begin to gnaw at his gut.

Marcia forced her gaze away from whatever was on her computer screen and finally looked at him. She ran her fingers through her perfectly coiffed silver hair and smiled. A smile on Marcia's face was an effort, and it showed.

Ollie was relieved when she let it go. "How are you this morning, Oliver?"

She was the only person, other than his mother, he could think of who called him by his Christian name. From her, it was fitting. And although with anyone else with whom he had a relationship of several years, Ollie would have been tempted to answer her query honestly and pour out his heart about his devastating weekend, he said only, "Good! How are you doing?"

Marcia merely smiled in response, and once again, Ollie thought how uncomfortable such an expression made his boss look. Marcia putting a smile on was like Miley Cyrus donning a nun's habit. He noticed a bit of her crimson lipstick on one of her front teeth. He ached to make a little tooth-rubbing gesture to alert her to the fact, but resisted. Instead, he sat back, spine stiff, and waited.

Marcia's dark eyes at last met his own and Ollie realized he could see a glimmer of humanity there and, maybe, concern.

Marcia folded her hands in front of her and Ollie concentrated on her nails, which were long without being too long, and sported a recent french manicure. She shifted in her seat.

"Just spit it out, Marcia. Did I do something wrong?"

She looked startled. "Wrong?" She chortled, and the laugh sounded eerily akin to choking. "You never do anything wrong, Oliver."

"That's good. So what do I owe the pleasure of this early morning quality time with my favorite boss?"

Ollie expected a smile and didn't get one.

"There's no easy way to say this, Oliver."

"Oh, shit," Ollie whispered and fought down an absurd desire to burst out laughing. What was that song? If it weren't for bad luck, I'd have no luck at all?

"I'm really sorry, but we're going to have to let you go. I meant to tell you this on Friday, but with the meeting with Consolidated at the end of the day, you'd gone home before I had a chance. I didn't want to call and ruin your weekend."

Ollie did laugh this time. Marcia cocked her head, plucked eyebrows drawn together quizzically. "Something funny?"

"Kind of. If you knew the sort of weekend I had, you'd get the joke. I won't bore you with the details. So, why now? Why me? My last review from you was glowing."

"Oh Oliver, it's not about your performance. It's just business. Belt tightening. As you know, we lost a couple of accounts recently: Flying

Monkey Games and Verde Body Products. They brought in a good bit of revenue, especially the games company. With them both gone and no new business on the immediate horizon, we're slimming down. It doesn't make me happy because I'm one of the ones who will have to take over your accounts."

"I'm so sorry for you, Marcia."

"I didn't mean you should feel sorry for me. I just meant to show you how deeply this cuts. You aren't the only one I am laying off today. About a quarter of our staff will be gone."

"We'll have to meet up for drinks."

Marcia looked alarmed. "What? You and me?"

Ollie laughed again and was surprised at how much he was laughing at this meeting, where he was being canned. "No, I meant the one quarter who are being let go. We can get drunk and commiserate together."

"Of course. Of course." Marcia glanced around her office. "I won't keep you. Take your time and clear out your personal stuff. HR has a severance check waiting for you. A month, plus any vacation pay you've accrued. Of course, we won't contest unemployment, but with talent like yours, I'm sure you'll land on your feet ASAP."

"ASAP. Sure."

Marcia returned to staring at her computer, and Ollie could tell she wanted him to leave. As much as he had never liked her, he could sense her discomfort and knew he should put her out of her misery. So he stood and said, "It's been great working with you, Marcia. I'll really miss you." He didn't mean a word of it, but he knew his statement would surprise her, and he had a devilish urge to shock.

There was that smile again! It was more akin to a grimace. "Me too, Oliver. And there's always hope business will get better, and when we start calling people back, you'll be at the top of the list. That is, if someone else hasn't already snatched you up."

Ollie stood.

"Thank you for all your contributions." And then with a nod to Amanda Priestly of *The Devil Wears Prada* fame, she said, "That's all."

Ollie wanted to snicker one more time as he left her office.

He returned to the office he'd occupied for the last several years, recalling the day he had moved into it, when Marcia herself had given him the news he had been promoted to creative director. It had been a happy day for him, the culmination of his dreams.

Wait. Rewind.

And once again he laughed, because the memory was false and he knew it. Although he couldn't put his finger on precisely what his dreams were, they weren't *this*. He had plodded along here, doing work he'd never really cared about.

He took stock of his office, the files on his desk, the print ad campaigns he had framed and mounted on his wall. His iMac was open to Yahoo News. He wondered what he should take with him. All that was really personal were the potted fern and the spider plant, both of which he had nurtured since his first day with the agency, so long ago.

He went out to the copy room and found a box with reams of paper in it that he emptied out, then brought back to his office. He carefully set each plant inside. They would brighten up his new and dreary home, a home he suddenly would have a lot more time to decorate and furnish, even if he didn't have the steady income.

But that was a minor worry. Not only did Ollie have a month of severance, three weeks' vacation pay, and his healthy savings account, he had his parents in Chicago, who would help their only son with any financial need. But Ollie would only rely on the wealthy Mr. and Mrs. D'Angelo as a last resort.

He stuffed a few more items into the box—a day planner he had stopped using several years ago, a few issues of *Entertainment Weekly*, an insulated lunch bag, a water bottle, and a bottle of Equipage cologne someone had once given him in a holiday gift exchange. He sat down at his computer and plugged a thumb drive in. He loaded all of his personal files onto it and removed it. He made sure he was logged out of any personal accounts, but knew IT would swipe the hard drive anyway.

He sighed. The dismantling of his life as Oliver D'Angelo, Creative Director, had taken less than half an hour. He turned his head and admired the one thing he realized he would miss about the office—its window and lovely view of Elliott Bay. Right now, a break in the cloud cover was allowing the sun to make a gilded light upon the slate blue water as a ferry glided across its calm surface.

He threw the thumb drive into the box and lifted it. He looked around once more and saw it—the framed photo on his desk. He sat down suddenly in his chair and picked it up. There they were, the happy couple. The picture had been taken last spring on a gorgeously sunny day. They had taken a stroll around the circumference of Green Lake and had stopped for cupcakes at Cake Envy. Ollie had asked the woman behind the counter if she would mind taking their picture.

They were at the table, heads leaned in close, laughing, dappled with sunlight. Walker had a smudge of chocolate just below his lower lip. Ollie was reaching up to wipe it away, staring adoringly at his man. Walker had eyes, though, only for the camera.

Ollie tossed the photo into the wastebasket.

He got up and turned off the light and started out, glad for an entirely different reason he had come in early, before most of his coworkers. This way he could avoid painful and awkward good-byes.

As he was about to exit through the glass double doors, he did an about face and hurried back to his office, where he rescued the framed photo from his wastebasket.

It was part of his history.

"Come on," he said to himself. "It's time to go."

On his way home, Ollie made a detour to stop at Fran's Chocolates. There, he bought himself a small box of salted caramels and a couple of coconut gold bars. He knew the candy would be gone by nightfall, and he might gain a pound or two from it, but if today wasn't worthy of a little indulgence and oblivion, what day was?

He also made a stop at the Westlake Whole Foods and bought himself the ingredients for a comfort food dinner—curried lentil soup with carrots. While in the store, a bottle of Washington State Syrah called out to him, singing, "Forget your troubles; come on, get happy."

In spite of the goodies he had purchased, Ollie felt the exhaustion peculiar to emotional shock set in on him as he entered his new apartment. Calling it home was out of the question, at least in these early days. The place was depressing, and the fact that it was empty made it even more so. He dared not even talk to himself because his voice would echo pathetically.

After setting down his purchases on the kitchen counter, he walked back to the main living area and pulled the blinds up. He looked down at 10th Avenue, which a bit farther south morphed into Broadway, the main drag through the gay ghetto of Capitol Hill. He wondered if he would ever feel a sense of home again. It didn't help that, while he was making his way there, the cloud cover had become complete, blocking out the sun and shrouding the day in somber tones of gray. A light drizzle, more of a mist, had begun to fall.

Everything outside looked dirty and drab. If Ollie had taken a photograph, it would have shown up in black and white.

Ollie wondered why he wasn't brought to his knees on the floor with grief and why he wasn't crying. Wouldn't these be normal reactions to one's world falling apart? Why wasn't he on the phone with his mom in Chicago, pouring out his almost laughable tale of woe?

Ollie did sit down on the floor then and smiled. He didn't smile because he felt particularly happy, but because he realized he *wasn't* sad.

Sure, he had lost almost everything in one fell swoop and was now faced with the prospect of starting over with almost nothing. But it didn't take long for him to emerge from the cloud of shock and confusion and realize the reason he didn't feel despair.

He was free.

Starting over did not represent a troubling, exhausting climb back to where he had been, but a chance to begin anew. And that prospect was liberating, exciting even.

How many of us have a chance to start over, really start over? Ollie realized his experiences with Walker and his job had taught him things, things that would need to be examined more closely, but on the surface he knew that he now had the chance to learn from what he had been through and come out on the other side a better person.

He could do anything.

Sure, the pain of losing Walker would linger. And the hurt, once the cloud of shock wore thin, would be more acute. He had loved Walker, or thought he did, and once the sting of betrayal had faded, he would most likely miss him. He'd miss the quiet nights when they snuggled on the couch together, falling asleep in front of some old chestnut like *It Happened One Night* and then crawling into bed together to make love in the darkness before drifting off again in each other's arms. He would miss even more taking care of Walker, making him dinner every night. Ollie loved the fact that somehow he had been gifted with an innate sense for food and how to make it wonderful. He had a natural knack for combining ingredients in just the right proportions or mixing things up in new and inventive ways.

Would anyone ever appreciate his cooking as Walker had? Would he ever again see that look of rapture take over someone's face when they tasted the first bite of something he had made?

There was a glimmer of a message in these thoughts, he knew, but he was too tired and too preoccupied with the rudiments of life to ponder it seriously.

Right now he needed to dig his slow cooker out of one of the boxes in the kitchen and get his lentil soup together. While it was simmering and making its spicy Indian-flavored magic, he would take his car and drive up to the Northgate part of town. He needed to get essentials like a few folding chairs, some sort of table on which to eat, an inflatable mattress and some bedding for tonight. Tomorrow he could visit a real furniture store and truly burn up the credit card. He hoped to have this place filled within days, no matter what the cost.

At least, he thought when he got back from Target, his little place— all his own!—would be redolent with the smell of curry, onion, and tomato, and he would have the comfort of dark chocolate and a good red wine to ease him into sleep.

Tomorrow he could begin to think seriously about what he would make of his new life.

Chapter FOUR

AFTER TWO weeks had passed and his mother, Lula, had not called back, Hank figured he was in the clear. He rolled over in his narrow single bed and glanced at his alarm clock. It was just past seven, and he was due downstairs in the kitchen in half an hour. He eyed the pack of cigarettes on the little nightstand next to the bed and wished he could have one, but knew if he took even one puff indoors, something terrible would happen. Alarms would sound. E.J. would rush in and spray him with that foamy shit that came out of a fire extinguisher. Hell, the world might end. Smoking would have to wait, no matter how much his mind and body demanded it.

He lay in bed for what he knew could only be another five or ten minutes tops and thought that whatever drama his sister Stacy had brought on herself must have gotten sorted. At least he hoped so. Even though he didn't personally know his sister's daughter Addison, it would break his heart to hear she had been put in foster care.

Lula wouldn't do that, would she?

He rolled toward the wall so he wouldn't have to look at, and be tempted by, his smokes. Foster care, he thought, was such a joke. He had known way too many kids when he was on the streets who had been ground up and spit out by the system, who were running from the very program that was supposedly in place to help them but in actuality put them in the line of fire for abuse of all kinds. He shivered. Addison was only four.

He wished there was a way he could help her. Wished he had the funds to buy a plane ticket, fly out to Pittsburgh, rent himself a sweet car to take him to Summitville, and ensure his flesh and blood, never mind the fact he had never laid eyes on her, was okay. Hank had a soft spot in his heart for young things: kids, kittens, puppies.

He had been tempted to give Lula a call over the past couple of weeks, see if everything had worked out okay. Stacy couldn't have been in *that* much trouble, could she, that she would be in jail for an extended period? Surely, she was out by now and being as much of a mom to her little rug rat as she should be.

But he hadn't called. He felt guilty because he knew why he hadn't. Sure, he could claim he was busy, doing things like learning how to julienne and make a *roux*, but that didn't mean he couldn't find a few spare minutes to call his ma. No, he knew it was because, if he were being honest with himself, he didn't want to get bad news. He didn't want to hear that Stacy was in jail, that little Addison had his mother tearing her hair out, or worse, that Lula had started the process to see that the little girl went into foster care.

Or that she was already gone....

He sat up, rubbing the sleep from his eyes. There was a communal bathroom down the hall with showers, but Hank didn't think he had time for such an extensive cleanup. After he finished the breakfast shift, he could shower. For now, a splash on his face and under his arms would have to do. Oh, and of course, he'd have to use a little wax on his faux hawk to get the red-dyed portion to stand up like a rooster's comb. Couldn't go out where others could see without his mane properly groomed and tamed, now could he?

He grinned, rolled from bed, and pulled on baggy black jeans, a plain white T-shirt that, when sniffed in the pits, didn't smell too heinous, and a black hoodie, which he knew would be doffed as soon as he started cooking downstairs. After sliding into his combat boots, he glanced again at the alarm clock and saw he had five minutes to get down to the kitchen. *Shit. There goes any time for breakfast. Guess I'll just have to eat standing up while I work.* E.J. was all about punctuality. On time meant being late to that woman.

He hurried from his room, clambering down the back stairs leading directly into the kitchen.

When he got to the bottom of the stairs, his heart just about stopped.

Sitting at the large stainless steel table that was used for everything from chopping vegetables to rolling out dough, was E.J. with two very special and very unexpected guests.

Hank wanted to turn and run back up the stairs.

His mother grinned when their eyes met. She rasped, in a voice gone deep as a man's from too many smokes, "Well, lookie here, it's my own little Sid Vicious!" She barked out a laugh. Hank was glad she thought her quip was funny; he had no idea what she was talking about. So what else was new?

E.J.'s gaze went nervously to Hank and back to his mother.

Lula got up and crossed the room, arms outstretched. "Give Mommy a hug!"

Hank stood frozen, unsure if this was really happening. Maybe he was still in bed and had yet to wake up. That made sense, didn't it? After all, his anxiety over his family situation and his own inaction could bring on a dream, or a nightmare, just like this. Couldn't it?

But his hopes that the appearance of his mom and what he assumed was his niece was a product of his subconscious mind were immediately dispelled as Lula pulled him into her grasp.

As bony as the woman was, she had a grip like a boa constrictor. She smelled of perspiration, Dentyne, and cigarettes. *Mom.* Hank's arms fluttered around his mother's form for several seconds, like panicked birds that didn't know where to go, until Hank had no other choice but to return Lula's embrace.

Finally, he had the presence of mind to ask, "Mom, what are you doing here?"

Lula took a step back but kept her hands on Hank's shoulders and her gaze locked on him. "Nice to see you too, Son. What a lovely surprise. How was your trip? Those are just a few of the things a mother might want to hear from a son she hasn't seen in years, but *noooo.*" Lula laughed. "It's okay, Hank. I know. I know. I should have called first."

Hank stared at his mother, trying to make her appearance real in his mind. She didn't look much different from when he had last seen her— maybe a little thinner, a few more wrinkles around her mouth, but otherwise she was the same Lula who, in spite of the mouth wrinkles, looked far too young to be his mom. Most people, if they didn't know better, would assume she was an older girlfriend or sister.

Lula was, after all, only fourteen years older than Hank. She still had a few years to go before she would see forty. She was pretty in her way, with amber-colored shoulder-length hair, green eyes, and a smile that was actually improved by the gap in her front teeth. She was tiny, barely reaching five feet, and Hank doubted his mother had ever looked down on a scale to see more than a hundred pounds. There had always been about her the air of an imp.

Demon is more like it, Hank thought.

"I brought little Addison all the way out here to meet her uncle." She let go of Hank and sat back down at the table, where Hank could see she had a cup of black coffee in front of her. "Damn Greyhound. I thought we'd die before we got out here. Horrible stinky bus, huh, Punkin'?"

The little girl nodded solemnly and stuck her thumb in her mouth. She stared at Hank with eyes that seemed too large for her face.

E.J. spoke up. "You didn't tell me you had company coming, Hank." She smiled at him, but he could see there was a threat in that smile. Visitors to Haven were supposed to be cleared in advance.

"If I had known, I would have." The sudden arrival of his mom and niece were still not in the realm of reality. He continued to process their appearance, almost as though they had appeared out of thin air. If they had, he would have been no more stunned than he was at this very moment.

E.J. forced herself up from the table, as if the act took a great deal of effort. "Why don't you take fifteen or so to visit with your family, Hank? I'll get the oatmeal and eggs going." E.J. wandered over to the stove. Once there, she turned and glared at him before pulling down a large pot from the rack above. Hank knew he would pay for this. E.J. was not fond of change or surprises. She was helping him out, sure, but a favor from E.J. did not come without its price.

Hank wasn't sure he wanted to sit down at the table. Doing so, he thought, might change his life forever. He had gotten very comfortable here at Haven. He'd become used to cooking and had begun to enjoy it, liking the faces of the other residents and those who wandered in off the streets as they dug into something he had prepared. For the first time in his young life, he felt a sense of accomplishment and pride, even if it was only serving up a plate of mac and cheese with chopped hot dogs in it. He had a paradoxical love/hate thing going on with the children he saw coming in.

He hated that they were homeless—it just about broke his heart—but it cheered to him to see that the work of his hands and the sweat of his brow were ensuring they did not go hungry, at least on that particular day.

As much as he wanted to, Hank had learned fast that he could not feed everyone who was hungry. There were just too many of them.

He had begun to envision a life as a line cook somewhere, bringing in a regular paycheck, maybe finding his own place to live. That light was still distant in the tunnel, but it glimmered at him every so often, encouraging him and making him see redemption was possible.

Taking a deep breath, he finally did sit down with his mom and Addison. For once, Lula was quiet. Hank could feel her watching as he took in his niece. Addison, although only four, seemed older. For one, she was big for her age, tall and lanky. Her reddish brown hair was soft, curly, more like cotton than silk. Lula had tried taming it with a bright teal barrette, but the effort was akin to taming a Bengal tiger with a flyswatter. Addison's hair practically threatened to explode into a tumbleweed at a moment's notice. Her skin was a lovely caramel color, her nose broad and flat. Her eyes made him think of brown sugar, melted and simmering with butter. At last, the somber expression she wore disappeared, dispersed like a cloud of smoke by a breeze as the little girl removed her thumb from her mouth and smiled.

Hank's heart clenched. She had the same gap in her front teeth that his mother did, and in the grin, he could see his twin sister. He reached out and grabbed her hand. Already, he was in love with this little girl. How could that be? They had not yet spoken a word. But he felt an urge to embrace and nourish her. She was his blood.

"You want to come over here and sit on Uncle Hank's lap?" Hank finally asked, his voice soft and encouraging.

"No," the girl snapped, leaning back in her chair and folding her arms across the fluffy bodice of the blue dress Lula had obviously forced her into. This was a child, Hank could sense, more comfortable in jeans and T-shirts than ruffles and lace.

Hank laughed, liking Addison even more for her abrupt refusal than if she had bashfully climbed into his lap. "Ah, you're gonna be a challenge." He nodded to her. "Well, whenever you're ready, Addison." He smiled warmly.

"Don't hold your breath."

Lula said softly, "She's not always full of so much piss and vinegar. She's out of sorts from the long bus ride. Do you think there's someplace we could clean up here?"

"I don't know, Mom. What are you doing here?"

Lula patted the oversize orange purse clutched in her lap, and Hank could guess the nervous gesture was because she wanted one of the cigarettes he knew was inside. He realized, all at once, that his mother was as nervous and uncomfortable as he.

He looked over at E.J., who was busy stirring a huge pot of oatmeal, and understood he was pressing his luck. He asked anyway. "Hey E.J., you mind keeping an eye on little Addison here? She could probably use a bowl of those oats with some raisins on top. My mom and I are gonna step outside for a few."

E.J. glared at him, somehow managing to smile at the same time. "Oh sure, you go on out, enjoy your ciggies. I'll take care of little Addison here. See that she's fed and looked after." She smiled bigger. "You go on. I don't mind a bit."

There would be hell to pay.

"C'mon, Mom. Let's go smoke."

Once outside, nicotine addictions dealt with, Hank faced his mother. The morning was chilly, making the cloud surrounding them even denser, strengthened by the steam of their breaths.

"I'll ask again. What are you doing here?"

Lula puffed nervously on her cigarette and seemed to be having trouble meeting Hank's eyes. Finally: "I told you. I can't take care of her."

Hank was about to snap back that he hardly could either when he noticed the tears standing in his mother's eyes and the pain apparent on her face. He was all ready to ask her if the reason was that Addison would interrupt her partying and annoy the latest in a long line of boyfriends. But he couldn't, not when he could see her anguish.

Hank put a hand on her shoulder. "What is it? Why?"

Lula looked away from him, staring at the blue-gray clouds hanging low on the horizon. She stepped away from him, and he saw her shoulders tremble. He began to reach out toward his mother when he heard her take in a great breath and watched as she stiffened her spine.

When she turned back to him, she was smiling. "I'm sick, Hank."

"What's the matter?"

"Big C."

It took several minutes for the news to sink in. Hank could only stand and think that he now understood the term "shell shocked." Finally, he forced himself to speak. "But you're only... what? Thirty-six? You're too young." Hank's stomach was doing weird things, churning, making him wish and not wish he had eaten something. If he had, it would probably be coming up right about now. He threw his cigarette on the ground and stamped it out angrily. "What is it? Lung cancer?"

Lula shook her head. "Breast. You know how you're always hearing people say, about the big C, that they caught it early?"

Hank nodded.

"Well, I *didn't* catch it early." She looked away quickly, eyes bright, making an effort to breathe, to calm herself. Finally, she won. "It had gone into the lymph nodes and progressed real quick." She smiled, but if Hank had ever seen a smile look sadder, he couldn't remember when. "Ran riot in there."

Hank came to his mom and took her in his arms. What was there to say? He had questions, but those could wait. Right now the simple melding of their two bodies, their arms wrapped around each other tightly, said more than words ever could. They stood like that for a long time, while Hank marveled at how small and vulnerable his mother felt, like a child or a little bird. She had always seemed so strong to him, as though no harm could come to her.

It shook his world to the core.

When they had both stopped weeping, he whispered a question he really didn't want to ask. But he had to know. "How long?"

Lula pulled back and looked out at him from hair that had fallen across her eyes. "Not long. Couple of months maybe." He could see the effort it took for her to swallow.

"You're kidding me, right?" Hank laughed. "Look at you. You're not sick. This is all just you punking me so you can unload that little shit in there on me, right?"

Please, Mom, please. Just laugh. Just say, "You caught me. Busted!"

But Lula only stared, not smiling. "I need to know that she's okay. Your sister isn't exactly mother of the year, and her being in jail kind of complicates things." Lula looked away, examining Haven's redbrick walls as though she had never seen bricks before. "That little girl has no one. I lied when I said I would put her into foster care. I could never do that. Even though she's a pain in the ass and has got the smartest mouth on her since, well, you, I love her." Tears welled in Lula's eyes, and she reached out and grabbed Hank's hand, squeezed. "Please, Hank, you gotta take her. Otherwise I'll be gone and she *will* go into foster care. I don't want to have my last thoughts be wondering about what's gonna happen to my little Addison."

"Ah, Jesus," Hank said. He groped in his pockets, pulled out two cigarettes, lit one for each of them. An idea came to him. "Can't they do something? I mean, isn't there stuff like, what do you call it, chemo? Radiation?"

Lula blew a stream of smoke into the air. "It was too late."

"Who's gonna take care of *you*?" Hank wondered, his voice coming out like a little boy's, sad and vulnerable, desperate for reassurance. Even if he did agree to take Addison—and he didn't know how he could manage that—what would happen to Mom? Where would she go? Who would care for her? He pulled her close, clung tightly to her, never wanting to let go.

If he just held her like this, close, she couldn't die.

It was Lula who pulled away first. She laughed. "We're a pair, aren't we? Being poor sucks. Hell, I'm not even 'wealthy' enough to say I sold the trailer so I have some funds. A trailer was movin' on up for us, right? Shit, I spent my last nickel on the bus tickets to get out here." She shook her head, drew in hard on her cigarette. "I was hoping you could take care of me, of us. For a little while."

It broke his heart. Her request was so plaintive, so sad. And so impossible. "Ma, I was fuckin' homeless before I got in here. I slept in parks. I don't know how I can help. I want to, but I just don't see how I can." He cocked his head, wanting to be the parent here but not having the means. "I got nothin'."

Lula shrugged, drew in some breath. "I don't know where we'll go, then."

A voice came from behind the screen door. "I do. You'll stay here."

They both turned. Hank had not seen E.J. come and stand at the screen door; he didn't know how long she had listened to them, but he had a good idea.

"We'll make room somehow."

And Hank bit down hard on his lower lip, so hard he tasted the copper of his blood. He was doing his best not to sob.

Chapter FIVE

MOM'S SPAGHETTI SAUCE AND MEATBALLS

(Serves 4-6)

- 1 29 ounce can tomato puree
- 1 12 ounce can tomato paste
- 1-1/2 teaspoons salt
- 1-1/2 teaspoons pepper
- 1-1/2 teaspoons sugar
- Pinch of baking soda
- 1-1/2 teaspoons garlic powder
- 1 teaspoon each oregano, basil, and onion powder
- 2 handfuls grated Romano or Parmesan cheese (approx. half a cup)
- 7 cups water or 1-2 cups red wine with the remainder water (I usually use the wine)

Note: Most all of the above ingredients can just be eyeballed. Mix everything in a big pot, add meatballs and pork and simmer for at least four hours. Highly recommended: brown some pork (ribs, chops, whatever's cheap), a little less than a pound, in the pan you're going to cook the sauce in. Just caramelize it. Once it's done, pull out, deglaze with a splash of red wine, and begin making your sauce.

Meatballs
- 1 pound ground beef (or beef and pork, or turkey)
- 1 egg
- 1 slice bread
- 1/4 cup milk
- Salt, pepper, garlic powder, parsley, onion powder, basil, oregano (just eyeball all of this)

Take a slice of bread, wet with milk, crumble into meat, and add seasonings and egg. Mix with hands, form into balls, brown in hot fry pan on stove in a little olive oil, and drop into the sauce.

"GO AHEAD, you do it."

Ollie looks up at his mother, her warm smile, her dark hair and green eyes as she stares down at the five-year-old expectantly.

"Like this?" Ollie asks and he upends the jug of milk over a couple of slices of white bread his mother has placed in the sink.

"Rub it in. Get the bread all nice and wet," his mother says.

"Like it's getting a bath?" Ollie asks.

His mother laughs. "Like it's getting a bath."

Once the bread is thoroughly wet, Ollie picks it up and holds it, dripping, over a bowl of equal parts ground beef, veal, and pork.

"Now grind it all up," his mother says. And Ollie squeezes the bread, squeezing and twisting it until it drops in damp crumbs to the meat.

"Very good." His mom pats his head. "What comes next?"

"The eggs?"

"That's right." His mom hands him the first egg, and Ollie awkwardly cracks it against the side of the glass bowl. Some of the white runs down the outside of the bowl. "That's okay," his mom says when he looks up at her, his lower lip out and eyes wide. "You'll get it right with this one." And she hands him another egg.

He does, cracking the egg and opening it over the meat and bread mixture so the yolk breaks when it hits. He looks down at the mixture, then back to Mom. "What's next?"

"You know what's next."

"Garlic?"

"Lots of garlic." She has already chopped the cloves fine, and she gestures for him to cup his hands. When he does so, she delivers the pungently smelling stuff into his palms and tells him to scatter it around.

They add dried basil, oregano, onion powder, and salt and pepper. "Now get your hands in there and mix it all up." She rubs his back as he combines everything, giggling at the wet mushiness of the mixture. She giggles too.

"Now the best part!" Ollie says. "Meatballs."

His mother pulls a chair from the kitchen table and sets little Ollie on it so he can work more easily. She rolls up her sleeves and says, "Let's get to work."

OLLIE AWAKENED from the dream with a smile. One of his favorite childhood memories was helping his Sicilian mother make her spaghetti sauce and meatballs every Sunday. He had done it throughout his life. He could now make her simmer-all-day, thick, rich, and delicious sauce with his eyes closed. Even though he used all the same ingredients in all the same proportions, it never tasted quite the same. Good, but just not quite the same. There was no substitute for a mother's love.

He rolled over on the air mattress, almost tipping out of bed. He'd be glad when the furniture store, Dania, delivered his real bed.

Outside the wind was howling, and it was at that point in the Pacific Northwest winter when it felt like the chill that had settled into your bones and the rain that never stopped would go on forever. Right now summer was just a dream, a false promise, as likely to come as lottery winnings. He could see out his bedroom window the top of a pine tree as it swayed in the wind. The sky was a somber shade of gray.

He picked up his phone lying on the floor next to the bed and pressed the home button to bring it to life. It was just past ten, and Ollie's first thought was that it was a little past noon in Chicago, so it was not too early at all to call Mom. The dream had induced in him a hunger to connect with her, to pour out everything that had happened to him over the past couple of weeks.

She was always the one who would listen, always the one he could turn to when he had something to share, whether the news was celebratory or bad. Mom always made him feel as though his news was the most special thing in the world to her. And indeed it was. Annette D'Angelo had grown up in a Sicilian clan where family was prized above all else.

Ollie realized, though, with a kind of little-boy despair, that he couldn't call her. It was the same reason he hadn't shared news of his break-up or the loss of his job with her in the past couple of weeks.

His mother and father were on a Mediterranean cruise, and it was almost impossible to reach them. Oh sure, Ollie had managed a few minutes here and there with his parents, listening to them babble on about Madrid, Barcelona, and the Parthenon in their excited voices, sharing with their son this trip of a lifetime.

He didn't have the heart to be Debbie Downer. They would be home later this week.

His parents were rich by most anyone's standards, yet they still behaved like the simple housewife and welder they had been when Ollie was the little boy in his dream. His father, Domenic, although everyone called him Chick, had turned his fascination for metals into a kind of alchemy, building on his ability to work tirelessly to transform a small metal-fabricating plant into something that eventually employed hundreds in the town north of Chicago where Ollie had grown up.

When Chick and Annette made their first million, they had moved Ollie, an only child, into a house in the upscale Jewish and Italian Chicago suburb known as Highland Park. Ollie had grown up not far from the famed musical destination Ravinia Park.

Now they were retired and enjoying their lifetime of hard work and sacrifice. Ollie was happy for them, but at the moment, a little jealous and possessive of Mom.

Right now, he needed her more than his Pop did.

"Oh grow up," he said, sitting up and swinging his legs out of bed.

Here were mornings lately: empty and without purpose. Ollie was not the kind of guy to relish lots of unfilled free time. The lack of anything to do upon awakening did not make him feel free, but rather unmoored, cast adrift. If his father had taught him anything, it was that a man worked hard—it was his purpose in life. One who didn't couldn't amount to much and certainly wasn't worth much. These lessons had sunk deeply within Ollie's fiber.

Yet he couldn't seem to make himself do what needed to done. Namely, get online, post an updated résumé to sites like Monster and LinkedIn, search for marketing and advertising jobs on Craigslist. Contact a headhunter. Work on his portfolio.

He couldn't bring himself to do it because he knew he didn't want it. When he had walked out of his office in Pioneer Square, he knew it was the end to something more than just a job. It was the end of a career.

And that *had* made him feel liberated.

That was why, when he emerged from the building, he repressed the urge to do a little jig. The chains had been cast off, he realized, even if he hadn't known they were there. He had been so comfortable with them through the years that they barely registered. But once gone, he realized their weight.

He could easily get another advertising job. He had dual degrees in English and communications. Years of experience. He could write great ad copy and had design skills. He could manage people and negotiate. He knew HTML, SEO, and a whole string of acronyms that would make him a very desirable catch on the open market… for any employer.

It was for these reasons Ollie had not done a single thing toward finding a new job. He had not even updated his résumé. He didn't even have enough interest in what was out there to peruse the online help-wanted boards.

If he sent out his résumé, if he looked even halfheartedly, he knew he would be hired faster than he could blink. It was not only his skill set and talents that virtually ensured employers would court him, it was the way of the universe. It was some twisted Murphy's Law—when you were not looking for something, it found you.

Ollie did not want to be found.

He didn't think he could stomach another meeting with some client, putting on a fake smile and pretending to feel passion for whatever product or service his client was trying to get out there. He knew now he couldn't care less about advertising. It was nothing more than sales—necessary, but drudge work nonetheless.

Some of his coworkers had been passionate about the field, and he was happy for them. But now that he was away from it, he knew that passion did not exist for him.

But what should he do with his life?

That was the question on his mind every day now. Yet nothing came to him when he tried to think of something else he could do, something he would look forward to doing, something that wouldn't feel so much like work.

Was it possible? Or did people just rely on their attitudes to get through their daily grinds, hoping they made it through happy and with a few dollars to retire on? As Peggy Lee once sang, "Is that all there is?"

Ollie got up and took a shower, threw on a pair of jeans, a black T-shirt, hoodie, and a pair of Nikes. He could at least go out. Espresso Vivace had a sidewalk coffee bar just down the street and, although the weather did not appear exactly welcoming, at least taking a short walk for his coffee and making eye contact with a few other human beings would get him out of the house, make him feel marginally human.

Espresso Vivace was surprisingly busy, given the late hour of the morning and the constant soul-sapping drizzle. Maybe coffee was the antidote for the latter, hence the reason for its popularity here in the Emerald City.

Ollie got in line. He couldn't help but notice the very broad, fleece-covered shoulders of the man in front of him. His dirty blond hair drew Ollie's gaze like a beacon.

He turned around and Ollie wondered if he had felt Ollie's focus on him, maybe a prickling sensation at his neck. He grinned. Ollie liked the man's gray eyes, the way they kind of matched the sky. He also liked the laugh lines framing them. They told a tale of happiness, something Ollie needed to see.

"Great morning for a duck, huh?"

Ollie was surprised at being spoken to. He had been pretty isolated these past couple of weeks, so the sound of a human voice directed at him, although welcome, was also a little unsettling.

"Hey, it's why we live here, right? The weather?" Ollie chuckled.

"Actually for me, it is. Although I do sometimes walk like a duck and quack like a duck, I am not, contrary to popular opinion, a duck. But I like the rain and the gray skies. Love cocooning inside." His pale eyes met Ollie's, and Ollie couldn't help but think, *what the hell's going on here? Is he flirting with me?* Ollie had been off the market for so long, he wasn't confident he'd recognize the signs. *Oh hell, you're a gay man. You know the look, the eye contact held for a little too long. It speaks volumes, more than words can say. Yeah, he's flirting.*

And Ollie didn't know how he felt about that.

He was still getting over Walker.

The guy interrupted his thoughts, startling Ollie. "What about you?"

"Huh?" Ollie was a brilliant conversationalist!

The guy smiled and revealed even more warmth. Ollie felt a tingle. "You like the rain?" he asked Ollie slowly, as though speaking to someone who was a little impaired. And, at the moment, Ollie would have to admit he was.

"As a matter of fact, I do."

They fell to silence and moved up a bit in line. The guy turned to him again. "Off today?"

"What? Oh, yeah." Ollie grinned. "Today and every day. Unemployed."

"Ah. Sorry to hear that."

Ollie laughed. "I'm not. I think there's a silver lining to that particular cloud. I just have to find it still."

The man nodded and turned when the barista, a black-haired Goth-looking guy called out, kind of rudely, "Next!"

"What are you having?"

"Huh?" There went that razor-sharp wit again.

"Can I get your coffee?"

"No, you don't need to do that."

"I know I don't need to," the man said in a hurry. "I want to. You're cute. Now tell me or I'll have to decide for you."

Ollie snickered as he pondered saying "I like my coffee like I like my men: strong and black." But he rejected the idea. He also didn't want to go into his usual complicated Starbucks order, so he just said, "Whatever dark roast they have, with room."

The guy turned and ordered for them both. Venturing out into the cold and damp was proving to be a very good idea.

After the guy handed Ollie his coffee, he introduced himself. "I'm Mike. I live a few blocks over on 17th. I stop by here most mornings for my fix." He smiled, and Ollie felt a little rush at the force of the smile. It was sexy, welcoming, and promising all at once. "It helps me start my day off. I work from home as an interior designer."

Ollie took his coffee and thanked him, wondering how it must be for Mike, working from home and maybe doing something for which he felt passionate.

"You like it?"

They started walking north on Broadway. "I love it. I never wanted to do anything else. Hell, I was rearranging my parents' living room in Snohomish when I was a kid. Mom used to consult me on slipcovers and wall art, even at ten." He laughed and Ollie felt wrapped up in the sound. "What did you do? I mean before you found yourself, as they say in England, made redundant?"

Ollie took a sip of his coffee. "Advertising. I hated it." And he realized he did, and had, for a lot longer than maybe he realized.

"Then perhaps the layoff, or whatever, was a blessing."

"Maybe." They walked on in silence.

Up ahead was Ollie's little redbrick apartment building with its courtyard and sad little pine in the middle of it.

He had nothing to do all day and this guy was cute. He was obviously coming on to Ollie. Why not? Even though something told him it was a bad idea and premature, he asked, "You wanna come up?"

A little glint appeared for a moment in Mike's eye. "I thought you'd never ask."

As Ollie led him inside the vestibule, he questioned what he was doing but told himself that it had been weeks since he'd availed himself of an orgasm, even by his own hand. And maybe, for a little while, hooking up with this cute but admittedly unknown quantity would help him get over being dumped by Walker, maybe even restore in him, just a bit, his sense of his own attractiveness.

Once inside the barren apartment, Ollie turned to Mike, embarrassed. "I have furniture coming later this week." Heat rose to his face. "But there's an air mattress in the bedroom."

Mike raised an eyebrow. "It'll be like camping. Hot."

They both laughed. Awkwardly, Ollie took his hand and led him to the bedroom. The first thing he saw was the picture of him and Walker in its frame, propped on the windowsill. He had an urge to rush over and place it face down.

Mike obviously saw it too. "You got a boyfriend?" There was a little hesitation in the question that said Mike didn't want to be part of some clandestine thing, didn't want to be an accomplice to infidelity.

And Ollie liked him better for that. But he also realized this was a nice guy he had brought home and quickies with strangers had never been his style. "Had. Had a boyfriend. He dumped me."

Mike gave a low whistle and he smiled, but sadly. "Wow. Lost your job and dumped by a hot guy all at once? You poor thing."

"Oh, come on, don't feel sorry for me." Ollie felt a hot rush of shame go through him. In an attempt to obliterate it, he grabbed Mike's other hand and pulled him close, so their chests touched. His heart thudded so loud Ollie was sure it overrode the sound of the wind outside. Suddenly, his desire for this man vanished, replaced by a feeling of pathos. He didn't want Mike to pity him.

He reached up with his mouth—Mike was tall—and kissed him. As his tongue found Mike's, tasting the coffee and that peculiar, wonderful essence that could only be described as essence of man, he thought of a song from the musical *A Chorus Line*. He couldn't remember the exact words, but they were something along the lines of reaching right down to the bottom of your soul and feeling... *nothing*.

Awkwardly, Ollie pulled away, looking up at Mike abashed and wondering how to put this fast-speeding train into reverse. He had a moment of clarity when he realized what he wanted was not sex but simply someone to talk to.

Mike groped him and pulled his hand away. Ollie was as soft as a spaghetti noodle boiled for a half hour. Mike shook his head and said softly, "We don't have to do this."

Ollie was about to rush in, tell him it was okay, that things would heat up once they got their clothes off, once Ollie had a gander at the lumbering hunk of manflesh before him naked, but instead all he said was, "Really?"

"Really." Mike moved away and picked up his coffee cup from the cardboard box of books next to the bed where he had set it. He took a sip. "I can just head right back out if you'd like. Go home and do what I should be doing: picking out fabrics and wallpapers for some rich bitch on Mercer Island."

"Or we could talk for a while?" Ollie asked, hopeful, his voice just above a whisper.

Mike smiled. "Or we could just talk."

And that's what they did. Ollie led Mike out of the bedroom, where the makeshift bed loomed like the unmet promise it was, and the two of them went back out into the empty living room and made themselves comfortable on the floor.

It wasn't so bad, really. Maybe, even without furniture, the little apartment was beginning to feel like home. Ollie liked the way the diffused sunlight shone in, gray and soft, but full of promise.

Without even knowing he was going to say it, Ollie blurted out. "Fact about me: I have no idea what I want to do with my life."

"And?"

"And I'm thirty-three years old. Shouldn't I be settled? In the midst of a relationship? A career? Instead, I'm like a kid who just graduated from college, maybe one who majored in something impractical, like philosophy or Latin, with no direction."

"What do you want to do?"

"Ah, there's the $64,000 question." Ollie wondered where that saying had come from. An old TV show maybe? One that was well before his time, anyway.

Mike asked again. "Think about it. What do you want to do? What's your passion?" He put a finger to Ollie's lips and Ollie felt a tingle, second-guessing his decision to put the brakes on morning sex with a stranger. "Really, Ollie. Take a minute. Think about it. What would you *really* like to do? Don't think about whether it's practical or not.

Sometimes, when everything goes to shit, it's life giving you an opportunity."

"That's just it. I don't know."

"You're answering too fast. Relax. Let it come to you." Mike leaned back against the wall, took a sip of his coffee, and closed his eyes. He appeared to be saying, "I can wait."

So Ollie did the same. First, he thought of everything he could do that had something to do with what he had done before, something that involved the employment of design and words. He could edit, he could write, he could direct people who did those things. Amazon was always hiring. He could be a tech writer at Microsoft.

But he knew those things would only leave him disillusioned and unfulfilled.

The answer was there. It had been waiting for him all the while, just biding its time, patient for Ollie to find it.

Once it popped into his head, he knew it was the right answer. It came to him with certainty. There was no doubt.

"I want to cook."

Mike looked over at him. "You mean like be a chef?"

"Um, maybe. I'm not quite sure just yet what the direction would be. Sure, I could be a chef, but there's also catering, cooking for people personally, even working in the foods department at a grocery store. I just know that one thing I've always loved to do is cook. It makes me happy. When Walker used to come home from work, he always wanted to order in, pizza or whatever, and I would protest and tell him I already had dinner all planned out.

"He'd argue that he knew I was just as tired as he was and why not give myself a break."

Ollie looked Mike level in the eye. "And that's just it: cooking *was* giving myself a break. It was a break away from a job I had never been happy in. When I got home, I could kick off my shoes, pour a glass of wine, put some jazz music on, and head out to the kitchen. It relaxed me to be mixing things up, tasting stuff, and making it all come together. Experimenting. Basil or thyme? Both? How about a little cinnamon and cocoa powder in the chili? And then there was the reward of watching Walker's face light up when he took the first bite." Ollie lowered his gaze to the floor, abashed. "It was almost as good as watching him have an orgasm."

They both laughed. "For real?" Mike asked.

Ollie nodded. "I should have realized this before. It's like this giant exclamation point right in front of me, and it was so big, I didn't even see it. Does that make any sense?"

Mike didn't say anything for a second, and then responded, "Does it make sense to you?"

"Yeah, it really does."

"Then that's all that matters."

Ollie went on. "I guess I always thought I wouldn't like cooking professionally. The pay is notoriously bad, but worse, I thought being on my feet and cooking for eight hours a day might take all the fun out of it. But I don't know that for sure. And I'm not even sure what exactly I want to do with this idea right now." He grinned at Mike. "But it's good to have a direction."

"Isn't there a saying about doing what you love and the money will follow?"

Ollie nodded eagerly. "I've heard that."

"Then follow your passion, Ollie." Mike leaned over and hugged him.

Even though the hug was simply, Ollie suspected, the friendly and logical conclusion to a conversation that had paid an unexpected dividend, Ollie felt the rising of another kind of passion as Mike held him close. When he made to move away, Ollie grabbed him tighter.

"What's this?" Mike whispered in his ear.

"This is me, following my passion." Ollie suddenly felt bold. The clarity he had just reached had changed his mood. Hell, it had redefined, in one fell swoop, his whole outlook on life. He reached down and gently stroked the denim mound between Mike's legs, sucking a breath in as he felt it rapidly harden.

"My goodness. Who knew vocational talk could be the music of seduction?" Mike unzipped his jeans and a very thick uncut dick popped out, its one eye looking imploringly up at Ollie.

"Well, would you look at that," Ollie said, a kind of wonder in his voice. He didn't know where it would lead, but finding his path had lent an unexpected joy to the day, a joy that erased his earlier trepidation about hooking up. He ducked down and licked away a drop of precome that stood poised at the tip of Mike's dick. "Tasty," he said softly, looking back up at Mike and smiling.

"It's just an appetizer. What do you say we go back in the bedroom and gorge ourselves on a real meal?" Mike pulled his shirt over his head, revealing a firm, broad chest covered in pale blond hair. His nipples poked out like gumdrops, and Ollie couldn't resist tasting them, which made Mike squirm, especially when he bit down on them, gently at first, then harder, harder.

"Is that your answer?" Mike asked, his voice, husky.

"No. This is." And Ollie moved his mouth from Ollie's chest down to his dick, swallowing it in one starving gulp. He moaned as he felt the head of it pressing against the back of his throat. Mike moaned too and then pulled him away, reaching under his armpits to pull him up. "The bedroom," he said, forcefully.

They shed clothes, leaving a trail like Hansel and Gretel behind them as they made their way to the bedroom and the inflatable mattress. Even though it was a short distance to the bed, both were completely naked when they threw themselves on the sheets.

"What do you like?" Mike asked the question most common to gay men, and perhaps lovers everywhere, since time immemorial.

"I like tasting… everything." True to his word, Ollie pushed hard on Mike's chest, forcing him to lie prone on his back, and began with a kiss. The kiss lingered, and Ollie's hands, like spiders, ran all over Mike's body. He realized it had been a long time since he had felt this way, consumed by passion.

This was fun.

Mike tasted warm, and his tongue was an agile dueler as it fenced with Ollie's own, twisting and contorting to meet his delightfully, raising the heat in the room. Ollie moved on to Mike's throat, licking and biting, tasting the slight salt of Mike's skin.

On down to the nipples once more. Now that he could tell from Mike's breathing, sighing, and groaning that the man liked things a little rough, he showed him no mercy, biting and chewing the tender flesh hard. Mike squirmed beneath him and at one point, cried out. Ollie stopped, looked up at him, and asked, "Want me to stop?"

"Don't you dare."

Ollie went back to his devouring of Mike, moving in a fluid and slick line down Mike's body, not just tasting but savoring every inch of him. He skipped over his cock, which stood at what looked like almost painfully hard attention, and moved on down to his thighs, his knees, and, finally, each toe, making Mike titter uncontrollably.

Then he moved back up to the equator and first licked Mike's balls, drawing the tender orbs in his mouth gently, one at a time. He worked his way slowly up to the head, pulling back the foreskin and pointing his tongue so he could scoop out the precome with it, rolling it around in his mouth, fully tasting him.

At last, Mike's rapid breathing and his sighs told Ollie he needed to stop this torture, despite how much Ollie was enjoying it, and give the man some relief.

He swallowed Mike down, so deeply his nose was buried in his pubes, then moved slowly up to the head, then down again. He continued this for a while, alternating every so often with swirling motions with his tongue, biting down gently just below the head, and squeezing with his throat muscles when Mike's penis was buried to the hilt.

At last, Mike gasped, "You want it?"

Ollie could only moan in what he hoped sound like assent. He wasn't about to miss a drop. He felt first the seismic tremors in Mike's thighs, trembling, and then the muscular pulse of his cock as it drew up his seed. Finally, Ollie was rewarded with a creamy burst of come that had the flavor of clean seawater. Even though he knew it wasn't the safest thing to do, he was beyond being practical and gulped down every drop.

Finally he pulled away, Mike's cock dropping, semihard and shiny with spit, onto his thigh. Ollie eyed it and sighed with contentment.

He reached down to stroke himself off and found that, during his ministrations, he had already come. He pulled his hand away, sticky and dripping, and offered it to Mike, who licked it clean.

"Tasty," Mike said and then kissed Ollie, their tongues exchanging each of their own sweet essences.

"I like to cook," Ollie said.

"You certainly do."

Mike slid down a little more and pulled Ollie onto his chest. They lay like that for a while and when Ollie heard Mike begin to breathe evenly and deeply, he poked him and asked, "Want some breakfast?"

Main Course:
SUMMER

Chapter SIX

LUSCIOUS TURKEY MEAT LOAF

(Serves 4-6)

- 1/2 pound button mushrooms, finely chopped
- 1 cup finely chopped onion
- 1 cup chopped bell pepper (a mix of red and green is nice)
- 2 cloves garlic, minced
- 1 tablespoon olive oil
- 1 teaspoon kosher salt
- 1/2 teaspoon ground black pepper
- 1 tablespoon Worcestershire sauce
- 7 tablespoons ketchup, divided
- 1 tablespoon brown sugar
- 1 teaspoon apple cider vinegar
- 1 cup panko bread crumbs
- 1/3 cup milk
- 2 large eggs, lightly beaten
- 1 1/4 pound ground turkey

Heat oven to 400 degrees F.

Line a baking sheet with aluminum foil then lightly oil the bottom. Chop vegetables (mushrooms and onion should be very finely chopped, garlic minced, and the peppers diced).

Heat onions and peppers in oil over medium heat until soft 3-4 minutes, add garlic and cook for one more minute.

Add chopped mushrooms with a 1/2 teaspoon of salt and a 1/4 teaspoon of pepper. Cook, stirring occasionally 8-10 minutes.

Dump cooked vegetables into a large bowl, add 3 tablespoons ketchup and 1 tablespoon of Worcestershire sauce. Cool for a few minutes.

While those are cooling, stir the breadcrumbs and milk together and let stand for a few minutes.

Add breadcrumbs and beaten eggs to onions and mushrooms, then mix well. Next, add turkey along with remaining 1/2 teaspoon of salt and 1/4 teaspoon of pepper. Mix well with clean hands. (It will be wet!).

Shape mixture into a loaf in the middle of prepared baking sheet.

Then combine remaining ketchup with brown sugar and apple cider vinegar. With the back of a spoon or a spatula, spread on top of meat loaf. Bake for 50 minutes or until an instant read thermometer reads 170° when inserted into the thickest part of the loaf.

"YEAH. I heard about your business from a friend of mine. Can you tell me a little bit about how it works?"

Ollie rubbed a hand over his dark, stubbled head and licked his lips. He pulled out one of his sparkly red vinyl chairs and sat down at his vintage gray Formica and chrome table. Fortunately or unfortunately, calls like this one were coming so frequently these days, he barely had time to get all the menu planning, recipe-trying-out, and cooking he needed to do done. If his business kept up like this, he'd need to hire a secretary.

And a sous-chef.

Ollie had to concede he was getting used to describing the concept behind Dinner at Home, the catering service idea he had come up with last winter. He knew he should create a brochure and some business cards, but doing so was veering too closely to his old profession, and he just couldn't bear it.

Besides, word of mouth was currently bringing him all the business he could handle. More than he could handle, actually.

"It's simple. I come over to your house, and I cook you dinner." He shrugged. "I don't do fancy. I don't do gourmet. I do basic comfort foods—feel-good cuisine, I like to call it." He chuckled. "I do use only organic ingredients, and I try to support local sources whenever possible. Menus vary by what's available seasonally."

"I love comfort food," the man on the other end of the phone said. "You mean like mac and cheese? Meat loaf? Stews?"

Ollie nodded and added, "Pot pies, garlic mashed potatoes, creamed asparagus, a nice whitefish filet with a crispy cracker crust and a squeeze of lemon...." He laughed. "Shoot. I'm making myself hungry."

His potential customer said, "You're making me hungry too. So what's your minimum?"

"My minimum?"

"Yeah, like how many people does it take to make it worth your while?"

"One," Ollie answered. He didn't really make much money cooking for one, but it gave him such satisfaction, since his single diners usually were lonely people and his coming by to make dinner was often a high point in their day. He did better with couples or families, of course.

"Really? You'd cook for just me?"

"I'd love to." Ollie rubbed the back of his neck and his hand came away wet. It didn't help that he was making three large pots of stock—chicken, beef, and vegetarian—in the middle of an August heat wave. Ollie felt like one of the many chickens he so expertly roasted.

"How do you afford to do that?"

"Well, I am not out there every night cooking for single people. I get families, sometimes big families, couples, and people who want to have dinner parties. It all works out. What I don't do are big parties."

"How come?"

"That's not my concept. Most other caterers do that. I'm here for the single person, the couple, or the small family who want a tasty, comfortable meal at home but don't always have time to make it for themselves." Ollie had said it a million times before, or at least it seemed like he had, but he said it again, "I'm the answer to those folks who are tired of heating dinner up in the microwave."

"So you're kind of like Mom, making a good, old-fashioned home-cooked supper?"

"Honey, I am a burly, bearded, and six-foot-tall Italian. If that sounds like your mom, you're in trouble. But you got the old-fashioned, home-cooked part right."

There was a momentary lapse in the conversation, and then the customer spoke up, "Can you come over tomorrow night? Wednesdays are always my most exhausting days. Hump day, you know." He snickered. "I usually come home, drop onto the couch, pass out, and then I call and order in a large pepperoni pizza."

Ollie thought, but didn't say, *And let me guess, you have the gut to show for it.* Instead, he said, "Actually, things have been going really good here lately, so normally I wouldn't be able to book you on such short notice. But I just had a client call me—a woman up in Shoreline who is a single mom to her two daughters—and cancel, so, sure, you want me to put you down?"

"I'd love that."

"How about a turkey meat loaf with a brown-sugar ketchup glaze, garlic mashed potatoes, and a nice tossed salad? Or maybe a hot vegetable? You like asparagus? I do a simple roasted asparagus that, I swear, will make you see God."

"Let's do the meat loaf. And yes on the divine asparagus. I want to see God, see if he's as cute as Cheyenne Jackson."

Ollie chuckled. He'd gotten another gay client. Word must be getting around. He hadn't started out to cater to the gay community, but it seemed as though more and more of his clients were of the friends of Dorothy variety, which was just fine with Ollie. Who knew? Maybe there would be a potential love interest among his clientele? Lord knows his schedule kept him from looking for romance, or even sex, lately. Chasing after clients, cooking, cleaning up, shopping, all kept him busy twelve to fourteen hours a day, seven days a week. He told himself once he got the business truly off the ground, he could slow down, maybe hire some help.

Ollie concluded the call with figuring out the best time for him to come by and if the guy had a sweet tooth or not.

"Sweet teeth, actually."

"What's that?"

"I don't just have one. I have sweet teeth. All of 'em."

"I make some awesome brownies, laced with caramel and studded with dark chocolate chips."

"Bring a big pan."

THE NEXT night Ollie bustled about the kitchen, getting ready for his latest client. He ran through a mental checklist to ensure he had everything he needed. All the food he had prepared was nestled into an insulated box, which would keep it warm on the drive over to Wallingford, where his new client, Sam Morris, lived. He had a plastic bag full of cutlery and a stack of Fiesta plates in bright colors, with sheets of paper towel between them and bubble wrap around them. He added a stack of linen napkins to the bag, and he was ready to go. From the start, Ollie wanted to be sure his diners were treated right, properly, hence the real flatware and china. No paper and plastic for Dinner at Home!

As he pulled up in front of Sam's house, his heart gave a little lurch. The house Sam lived in, a gray and slate blue painted Craftsman bungalow with a view of Lake Union and Gas Works Park, took him right back to the similar house he had once shared with Walker.

He sat in the car for just a few minutes so he could compose himself before putting on a happy face and going inside. Since last winter, he had thought less and less of Walker, even though there had been little beyond building his business and cooking to fill his time. Oh sure, Ollie was human, so there had been the occasional hookup, culled from Scruff or Adam4Adam, but none of those were memorable, and certainly none had led to anything even remotely resembling a date. He thought of those hookups as little more than glorified assisted masturbation.

Still, if you had told him even as recently as an hour ago, when he was drizzling lemon juice on his roasted asparagus, that he had missed Walker, or indeed even thought of him, Ollie would have laughed.

Yet sitting here, he knew he had never truly gotten over the man. Being back in their old neighborhood and sitting in front of a house so similar to the one they had occupied brought it all back. The comfort of home….

He didn't know if he missed Walker the man or simply the idea of him and all he represented, but it hurt. Being here now brought to the surface the feelings he had managed to successfully bury over the past few months.

Ollie knew, deep down, what it would really take to get over Walker was a replacement.

Now, now. This is neither the time nor the place for self-pity. After you get your work done, if you're still feeling blue and lonesome, you can go home and cry into a nice glass of Riesling, or maybe just a hearty lager. You can dull the pain with a wank or go online and grab the first available lovely who turns your head and is willing to "travel." But right now, you have dinner to serve.

The pep talk worked. Ollie hoisted himself from his car and stacked everything he would need atop the insulated box containing the hot food.

He forced himself to smile as he approached the front door. He set his stuff down and rang the doorbell.

When Sam Morris opened the door, Ollie tried his best not to let the smile falter. He wasn't expecting a guy in a wheelchair. Sam Morris blinked up at him, the sun in his eyes.

"What? Weren't expecting the wheels?" Sam chuckled and moved back to admit Ollie.

Ollie hoisted the box up and entered. "No, no. What makes you say that?"

Sam whirred ahead of him, leading Ollie toward the kitchen. "The look on your face, buddy. A mixture of shock and pity." He turned to look over his shoulder at Ollie. "No worries. I've seen it before."

Ollie entered the kitchen, which had been painted the color of a Granny Smith apple, contrasting wonderfully with the dark-cherry cabinets. He began setting things up, his hands trembling the tiniest bit. Damn him and his expressive face! He had never been able to lie because his face always gave him away. It wasn't that he felt sorry for the guy; he just wasn't expecting a handicapped person.

"You wanna know what happened?" Sam said brightly, as if he were asking Ollie if he wanted to know how he came to choose the color for the kitchen walls.

"No, of course not." Ollie began unloading the food onto the countertop. "It's none of my business."

"Look. You can walk and I can't. It's not going to change anything if you tiptoe around pretending I'm not in a wheelchair." Sam sniffed the air. "Jesus. That smells good."

"It's the barbecue sauce I make for the meat loaf. Yum!" Ollie set out a plate, napkin, and cutlery. "So what happened?"

"Tennessee Walker."

"Beg your pardon?"

"A horse is what happened. A horse on a trail ride that got spooked when we went through a picnic area of a park and a little poodle ran for him." Sam laughed. "I still remember its owner calling it back. The damn thing's name was Killer! Doesn't that beat all?"

"In here or in the dining room?" Ollie asked, picturing a poodle named Killer.

"Let's eat in the dining room," Sam said. He wheeled through an archway and switched on a light. Ollie loaded up a plate for Sam and followed him into a charming dining room, complete with a stained glass window over the buffet and a mission-style table and chairs.

Sam pulled himself up to the table and Ollie set the food before him. Sam looked up at him. "This looks amazing." And it did: the garlic mashed potatoes were fluffy, the roasted asparagus had just the slightest amount of caramelization, and the two slices of meat loaf glazed with the brown sugar, molasses, and ketchup barbecue sauce, positioned just so on a sky blue Fiesta plate, looked like it was ready to be photographed for the cover of *Bon Appétit*. "But aren't you having any?"

Ollie never ate with his clients. It just seemed somehow wrong. He was there to serve them, not be a part of things. He smiled tentatively. "I don't usually do that."

"Don't be silly. You made more than enough." Sam reached up and gripped Ollie's hand. His grasp was stronger than Ollie would have imagined, then he realized how much upper body strength the man must have. It was Sam's eyes, though, that changed Ollie's mind about associating too closely with a client.

It wasn't the color, although the pale blue of them was startling, it was the plaintive look Ollie saw there. With only a pair of eyes, Sam managed to tell Ollie how much he wanted company—and how infrequently he'd had any.

"I don't usually dine with clients," Ollie said softly, letting an impish grin float around his lips. "But it smells so good...."

"Go on," Sam said. "I won't mind."

Ollie went into the kitchen, loaded up a plate, and returned.

"That horse reared up like you see in some old Western and threw me flat in my back. Broke my spine." Sam took a bite of the meat loaf. "Good Lord, this is obscenely good." He swallowed and said, "Fortunately, I just ended up a paraplegic and not a quadriplegic, like poor Christopher Reeve."

"Lucky," Ollie said, because he didn't know what else to say.

"Oh yeah. Lucky me. I should play the lottery." Sam snickered. He put his hand over Ollie's when he presumably saw the color rise to his cheeks. Ollie could feel the heat in his face. "Don't worry about it. I'm just glad to be here… with you."

Ollie smiled, taking in the full measure of the place and saw how perfectly kept it was. He imagined Sam had a cleaning person who kept it spotless. But he wondered if anyone ever came over who wasn't paid to do so.

"I'm glad to be here too." He had a bolt of inspiration. "Since I'm eating with you, there's no charge for tonight."

Sam shook his head, his lips set in a firm line. "No way, buddy. I do not want your charity or your pity. I have a job that pays me well and some smart investments that pay me better." He took a bite of his mashed potatoes and closed his eyes for a moment, and Ollie was thrilled to see the look of pleasure that crossed his face. He opened his eyes and met Ollie's gaze. "Now, what's your story, young man?"

Ollie told him everything—starting with his having lived, once upon a time, just two streets over, and up until tonight, when he was trying to make his dreams come true. They talked far into the night, at last ending up on Sam's front porch, watching the summer light as if faded from gray, to purple, to an inky violet. Fireflies appeared. The two of them ate brownies, drank red wine, and shared their lives.

At one point, Sam asked Ollie if he had a boyfriend.

"Nah. No one special anyway." Ollie felt familiar heat rise to his face once more at the lie. "No one at all, actually."

Sam made a "tsk" sound. "A big, handsome guy like you? I would think you'd be beating them off with a stick." He paused for a moment. "Or at least your hand." He snickered at his own joke and Ollie joined in, although the statement made him feel self-conscious. His hand was actually his most frequent lover, spending the night and everything.

Sam cocked his head and took a sip of his wine. "No, really. You're gorgeous. Just the kind of man I like—with some fur and some meat to hold on to. And you can cook! Christ Almighty, it's a crime that you're alone. Why, if I didn't have my Ralph, I'd be putting the moves on you myself."

"Ralph?" Ollie asked, unable, he knew, to keep the surprise from his voice. "You mean you have someone?" He didn't mean to sound as amazed as he knew he did. He felt ashamed. But it was just that he had seen Sam as this lonely creature, pathetic, and suddenly it seemed as if he might have more going on than Ollie.

"Don't sound so shocked!" Sam punched Ollie's arms. "I'm not *that* unfortunate looking!"

"No, you're not at all," Ollie said. "You're pretty cute." And Sam was. Ollie just hadn't noticed it until now, when he was able to separate the man from the wheelchair in his head and see that his sandy hair, blue eyes, broad shoulders, and pecs that stood out nicely behind the thin white cotton of his T-shirt all conspired to paint a portrait of a very sexy guy.

"Pretty cute?" Sam scoffed. "I'm gorgeous and you know it. Eat your heart out, buddy."

Ollie chuckled. "So where's Ralph?"

Sam held up a hand. "And I know you're wondering. Everyone does. But, although the legs don't work, what's between them functions just fine."

"Great!" Ollie chirped, thinking it was time to be getting home.

"Ralph's in Chicago. He's in sales and travels out to the Midwest pretty often. He's the cook in the family, and I couldn't face another Lean Cuisine, so I'm glad I found you. It's nice to have real food for a change." He engaged Ollie with his gaze. "It's nice to have company."

Ollie had been right—Sam was a very lonely man, at least for tonight. Although his disability didn't slow him down much, Ollie knew it slowed those around him, who most likely either treated him with too much care or too little, made uncomfortable by his difference. But Ollie was glad he could be someone who, finally, saw past the wheelchair.

Ollie was also glad he could stay, glad he could bring some warmth and comfort into a lonely person's life, even if he was only lonely for one night.

It was the whole idea behind Dinner at Home.

Chapter SEVEN

HANK KNEW this was the wrong thing to do for so many reasons. For one, he was leaving little Addison by herself. There was no excuse for that, even if it was late at night and the little girl, stomach empty but tired, had been fast asleep when he had crept out of the little fleabag room they shared half an hour ago. Hank promised himself he'd be back before she woke up, and she would never know he'd even gone. Where was the harm in that?

Except visions of Addison waking, alone in a gloomy room, the only illumination a sock-monkey nightlight Hank had plugged into the wall, dogged his every step. He pictured the terrified look on the little girl's face. Would she cry out for him? Or would she remain silent, keeping her own counsel, brown eyes wide with fear and thinking this latest desertion was par for the course?

He didn't know which option was worse.

For another reason, he needed money. He needed cash so he could feed her. Since he had lost his job as a short-order cook at Myra's Diner over on Broadway, he barely had enough cash to pay their weekly rent on the roach-infested room the two of them shared in the Central District.

The room, barren and dirty, had been the best he could do.

He had thought, once he got the job, standing over a hot grill and flipping burgers all day, making omelets, frying bacon, that he could support the two of them once their time at Haven had run out. No one was allowed to stay at Haven for long, even such hard-luck cases as Hank and his niece.

He had been wrong. Even before he had argued with his boss Chuck, calling him a "fucking loser," and been fired on the spot, Hank quickly learned that the minimum-wage job would barely cover the rent, let alone pay for such luxuries as food and clothing.

How did people do it? How did they get by, managing not anything fancy, but just keeping their heads above water and getting the basics? It was a mystery Hank didn't know how to solve. The pressure of figuring it out was always with him, causing him to want to retreat back into the demons of drugs and sex-as-commerce that had almost ruined him. All it took, though, to banish those thoughts was one look at the innocent face of Addison, who relied on him and had no idea what her uncle's history included. That trust and faith about broke his heart, but it also ensured he stay responsible.

Was what he was doing tonight responsible? *Yeah, right.* He laughed bitterly.

But he had no job anymore. The loss of the position, meager as it was, was not his fault. Not really. He just couldn't keep his big mouth shut once he had seen Kelly, that acne-scarred waitress, drop some sausages on the floor during a breakfast shift, giggle, put it back on the plate, and serve it to a customer with a big smile. Hank had to squeal on her. He had first snatched the plate away from the old man who already held one of the dirty sausages aloft on his fork, ready to bite into it.

Hank had been sure Kelly would be fired. But it was he who got the axe.

"What? You think I'm rich? That I can afford to throw away good meat? I'm sure Kelly brushed it off before she served it," Chuck had told him.

And so now he found himself prowling around Capitol Hill looking for an opportunity to steal something, anything, that could be traded in somehow, somewhere, for cash so he could buy them something to eat. He didn't care so much about himself, although he had a hard time denying the painful emptiness in his gut and its constant growling, but Addison was just an innocent little girl, and she depended on him.

Up ahead, he saw a gift from God. Someone had left the door to his or her car open; the light in the car was even still on. How could this be? *Probably some drunk escaping home after a night at the clubs farther south on Broadway.*

He crept up to the vehicle, looking nervously around. He slid quickly back into the shadows as a pickup truck rumbled by, its engine sound lonely this late at night.

He returned to the car and saw there really wasn't much worth stealing. The car was a later model, some sort of Japanese deal that was so common around town, probably a Subaru. But all it contained was a big plastic box in the back seat and some dishes and shit next to it.

What could he do with dishes? He had nothing to eat off them!

He saw the car had a fairly serious stereo, but he was not enough of a criminal to know how to take something like that out quickly. His efforts would probably yield only a ruined stereo, worthless.

He decided there must be something in the car, even if it was only spare change in the glove box, so he slid inside and closed the door. He was so busy rummaging through the car, thinking now that its dome light was extinguished, he'd be safe, that he barely heard the guy creep up.

Hank cried out when the door was yanked open and the light came on, exposing Hank like the cockroach he felt he was.

"What the fuck do you think you're doing?"

Hank looked up into the dark, angry eyes of a burly, bearded man, glaring down at him. He didn't know what to say. Words, and the ability to form them, completely escaped him. His mouth dropped open. All he could do was stare.

"Well? What do you have to say for yourself?"

Hank shook his head in an effort to clear it. "You left the car open."

The guy laughed. "So it's *my* fault?" He shook his head slowly. "That's rich. Blame the victim. Yeah, I left the car open, but only for a minute while I carried things in from my work. I didn't expect some asshat to come by and make himself at home. What the fuck's wrong with you, anyway?"

Hank had lived on the streets, been in situations much uglier than this, but his fear, his exhaustion, and his hunger all joined forces to make him feel hopeless, as if he had sunk to the very bottom of whatever hell he was living in. Not only had he been stupid and careless, he had taken a chance on a situation that didn't even promise much of a reward. What if the guy called the cops? What if he couldn't get away from him before the police arrived? What would happen to Addison if he were taken into custody? She would awaken, alone, terrified, and hungry in the morning and there wouldn't be a single thing Hank could do for her.

He had only intended to leave her for a short time—bad idea.

It was all too much. He hated himself as he felt the hot liquid rush in his eyes and the lump growing in his throat, expanding, threatening to break through the tender flesh. The only release was one he couldn't control. The tears had been coming for days, weeks, and maybe even months now. Watching his mother die, the downward spiral of his life, the added joy and terror of having a child depend on him all coalesced, descending on him like an emotional tornado.

He lowered his head, covered his face with his hands, and wept.

"Oh Jesus Christ! *Really*? You think that's gonna help?" The man reached down to Hank and angrily snatched his hands away. He recoiled when he saw real tears on Hank's face and a look of concern creased his features. "You weren't faking," he said softly.

The man's posture assumed a position of defeat and he leaned a little into the car, one hand on the roof for support. "C'mon."

Hank sniffed, trying to rein in the tears.

"What do you mean? Where?" His sorrow was suddenly replaced by fear. He knew he was vulnerable, and he was savvy enough to know that people took advantage of vulnerability. They pounced on it when they saw it and turned it to their own advantage.

The man threw up his hands in defeat... or disgust. Hank wasn't sure which. "C'mon into my place. I'm not gonna hurt you. I'm not gonna call the cops, although I probably should." He bent down so his face was level with Hank's. "My name's Ollie. Just come on in for a minute, tell me what's making you cry at—" He looked down at his watch. "—two o'clock in the morning."

"You sure? I should probably just go." Hank leaned forward. It had been a long time since he had seen such kindness in anyone's eyes. He knew he should just place a hand on this Ollie's chest, push him hard, and run down the street.

"Go do what? Find another car? Or maybe a house or apartment to break into?" Ollie shook his head. "Is that what you really want?"

"No," Hank said honestly.

"Then come with me." Ollie turned and began walking toward the courtyard of the small redbrick apartment building behind him. He didn't look back, and Hank knew he was leaving him to make up his own mind about what his next move would be. Hank realized he *could* have simply run away. The fact that Ollie had left the choice up to him demonstrated something. He wasn't sure what at this point, but it made him feel better; it helped the stupid tears to ebb.

So he got out of the car and followed.

At the front door, Ollie paused, keys in hand. "I'm an overly trusting idiot and have been told my heart's too big for my own good." He laughed. "And it's all true. If you have a gun, a knife, or whatever, I hope you know you can take whatever you find in here. Just don't hurt me."

Ollie unlocked and opened the door. Smells of cooking drifted out, warm and comforting, making Hank's mouth water and his stomach growl—loudly. He placed a hand over it and grinned at Ollie, embarrassed.

Ollie didn't smile back. He cocked his head. "You're hungry?"

"Oh God, you don't know." Hank swallowed painfully, his throat dry, hating to be found so weak and wanting. His mind rushed to Addison, and he realized, again, how important it was that he get home soon to her.

"Why don't you come into the kitchen and sit down? I'll fix you something to eat."

"You don't have to do that, man. You don't even fuckin' know me."

"I know you're hungry. And I suspect, because I have great and powerful deductive reasoning, that your breaking into my Subaru had something to do with that." He opened the refrigerator and started rooting around in it. Although Hank couldn't see his face, he could hear Ollie.

"And I'm a cook. It's your lucky night. I have leftovers out the whazoo. Name your pleasure. I have mac and cheese with roasted peppers and bacon, my famous Mexican casserole with salsa, black beans, corn and roasted chicken, a little veggie beef soup, half a pork tenderloin with a bourbon brown-sugar glaze…."

Hank wanted to get up and shove the man out of the way and simply kneel before the refrigerator, stuffing what sounded like manna from heaven into his mouth.

"What do you want, buddy? I can heat any of this stuff up in two minutes in the microwave."

Hank put his head down on the table and sobbed. He heard the refrigerator door close and felt Ollie's shadow fall over him. "Oh for

Christ's sake, kid. Get a hold of yourself! It's just food." He chuckled and Hank could feel Ollie kneeling down beside him. Ollie slid a hand onto his shoulder and rubbed. "What's the matter?"

Hank managed to ebb the flow of tears once more, embarrassed and ashamed. "It's just that I'm so hungry. I've never been so hungry."

Ollie stood up. Hank watched him pull what looked like a glass dish of mac and cheese from the white refrigerator. He put it in the microwave, pressed a couple of buttons, and the machine was humming, giving Hank a warm late-night supper.

This would seem like such a blessing if it weren't for Addison.

Ollie said, "I'm sorry. We'll get something hot into you in just a couple of minutes."

"I'm not alone," Hank said.

"What's that?" Ollie paused before the microwave, glass dish in his hand.

"I said I'm not alone."

"I don't know what that means. You look alone to me."

Hank stared out the kitchen window at the darkness pressing in, like something palpable. He felt like he and Ollie were the only two people in the world. "I have a little girl. Her name is Addison."

Ollie laughed. He set the dish down on the counter and scooped some of the mac and cheese onto a plate, an orange one like the one Hank had seen in Ollie's car. Steam rose from the pasta invitingly, and Hank was torn between wanting to devour the food and finding a way to bring it home to Addison.

Ollie set the plate down before him, with a fork alongside. Hank couldn't help himself. The biological imperative that was hunger took over, and he started shoveling the food into his mouth. He didn't know if it was because he was so hungry, but it tasted like the best thing he had ever eaten, nothing like the powdered milk, cheese, and dried pasta concoction he would make up in a vat at Haven.

Ollie pulled out a chair across from him, the chair making a scraping noise on the redbrick-patterned Linoleum. He watched Hank eat for a few minutes. When Hank looked up, there was an amused grin on his face. Finally, he spoke. "So what's this about a little girl? Because I gotta tell you, you do not by any means look old enough to have a child. What are you? Eighteen?"

"I'm twenty-two," Hank said, somewhat indignantly, between bites. "She's my niece, actually."

"Where is she?"

"In some crap room I can't even afford, down in the CD. I thought—" Hank pushed the empty plate away. Ollie got up and loaded it up once more and set it in front of Hank. He dug in again. "I thought I could slip out for an hour or so while she slept, steal something I could sell real quick and get her something to eat." Hank looked down at the food, a sudden pang of guilt twisting in him like a knife. How could he sit here and wolf down food when Addison was alone in that room, with only the roaches to keep her company, her belly so empty it ached?

Ollie shook his head. "Good Lord, kid, you're like something out of *Les Misérables*."

"What's that?"

"Never mind. Just finish up."

Hank ate a little more, but slowly. He regarded Ollie out of the corner of his eye. The man seemed to be thinking.

Ollie appeared to have come to a decision. It was the way his features softened and he relaxed in his chair that told Hank that.

"Once you're done there, I'll fix up a plate for Allison."

"Addison."

"Addison. And we'll take you back to that crap room and see that it's there for her." He smiled. "And for you. I'll be right back." Ollie left the apartment, leaving Hank alone to look around and ponder all he could steal. An iPad lay on the coffee table, an iPhone next to it. There was a watch with what looked like a white gold band on the kitchen counter. There were any number of things he could grab and be out the door in seconds.

But he stayed put.

When Ollie returned, he carried the big plastic box Hank had seen earlier in the car. "This is my insulated box. We can pack this up. I have a lot of food in the fridge. You tried to rob the right guy, my friend."

Hank hung his head over his plate that was, once again, empty. "I'm sorry about that, man. I'm not usually a thief, but I just couldn't see any other way to get us some food, you know?"

Ollie shook his head, his features creased by sadness. "I can't say that I do know."

"Good for you. No, I mean it."

Ollie busied himself at the counter, pulling out dishes of food that he loaded into the box. "You about ready?"

Hank stood. "You sure you want to do this?"

"I am not sure of anything. Maybe this is all a dream. You really have a hungry little girl back at the place you call home?"

Hank nodded.

"I can't *not* do it—" Ollie stopped suddenly. "What's your name, anyway?"

"Hank. Hank Mellinger."

Ollie grasped his hand, his grip delightfully solid and firm. "I'm Ollie D'Angelo."

"Nice to meet you," Hank said weakly.

"Likewise. Shall we go?"

"You don't have to do this."

"Are you really gonna stand on pride? After all you told me?"

Hank grinned and shook his head at his own stupidity. This was a gift. "Guess not."

"Okay, then stop asking me if I mind. Let's get you guys taken care of." Ollie blew out a big sigh. "Listen, Hank, I have always been lucky. I came from a hard-working family that happened to strike it rich, or at least what most people would consider rich. I never wanted for a thing. I always had a safety net, no matter what I did. Mom and Pop were always there to catch me if I went down the wrong path. I have a sneaking suspicion you can't say the same."

"Not hardly."

"Then come on," Ollie started toward the front door.

As they headed out into the quiet that comes just before dawn, Hank turned to Ollie and said, "Listen, man, someday I'll pay you back for this. We'll be square."

Ollie only smiled and held out his car keys. "Get the doors, would you?"

Chapter EIGHT

SATISFYING BANANA GINGER CARAMEL PUDDING

(Serves 8-10 or one very hungry little girl)
- 3/4 cup sugar
- 2 tablespoons cornstarch
- 3 cups milk
- 4 egg yolks
- 1 teaspoon vanilla extract
- 1/2 stick butter
- 3 medium ripe bananas, sliced
- 1 small box Ginger Snaps (you'll need about 12-16)
- 2 tablespoons caramel topping of your choice

Mix together sugar and cornstarch and add milk. Cook in the top of a double boiler or over low heat, stirring constantly until it thickens—don't leave it alone! Beat egg yolks and temper with a little of the hot custard; stir. Add egg mixture to custard pot and cook 2 more minutes. Take off heat and add vanilla and butter. Let cool. In a 9x9 inch ovenproof baking dish, alternate pudding, bananas, and ginger snaps, beginning with pudding and ending with pudding. Drizzle caramel over the top.

OLLIE PULLED up in front of a nondescript wood-frame building. Even if it were daylight, he thought, the peeling boards of this so-called house would be a color he could never describe. It just looked dirty, tired, and rundown. There was plastic sheeting on some of the windows; others were boarded up. The intact windows looked like dark eyes, staring out uninvitingly. Cans and other trash littered the weed-choked front lawn.

The street they were on was narrow and crowded with vehicles that looked like they were on their last legs. At the corner was a convenience store with a big iron gate covering its front. A couple of men in hoodies and denim stood outside, hands in pockets, cigarettes clamped in their mouths.

"This is home?" Ollie asked, his words catching in his throat. He was horrified to imagine a little girl walking down this street. The notion turned his stomach.

"Well, I wouldn't call it home. But it is where me and Addison stay, at least for now."

Ollie sighed. The sky was just beginning to lighten in the east, a barely discernible line of gray. As they got out of the car, he rubbed his bare arms against the cool air. Even in summer, Seattle was chilly at this hour.

He started to hoist the insulated box from the back seat.

"Let me get that," Hank said. He reached over Ollie and grasped the box by its handles. "Again, this is so nice of you. I can't thank you enough."

As they turned toward the building—Ollie couldn't bring himself to call it a house—he noticed a light come on in an upper story window.

Hank saw it too. He looked over to Ollie and smiled. "That'll be Addison. There's gonna he hell to pay."

"How old is she?" Ollie asked, thinking maybe this "child" was close to Hank's own age, since he seemed to fear her wrath.

"She's four."

Ollie barked out a short laugh. "You're scared of her."

"Oh, if you only knew! Come on." Hank led Ollie toward a flight of stairs at the side of the old building.

At the landing, Hank fumbled with the keys he had hanging from a chain off the belt loop of his jeans and unlocked the door. A smell of mildew immediately wafted out of the little room, which Ollie could see had once been the attic. Despite the early-morning damp and chill, the attic felt hot when he stepped into it behind Hank.

The room was barren. Slotted wooden walls sloped down on either side. The wood had never seen a coat of paint and looked old and rotting. Ollie wondered what lived inside those walls and shuddered. The floor was the same unfinished wood. There were two sleeping bags on the floor, bags that looked like they had been cadged from the Salvation Army, or worse. Between them was a plastic crate topped with a lamp with no shade. Along one wall was a dorm-size fridge. Above that was a counter with a hot plate. The shelves contained a couple mismatched plates and a stack of silverware; there was a cracked measuring cup.

The one window was high up and grimy, situated between the eaves. Ollie doubted it let in much light.

He was overwhelmed with a feeling of both claustrophobia and sadness. The heat was already causing a line of sweat to form at his hairline.

But he didn't see a little girl. At least until he heard a toilet flush and the door at the back of the room open. Framed in the open doorway stood the most beautiful child Ollie had ever seen. The word cinnamon came to mind as he met her dark-eyed and somber gaze. Her hair was deep red and in tight little curls; her skin was the color of creamy hot chocolate, perfectly complementing her brown eyes, which were so dark the irises appeared to have swallowed up her pupils. A constellation of cinnamon colored freckles spread across her nose and cheeks. Her lips were full, but right now were thinned in a line that Ollie could only imagine was fury.

There was something very grown up about this four-year-old, and that made Ollie sad. It was like she had already missed the fairy tales and princesses stage and gone straight to world-weary adult. Yet there was something weak and vulnerable about her too. Her little matchstick limbs, sticking out from an oversized T-shirt, were so pathetic and malnourished-looking, Ollie's heart gave a lurch.

She crossed those stick-like arms across her chest, and when her voice came out, it was deep and sounded anything but vulnerable. "Where have you been?" she demanded, ignoring Ollie to stare at Hank.

Hank shrank back a little, and Ollie could understand why. This little girl had something about her, something his Sicilian mom would call *faccia tosta*, but that his simple, hard-working papa would just refer to as "brass."

"I was out trying to get us something to eat, Addison. I didn't think you'd wake up."

"You didn't think too damn hard."

"I'm sorry. It won't happen again."

And all at once, the brave façade began to crumble. Like any little kid who was scared and upset, Addison's upset was first manifest in her upper lip, which protruded at the same rate as her frown deepened. Her eyes became shiny with tears. Although she tried to retain her bravado, her next words came out whispery. "I was scared." She lowered her head and her shoulders shook.

Hank rushed to her and gathered her up in his arms. She stood stiffly, allowing herself to be hugged, staring at Ollie. At last she appeared to compose herself, and she shoved Hank away. "Who's this?" She nodded toward Ollie.

"This is a nice man." Hank got to his feet and moved to stand next to Ollie, placing a hand on his shoulder. Ollie could feel that hand trembling. "He's brought us some food. His name's Ollie."

"Food? Really? That's good because I'm starving." Addison moved forward, gaze searching for the promised food. "I don't see any damn food."

Ollie squatted down beside the insulated box. "It's all in here. What do you like?"

"I'm not picky, mister. I'm just hungry."

Ollie looked at Hank, who nodded for him to continue. Ollie was at a bit of a loss. His catering business included children, of course, but the comfort foods that were his specialty usually just meant smaller portions for the kids. Where to start? He remembered when he was a kid and decided the best place to start was at the end.

"You like banana pudding?" Ollie smiled. He withdrew a bowl of the pale yellow fluff from the box. Broken into it were ginger snaps. A line of caramel ran through the pudding. "This is my specialty."

Addison approached him warily, as though he were a wild animal and might bite. Ollie removed the plastic wrap covering the top of the bowl and set it down on the floor. He held the bowl out to her, relying on the delightful sweet smell of bananas and caramel to charm her. He could feed her something more nutritious later, he thought; right now he was all about winning her over.

Addison stood for a moment, a finger in her mouth, swaying, just a foot or so away from the proffered bowl. Finally, as though pushed by invisible hands from behind, she stepped quickly up to the bowl, removed her finger from her mouth, and plunged it into the pudding.

With a big scoop of pudding on her finger, she stuffed it back into her mouth.

And closed her eyes. The expression on her face was one all cooks long for, and it could best be described as rapture. "Mmmm," Addison said, her voice a growl too low for a little girl, but there was no mistaking the pleasure wrought from her very first bite of Ollie's special banana pudding.

"Here, home slice, let's not eat like animals." Hank groped around on one of the shelves above the hot plate and produced a spoon. Addison snatched the spoon from Hank's hand, the bowl from Ollie's, and sat herself down on the bare floor to begin shoveling pudding in her mouth. She didn't stop until the bowl, which contained about four servings, was empty.

She belched and wiped her mouth with the back of her hand. "That was good, mister. What else you got?"

Ollie chuckled. "How about something good *and* good for you?" Ollie rooted around in the box and pulled out the container of vegetable beef soup. He looked at Hank. "Can I heat this up on the hot plate?"

Hank grinned sheepishly. "You could, if I had a pan. Usually, I just stick a can of something on the coils and heat it up."

"Oh, never mind," Addison said impatiently. She snatched the container from Ollie's hands, opened it, and dug in with the spoon she still held clenched in her little fist.

Hank plopped down on the floor. "She obviously needs some lessons in manners."

Addison glared at him. "*She* is obviously starving, no thanks to you, Hank!" Addison slurped up another spoonful and deigned to look at Ollie. "Thank you, mister."

Ollie grinned. "It's Ollie."

"Thanks, Ollie." She rolled her eyes. "Whatever."

The three of them were now sitting on the floor. Hank put a hand on Ollie's knee. While Addison devoured the soup, he told Ollie that they were really very grateful.

Ollie felt warmed by his gratitude, yet wondered what the rest of the day would bring. He couldn't continue to feed them every day. Their stomachs were full now, but what would happen when they were empty again? Where would they go? What would Hank do? What risks would he take? He turned to eye Hank and noticed, for the first time, now that all the drama had begun to settle, that he was a very attractive young man... in a grungy sort of way. Somehow, in spite of the obvious lack of funds, Hank had managed to acquire quite a few tattoos. One arm was encased in a sleeve that was a riot of yellow stars, green vines, and the purple heads of what looked like dragons. The words "love" and "hate" were tattooed on his fingers. On his neck, he sported some sort of tribal symbol. And then Ollie spotted his other forearm and saw the Santoku carving knife there. Near it was a wooden spoon.

Ollie reached over to touch them. "You like to cook?" He cocked his head.

Hank barked out a laugh. "Yeah. Got a little training over at Haven?"

Ollie shook his head and shrugged.

"It's a homeless shelter. They taught me the basics, good enough to get me a job as a short-order cook over at Myra's?"

Ollie nodded. He'd heard of the place—typical greasy spoon.

"Too bad I couldn't hold onto it." He snorted out a burst of cynical laughter. "My standards were too high. Maybe the boss could look the other way if a waitress dropped food on the floor and then served it, but I couldn't."

Ollie shook his head, glad he'd never eaten there. They fell to silence while Addison finished her soup. At last, she shoved the bowl away and it too was empty. "I'm tired," she announced. Outside, the sun had risen. And so had the heat in the little apartment. Ollie watched Addison crawl on top of her sleeping bag and lie down. After a moment, she eyed Ollie and Hank with a kind of fierceness. "What? You two gonna watch me while I sleep? That's creepy, but whatever."

Hank touched Ollie on the arm. "You wanna step outside? She's probably been up half the night worrying, and now that her belly's full, maybe she'll get a little sleep. If nothing else, it's an escape from the heat."

"Sure."

The two of them stepped out onto the landing that fronted the door. Hank groped in his jeans pocket and brought out a battered pack of Marlboro Reds. He opened it, and Ollie could see that inside were basically a bunch of butts in varying lengths, their ends blackened. Hank shook his head. "Hey, who can afford smokes? I admit it, I pick up half-smoked butts from the sidewalk. Surprising what people throw away." Hank looked away from Ollie as he lit up, blowing the smoke toward the curdled-milk sky.

Ollie stared at the back of the man's head. Hank had the same red hair as his niece, although his was buzzed close to his skull save for a line running down the middle that was a little longer. This, Ollie believed, was called a faux hawk. In spite of the scrawny build, Ollie noted there was a wiry strength in Hank's body. His shoulders were broad and the arms sticking out of his cut-off sleeves were sinewy.

Ollie smiled to himself as he realized he thought the guy was hot. *No. No. No*, he told himself. *Number one, you don't even know which way this guy goes. Odds are, he's straight. And number two, what kind of perv thinks about how hot a guy is in a situation like this one? You're supposed to be helping him, not lusting after him.* Ollie shook his head, knowing that sexual attraction had never been tempered by goodwill or even common sense. The body wanted what it wanted. Still, Ollie knew he'd be better off if he shoved any such thoughts deep down inside.

Hank finished his cigarette and pitched it over the side of the landing, where, Ollie was sure, it would join thousands of other fallen comrades. "I guess you need to be gettin' back home, huh? I mean, you have a job and shit, and I've kept you up all night."

"It's okay," Ollie said quickly and realized it really was. Helping these two out had brought him unexpected joy, and whether they knew it or not, lifted Ollie's life out of the run-of-the-mill. If someone had told him, when he was loading up his car and preparing to leave his last client in Wallingford a few hours ago, everything that would transpire, he would have laughed and called them crazy.

Yet here he was. And here Hank was. He leaned to look inside, and there Addison was, on her back, mouth open and snoring.

He turned back to Hank, looking him in his gray eyes that verged on silver and asked, "What will you do?"

Ollie could see some sort of internal conflict going on within Hank. He didn't speak for several seconds. Finally, he shrugged. "I don't know. Keep lookin' for work. That little girl in there depends on me." He sighed. "*I* depend on me." He returned Ollie's gaze. "Not sayin' this to make you feel sorry for me or nothin', but I got nobody. It's all on my shoulders."

"It doesn't have to be."

"Yeah. Right. Charity's gonna have to be a last resort. I'm not eating on the government's dime unless there's no alternative."

Ollie thought that right now, there was really no other alternative, but he kept the notion to himself. He liked Hank even more for at least having the desire to keep his own head above water, without help. Of course, he wasn't sure how stealing fit into that noble equation, but desperate times called for desperate measures, right?

"So you wanna work for your keep? Earn it?"

"Yeah." Hank groped around in the pack and lit up another butt. Ollie noticed the weariness around Hank's eyes. "Does that surprise you? I'm not a fuckin' thief." He shook his head, took another drag. "I've done some bad shit in my life, but that doesn't mean I don't keep trying." He shrugged. "None of us is perfect. But all of us can keep trying, right?"

Ollie nodded. "That's for sure. So what kind of work are you looking for?" Ollie knew where he was going with this and questioned his sanity. There was a common sense streak in him that told him to slow down, that he should think about things before he made a move. But there was another part—perhaps one that very much looked like a heart—that said he needed to move now because these were two people whom maybe God himself had thrown in his path to help. And they did not seem to have a lot of time to wait around while Ollie "thought things over" or "looked before he leapt."

They needed him now. That much was clear. Who knew what kind of trouble Hank might have been in right at this very moment if someone other than Ollie had caught him trying to steal the night before? Would he be in a prison cell somewhere? Would Addison be wandering these mean streets, searching for her uncle? Ollie shuddered.

Hank snapped his fingers in front of Ollie's face, snapping him back to reality. "Dude. You there?"

Ollie laughed. "Sorry."

"I was just saying I love to cook. I'd love to be a chef someday, work in some fancy restaurant, dreaming up menus and food combinations no one has ever seen before." Hank sighed. "But I'd settle for more short-order work, if it was all I could get. Why? You know someone who's hiring?"

Ollie felt like he stood at the tip of a precipice. Everything could change in an instant with his next words. This was one time when he truly understood the head and the heart being at war. The head was telling him he barely knew this guy; their acquaintance was fewer than a couple of hours old, and that same acquaintance was forged under dubious, if not criminal, circumstances. But his heart reminded Ollie that he had good instincts. And wanting to help someone was never a bad thing. He wasn't, after all, considering more charity for Hank. He was thinking about asking him to work with him.

After all, he needed the help. Dinner at Home had taken off in ways he hadn't imagined. Who knew there was such a market out there for small home-cooked dinners? When he had started, he wasn't sure he could support himself, but he had gone beyond that and was already approaching the kind of money he had made as a creative director.

He had found a niche no one else had yet capitalized on. And to grow even more, he would need help.

But this kid? He could be more trouble than he was worth. *Think about it, Ollie. Go away for a day or two. If you still think it's a good idea, then come back here and make the kid an offer. Part-time to start, see how he works out.*

Ollie cleared his throat. "Yeah, I know somebody."

Hank's expression brightened. "Yeah?"

Ollie put a thumb to his chest. "Me. And I need full-time help." Ollie launched into the elevator speech of what Dinner at Home did, how long it had been around, and its astonishing success in only a few months. "Even I can't believe how fast it's grown."

"I don't know why you're surprised," Hank said. "That shit you cook is awesome."

Ollie closed his eyes for a moment, then spoke slowly. "Um, if you are gonna work with me, the first order of business is to mention that we do not call food 'shit.' Shit is the byproduct, what comes out later. But what goes *in* needs to be referred to more delicately and with a little more, um, flavor."

Hank laughed. "Gotcha. So, how does this work? Do I need to fill out an application? Or what?"

"I haven't gotten to the application stage yet. You said you knew how to cook. I need help. I have no time off. In fact, I should be shopping for tonight's appointment right now. Can you help me?"

Hank grabbed Ollie and hugged him. Ollie was taken aback, but felt a rush of heat as the other man's body pressed up against his own. "Thank you, man. I'd love to be a part of Dinner at Home. When can I start?"

And then reality intruded and Ollie questioned once more what he was doing. He peeked into the little hot box where Addison slumbered. "You could start tonight, but what about her?"

Hank looked over his shoulder. "Yeah. That's kind of my Catch-22. I need a job to support her, but then if I go off to work, who takes care of her?"

"Exactly." Ollie could not advocate leaving a four-year-old to her own devices, even if her guardian was off making a living.

Ollie stood in silence for a while with Hank. Around them, the day was springing to life. Traffic rumbled along the street below. Voices began to emerge from the sidewalk. The heat seemed to rise a couple of notches, the sun burning away a morning caul of fog that had hovered below them while they talked.

"So maybe this won't work?" Hank said, the defeat already clear in his voice.

"What did you do when you worked at that diner?"

"That was mostly days. There's a daycare over at Haven? The place I was telling you about? They'd take her for the days." Hank looked around, desperate. "Your work's mostly at night?"

"Dinner at home. Yeah." Ollie scratched his head. "I can't hire you if I know she's by herself while you work."

"Give me some time?" Hank asked.

"Buddy, you don't have time." Ollie shook his head, every fiber of his being telling him this was a mistake, but saying it anyway. "Start tonight and bring Addison with you. Tomorrow, though, you look for someone to take care of her, to help you out."

"Sure, sure! Thank you so much!" Hank seemed like he was a kid again, one who had just gotten an ice-cream sundae with a cherry on top.

And Ollie felt like he was making the worst mistake of his life. He only hoped time would prove him wrong. Damn him and his soft heart!

Chapter NINE

HANK AWAKENED and looked around him, reassuring himself that the last two weeks had, indeed, happened. So much had changed in a mere fourteen days that he fully expected, still, to get up each morning and find his good fortune had been nothing but a dream, a byproduct of hunger and wishful thinking.

He sat up in bed. Yes, a real bed, with sheets and a quilt that slithered to his waist when he sat up. Although his room was still shrouded in a kind of half-light, he could make out what was fast becoming familiar: the white dresser, with its chipped and peeling paint that made it look loved and not old, the rocking chair in the corner, the bedside table with its reading lamp, and the book Ollie said he should read beside it, Mark Bittman's *How to Cook Everything*. He peered down at the braid rug on the distressed hardwood, over at the walls, covered with framed covers from *Cook's Magazine* (another of Ollie's ideas).

Best of all, he looked to his window, a picture frame that looked out on... well, the house next door. But still, it was a lot more than he'd had in the rat hole of an attic he had been living in until so very recently.

The bedside alarm clock told him it was just past six. He'd need to get up soon and make breakfast so he and Ollie could begin their workday.

He put his feet to the floor and stretched, dying for a smoke, but knew Ollie would have a fit if he lit up inside. He snatched the pack of Marlboro Reds off the nightstand and crept downstairs. Ducking out onto the front porch in only his boxers, T-shirt, and bare feet, he cupped his hands over the lighter and cigarette as he lit up. He blew the smoke toward the lightening sky, enjoying the silence.

But not for long. The door squeaked open behind him. Ollie's voice caused Hank's back to stiffen. "My most fervent hope," Ollie said, in what sounded to Hank like a proclamation, "is to come down here one morning and find you just enjoying the morning with maybe only a cup of steaming coffee in your hand."

Hank turned toward the man and grinned. Ollie looked well rested, eyes shining and clear, beard heavy, sexy in only a pair of flannel sleep pants. His chest could hardly be described as bare, covered as it was with a blanket of fur that Hank, in weaker moments, had fantasies about running his fingers through.

But Ollie didn't know that. Knowledge like that would complicate things. Although Hank knew Ollie was gay, the subject of Hank's own sexual orientation had yet to come up. He assumed Ollie just went to the default most people did and presumed Hank was straight.

And that was just fine. Meth and trading his body for the drug had essentially spoiled Hank's view of sex. Although he still longed for the connection, there were too many bad and shameful memories attached to the act for him to seriously consider it. Besides, he was too busy to think about sex and love right now. Too much to take care of. Too busy forging a life for Addison and himself. Sex and love were still an out-of-reach luxury, something for the rich folks.

Hank blew a stream of smoke out of the side of his mouth and said, "It's nice to have a dream."

Ollie shook his head. "Ah, I don't have to tell you all the disadvantages and the risks you take every time you put one of those things in your mouth."

"Compared to the kind of shit I used to do, this little vice doesn't seem so bad."

They were quiet for a moment, enjoying the look of their tiny front lawn here in the Central District, just a few blocks over from the rooming house where Addison and Hank had once stayed. Right now, mist was rising off the dew-soaked grass, and it told a tale of another unseasonably hot day.

Ollie had rented the house shortly after he had hired Hank, saying he needed the space and that the house came with a large kitchen, with an island, a range, and double ovens. It was practical, he had said. But Hank knew the truth, although he had never let on to Ollie: the house had been rented to get Hank and Addison out of the firetrap where they were staying, the roach-infested, stinky, toilet-rarely-working dump.

Whatever Ollie's real reasons were, Hank was glad to be here. He had never, in his whole life, lived in a house. Even when he was growing up with Lula, they had lived in a series of rented apartments (always run down) or, if Lula was really flush, they had taken up residence on the outskirts of town in one of the finer trailer parks.

A house, even this simple, aluminum-sided job, was a palace to Hank. To have his own room and this porch to slip out onto to think were luxuries that were so far out of reach for most of Hank's life that he had never let himself dare imagine them.

"Penny for your thoughts." Ollie stepped up next to him, waving Hank's smoke away with his hand.

Hank wanted to say something along the lines of "I was just thinking how lucky we are to be here. What started out as a very bad idea, robbing your car, turned into something good. You're like an angel sent down to rescue Addison and me. I don't know how I can thank you... ever." But that all seemed too sappy, and not the kind of words that would come out of Hank's mouth. He knew that Ollie would check behind him for a ventriloquist if Hank ever dared utter such schmaltz. So what he said was, "Just thinking about all we have to do today."

"It never stops, does it?"

Hank shook his head. "No. And that's good, man. Job security." He grinned.

The door creaked open again, and Hank expected Addison to come out in her nightgown, rubbing her eyes, glaring at him, and giving him the same grief about smoking that Ollie had.

But it was not. It was Rose, another of Ollie's "new hires." The young girl was as shy as they came. Hank was surprised to see her get her nerve up enough to join them on the porch. Even now she stood before them looking as though she wanted to disappear into the aluminum siding behind her, shrink into it if there were any way she could.

But Rose had come with good credentials and a lot of need, which was why both Hank and Ollie had been happy to find her. She had just finished a training course in cooking *and* early childhood education at a vocational school in White Center that spring, and she solved the problem of one more hand for cooking as well as childcare for Addison when Hank and Ollie were off doing meal set-up and delivery.

Hank and Ollie still didn't know her full story. She had come to them when Hank suggested Ollie call up Haven to see if any of the residents there were taking their cooking training and looking for a job. Rose was fairly new, quiet to a fault, but E.J. had said that she could work "magic" in the kitchen, transforming simple ingredients like brown rice, beans, tomatoes, and herbs into something wondrous and filling, all for pennies on the dollar.

She had been with them three days now. In exchange for a room in the house, all the food she could eat, and a minimum-wage salary, Rose helped out with the prepping of meals in the kitchen and took care of Addison while the two men scooted around town delivering comfort and food to Seattle's hungry populace.

There was something about her that made Hank want to reach out and hug her. The only thing that stopped him was the fear that if he *did* touch her, she would run off screaming, never to be found again. Someone, at some time, had hurt her badly, and it showed in the way she kept her green eyes cast downward, her shoulders hunched, and in her slow, deliberate movements. Hank wondered if she was afraid if she moved too fast, she might be hit, or worse.

Underneath the mousy exterior and frizzy hair, though, if Hank looked very, very closely, he could see a beautiful young woman. In spite of her fierce shyness and quiet demeanor, she had a body he knew straight men would go nuts over. She was curvy in all the right places and was very well-endowed up top, although she tried her best to hide these attributes with baggy, formless dresses, T-shirts, and jeans. She never wore make-up.

It was as though she wanted to never be noticed.

Hank looked at her face, though, and was reminded of the few religious paintings he had seen in his life, those of the Virgin Mother and of saints. There was, underneath the temerity, a glow to her skin and a clarity in her eyes that was almost mesmerizing. The word that came to Hank's mind was purity.

It was when she was alone with Addison, though, and not realizing anyone was watching her, that Rose's true beauty and personality came out. Around the little girl, she could be herself, and the two of them would laugh together, whispering jokes only the two of them could understand. Rose would hunker down on the floor with Addison and become a little kid again.

Hank wondered if it was because she had never had a chance to be a kid herself.

But she could just as easily mother Addison, making sure she ate properly, brushed her teeth at night, and wore the appropriate clothes. Rose had no compunction about informing the little girl that her often smart mouth was out of line. And woe be it if one of the neighborhood kids dared tease Addison. Then, Rose's shyness melted away like a Popsicle on a hot day, and she would be on the offender like a lioness protecting her cub.

Someday, Hank thought, he would get her story, and he suspected that they would have a lot of notes to compare.

"Good morning, Miss Rose," Ollie said, smiling.

Her eyes flickered up to him for a moment, then back down to the floor of the porch. "Morning," she whispered, looking quickly at Hank.

"Sleep okay?" Ollie asked her.

She shrugged, smiling. She looked like she was gathering up her courage. Finally, she spoke and both Hank and Ollie had to lean in close to hear her. "I was thinking of maybe making some breakfast for us. If that's okay, I mean." Rose backed toward the door.

Hank spoke up, "That would be really sweet, Toots. Can you do us some bacon and eggs?"

Ollie eyed him, and Hank could see the question on his face: *Toots? Really?* But Hank thought giving the girl a nickname might make her feel more a part of things. He could practically count on two hands the number of words she had spoken since coming to them, including the ones this morning.

"Sure. Toast? Coffee? Potatoes?"

"Yes, yes, and yes," Hank said. "Just scramble 'em up; it's easier."

Rose nodded and rushed back inside as if they had been holding her out on the porch against her will.

Ollie turned to Hank. "I'm just glad we don't have to take her out on calls. I think she'd die of fright."

Hank nodded. "I've seen girls like her before, on the street. I hate to say it, but I'm guessing something very bad happened to her at some point."

"Well, that much is obvious. I hope some time with us will help her realize that not everyone wants to hurt her." Ollie shrugged. "If that *is* what she's afraid of. E.J. didn't know much about her and couldn't get a whole lot from her."

"But she's great with Addison. It's nice to be able to go off to work with you and not have to worry about Addy. I know she's in good hands."

"Oh God, Addison adores her, follows her around like a puppy. We were very lucky to find her." Ollie looked out at the morning as a car rumbled by, blaring hip-hop so loud it was rattling the vehicle's frame. He looked back at Hank. "I was very lucky to find you."

Hank laughed, embarrassed both by the praise and the frankness of Ollie's stare, which, if Hank didn't know better, he would say was provocative. It made him feel exhilarated, horny, and bashful all at once. "Ah, get out of here, you big homo."

Ollie laughed. "Hey, I don't lie about who I am. I see a good-looking man and I'm not ashamed to let him know." He raised his eyebrows at Hank, which caused heat to rise to Hank's cheeks.

"That blush just makes you look more handsome."

The heat went up a few notches and Hank had an urge to laugh. "Shut up. I'll file a sexual harassment claim against you."

"You can't harass the willing." Ollie winked. "We should probably be getting inside, see if Rose needs help. We could at least set the table, maybe pour some OJ."

Hank watched Ollie as he hurried away, his figure changing to a silhouette as the screen door slammed behind him. Hank could still make out the broad shoulders and his confident walk. Did Ollie know Hank was gay? Was that little exchange his way of telling Hank it was cool and to come out, come out, wherever you are?

Hank followed him inside, wondering where such knowledge might lead.

Chapter TEN

SLOW-COOKER POSOLE

(Serves 4)

- 2 cloves garlic, minced
- 1 medium onion, chopped
- 1 poblano pepper, diced
- 2 stalks celery, sliced
- 4 tomatillos, peeled and quartered
- 1 pound boneless, skinless organic chicken thighs
- 2 cups chicken stock
- 14-1/2 ounce can hominy (I prefer gold, but white is fine too)
- 14-1/2 ounce can diced fire-roasted tomatoes (with chiles or other Mexican seasoning)
- 4 ounce can sliced jalapeños, with juice
- 2 tablespoons ground cumin
- 1 tablespoon dried oregano
- 1 teaspoon red pepper flakes or more to taste
- Salt and pepper to taste

Sauté garlic, onion, pepper, celery in pan for 5 minutes, add tomatillos and sauté for two more minutes.

Combine the above with remaining ingredients in the slow cooker and cook on low for 7-8 hours (or high 4 hours).

At end of cooking time, pull out thighs and shred with two forks, return to pot. Test seasonings, adding more salt and/or pepper if necessary. Garnish with chopped cilantro, sliced radishes, cubed avocado, and lime juice.

"WE'RE A little early. You want to have a smoke before we go up?"

Hank eyed Ollie across the seat from him in the car, his mouth open in surprise. "Seriously? You're inviting me to smoke?"

"Well, you know I'd rather you quit. But with the traffic and all, I gave us too much time, and I am not going to barge in on a client—" He glanced down at his bright orange watch. "—twenty minutes before we're supposed to be there."

"Is this some kind of trap?" Hank fingered the pack of Marlboro Reds in his pocket, and the itch to have one commenced.

Ollie chuckled. "No. Just a way to pass the time."

Hank needed no further encouragement. He hopped out of the car, headed toward the rear of it, leaned against the fender, and lit up. Ollie joined him. "I'll never get it."

"What?"

"So many cooks, chefs, whatever, smoke. It deadens your taste buds; it messes up your sense of smell."

"Whatever. I enjoy it. I'll quit one day."

"Is that a promise?"

Hank nodded, blowing a stream of smoke toward the sky. "Who we got tonight?"

"Didn't you check the roster before we headed out?"

"Come on, Ollie, just fuckin' answer me."

Ollie shook his head, which made Hank grin. He didn't know why, but Hank loved getting under the man's skin. A thought arose, unbidden: *you'd like to get under his pants too. And touch some of that skin you love to get under.* Ollie pulled Hank away from a detour into fantasyland by responding, "We have a Mr. Michael Sharpe. He came to us through the offer I ran on Amazon Local. Wanna know what we're serving too?"

Hank rolled his eyes. "I made the fuckin' posole myself."

"That you did, and a very good posole indeed. I liked how you made it leaner by using the chicken thighs instead of pork. Great idea." Ollie glanced down at his watch once more, and not only did Hank covet the watch again, but he couldn't help but admire the thick, dark hair on Ollie's forearms.

Jesus, I'm getting a woody!

"I think we can go in now."

Hank felt heat rise to his cheeks, as if Ollie had been reading his mind. He didn't trust himself to speak, seized by an irrational fear that his voice would come out high and squeaky like a little girl's. He threw his cigarette on the ground and stomped it out.

"Don't leave that there," Ollie said.

"Really? Oh for Christ's sake." Hank picked the cigarette butt up off the ground, brushed it off, and stuck it in his pocket. "Anything else?"

"Yeah, you can grab the insulated box out of the back. I'll get the plates and stuff."

The two lugged everything up to the little neon pink bungalow with its canary yellow front porch. It looked out of place here on 17th in Capitol Hill, not only because of its hey-look-me-over color palette, but also because its neighbors were a mix of apartments and commercial properties.

"What is this guy? A fag?" Hank snickered.

Ollie blew out a sigh that sounded annoyed to Hank. "I don't know. I didn't ask him when I was taking his order. Is that important to you? Should we start prequalifying?"

"Jesus, I just meant the bright pink house," Hank said, voice barely above a whisper. Maybe it wasn't so smart to use the term "fag" around his boss, especially since his boss was one. *And you too, Mr. Hank; you're one too, although right now that's probably your own dirty little secret.*

Ollie said, "Sorry. I didn't mean to sound harsh. It's just that our clients' sexual orientation is none of our business." He lowered his voice. "Beside, genius, it's summer, and the guy's windows are open. What if he heard you?"

"I'm sorry."

"I'm a *fag* as you put it. Do you hold it against me?"

"No." *But I'd like to*, Hank thought, *I'd like to hold it against you. More than just hold it, rub it, stick it somewhere....* He burst out into nervous laughter.

"What's funny?" Ollie asked, grinning, wanting to be in on the joke.

"Nothin'. Just ring the doorbell, this box is freakin' heavy."

When Michael Sharpe opened the door, Hank immediately became aware of two things. First, stereotypes be damned, the guy was a fag. Straight men did not wear scarlet satin kimonos. Second, Michael Sharpe was gorgeous. He had a mane of sandy brown hair flecked with strands of gold that almost begged for lascivious fingers to run through them. His eyes were pale and arresting, ranging from gray to blue depending on how the light was hitting them. And the body that the kimono clung to? Kimono or not, it was all male and very hot: broad shoulders, a shape that formed a perfect V, strong calves covered with golden down jutting out from beneath the robe's hem.

Hank was taken aback, and his heart fluttered a little faster. They served hot guys before, but this one took the freaking cake.

But the little cloud of lust that had enveloped Hank was quickly dispelled when he noticed Ollie had what was most likely the very same reaction to the guy, who Hank now realized looked a lot like the guy who played the title character in *Thor*, a movie he had managed to sneak into a couple of years ago.

Hank hung back and observed, with rising nausea, the way the pair's eyes were locked on one another, their smiles.

It was as if Hank wasn't even there!

What? Ollie likes this guy? Hank shook his head almost without realizing he was doing it. He hated the feelings within him that had arisen and taken over—an almost hot sickness that he recognized as jealousy.

But you got no right to be jealous, dude!

"Mike!" Ollie called out, with what Hank recognized as familiarity. Hank rolled his eyes, thinking how fucking wonderful it was that Ollie already knew the guy. *That's just too perfect!* Why hadn't he told him? "You never called me. You said you were gonna call." Ollie stuck out his lower lip like a little kid. Hank rolled his eyes.

Hank watched, with a smirk of satisfaction, a look of confusion fall across Michael Sharpe's face. Mike let out an embarrassed laugh. "I know, I know. I was going to, and then I got busy. And I was going to again, and then I kind of met someone. And I was going to *again*… and it seemed like the dating statute of limitations had run out." Mike shrugged, offering up a smile that, if Hank weren't feeling so nauseated and, well, mad, he might have found adorable. Hank watched as the wheels turned for a moment in Mike's head. "But I *did* call. Last week, for dinner. That's good, isn't it?"

"I guess it'll have to do." Ollie put a foot over the threshold, and Mike stepped back so he could enter. He barely gave a second glance to Hank, who trailed behind the two men, lugging the heavy insulated box. He felt ignored and worse, like some pack animal.

"Kitchen's this way." Ollie and Hank followed Mike as he led them toward the back of the house. Hank couldn't help but notice how the inside of the house matched the outside, at least in its explosion of bright colors: lime green, yellow, sky blue and other colors all somehow merged to work together and to induce in Hank a kind of momentary joy.

But the joy didn't stand a chance of lasting for long, not when the two other men were making goo-goo eyes at one another.

Mike said to Ollie, once they reached the kitchen, "I should be kicking myself for not calling. I forgot what a hot man you are."

"Aw, get out of here."

"And you can cook too. We talked about that, remember?"

Ollie nodded. "I remember. You were actually the one who told me to think about what I really wanted to do."

Hank slammed the insulated box down, too hard, on the dark black-and-green granite countertop.

"And this was what you decided to do?" Mike asked.

"This is it. Dinner at Home. A unique catering service for people who want a good meal at home with no fuss."

"Are you reciting from your marketing materials?" Mike asked, laughing.

"I am, actually. The business has really taken off. I didn't expect it to grow as fast as it has."

"Well," Mike said, "you obviously found a niche. I'm living proof of that."

"Yeah, I've already hired two people." Ollie nodded toward Hank. "This is Hank."

"Hey," Hank said. He shot a brief look at Michael Sharpe, then returned his gaze to the kitchen counter.

Mike nodded but never really stopped staring at Ollie. "So yeah, I am sorry I never called you after we hooked up."

Hank felt his jealousy twist into a low-simmering rage. *Stop it! You have no right to feel this way. Ollie doesn't even know you're gay, let alone that you have feelings for him.* Hank slammed open the box and began banging the dishes on the counter.

"Hey! Careful there," Ollie cautioned.

The savory smells rose up to meet Hank, but instead of delighting him, they turned his stomach. He had an urge to just say "Oops!" and shove the ceramic casserole dish of posole—a Mexican stew that boasted chicken, hominy, and tomatillos, among other things—onto the floor.

Mike went on, "Time just got away from me. It's not that I didn't want to call you." Mike edged nearer to Ollie, and Hank wanted to scream when he saw the way they flirted with each other. Shameless! What was next? They were going to start making out?

Ollie said, "It's okay. I know how these things can go." He grinned. "But it's not too late."

Oh no. This is so *not going there!* Hank cleared his throat. "Sorry, boss, but this shit is gonna get cold unless we serve it soon."

Ollie cut a look to Hank that was all glare. Hank knew perfectly well that Ollie despised food being referred to as shit. It was one of the first lessons Ollie had taught him. But this was just a slip, wasn't it? Hank called all sorts of things shit, good and bad. "It can wait," Ollie said slowly, then returned to Mike, all smiles.

"As I said, it's not too late."

Mike smiled bashfully, tugging on his ear lobe. "I could go for seconds."

Oh, aren't you just adorable? Hank started to dish up a bowl of the posole, resisting a mighty urge to spit in it. No one would notice anyway, since neither of the men was looking at him. He held himself back by opening the Tupperware they had brought with garnishes for the stew, things like lime, sliced avocado, radishes, and chopped cilantro and red onion.

"So Ollie, what are you doing this coming Friday?" Mike asked.

Hank blurted out, "He's cooking dinner for a family up in Shoreline, with me."

"Hank!" Ollie hissed.

"Well, it's true, boss." Hank smiled as if he had no idea he was causing any trouble. He then echoed something Ollie had asked *him* earlier. "Didn't you check the roster?"

Ollie stared at Hank for a full minute, maybe more. Then he turned back to Michael. "He's right. We're doing a small dinner party that night."

"Hey, I'm a night owl. Maybe after? Late date?" Mike asked hopefully. "Drink at the Pony?"

"That sounds great," Ollie replied. "It'd be nice to unwind after that."

Hank was wondering if Ollie would include him. He didn't have to wonder long. Ollie looked at him, wearing a very sweet smile. "You wouldn't mind taking care of clean up and putting the stuff away after the dinner party, would you, Hank?"

Hank wanted to scream. But he took a deep breath, internally counting to ten, then smiled back, just as sweetly, and said, "Not at all, boss." Hank erased the sweet smile quickly, for fear it would break his face clean in two.

Ollie turned back to Mike. "Then I guess we have ourselves a real date, then."

Mike looked wistful. "A real date. Sigh. And not just a morning hookup on an air mattress?" He winked.

Hank was ready to leap over Mike's kitchen table and strangle the guy. He told himself he had no right to his feelings. But right or not, he couldn't deny them. Right now, he was feeling a curious mixture of gut-twisting yearning and rage. He knew he needed to get hold of himself, to somehow see this dinner through. This was, after all, his job. He had Addison to think of, as well as his own future.

Things had been going so well. Until tonight.

Mike clapped his hands together. "Well, I should leave you guys to it. My sister's going to be joining me for dinner. And by sister, I do mean biological sister, Ellen, and I need to go get dressed. Just set it all up in the dining room, if you don't mind. Feel free to rustle through the drawers if you need anything." Mike slipped out of the room, and Hank listened as he mounted the stairs. There was a creak, and a door closed.

Ollie must have been listening too. He whirled on Hank, a low fury in his words. "What the hell's wrong with you?"

Hank took out a foil-covered paper plate of homemade flour tortillas. He grabbed the cast iron skillet they had brought and set it on Mike's stovetop, turning the burner to high, so he could warm and lightly toast the tortillas.

He ran a hand over the cast iron, testing the heat. He didn't look at Ollie. He *couldn't* look at Ollie, actually. His emotions were too fucked up to analyze why, but for the moment, all Hank could do was stare down at the black metal, becoming shiny as the oil it was treated with became liquid. "I don't know what you're talking about."

Hank could feel Ollie step close, so close he was practically pressed up against his back. He spoke in a low voice, barely above a whisper. But just because his words were soft did not mean they weren't also hard. "You know perfectly well what I'm talking about. You acted like an ass in front of a client." He softened his tone a bit, and Hank dared glance over his shoulder at Ollie for a fraction of a second. Ollie went on. "What I don't understand is why. Do you have a problem with my being gay?"

The question was so unexpected and so ironic that Hank couldn't help the snort of laughter that escaped.

Ollie must have thought Hank was laughing at him. Hank could feel him move away. "Honestly, Hank, I never figured you for a homophobe."

"I'm not." Hank turned and stared at him. *Should I tell him? No, no, not now. It'll just look like you're kissing up to him.* "I have no problem with your lifestyle." Hank thought he was saying the right thing.

"Lesson number one in Gay 101: I do not have a life*style*, I have a life. Remember that."

Hank nodded.

Ollie stood next to him and threw a tortilla on the hot pan. Neither of them said anything for a long while, long enough anyway to get through the whole bag of tortillas. When they were all nicely warmed and a little browned on the edges, Hank took them and put them on a plate, covering them with a dishtowel. He went into the dining room and set the plate on the table.

"You want I should put the garnishes all in separate bowls?" Hank asked.

"That would be nice. Presentation is everything."

"I know," Hank said, echoing one of the lessons Ollie had taught him. "We eat first with our eyes."

As they worked, Hank couldn't deny the tension in the air. It was something he had yet to feel when he was with Ollie. One of the things he loved about them was that, even after just a few weeks, the two of them worked so harmoniously together, almost like they were two halves of the same whole. After only a very short time working for Ollie, Hank could do most of the things required of him without even being asked. Ollie had once even commented that he got things done practically before Ollie had even thought of them.

Tonight that harmony slipped out the back door, when Mike and Ollie were making goo-goo eyes at one another and Hank was watching them doing it. Now, Ollie and Hank were bumping into one another as they moved from the kitchen to the dining room. Hank dropped a couple of limes on the floor that Ollie almost slipped on. Worst of all, the knife Hank was slicing up the avocado with got away from him, fell to the floor, and almost landed on Ollie's instep.

At that point Ollie said, "Just slow down and breathe, Hank. This isn't a race. We have plenty of time." Ollie peered up at the ceiling from which issued the sound of a low drone. "He's still in the shower. I can hear it running."

Hank turned to the counter to finish dicing the avocados and to add a squeeze of lime to them so they wouldn't brown. "I bet you'd like to join him," he whispered.

"What was that?" Ollie asked with just the tiniest hint of annoyance in his tone.

Hank thought fast. "I said, 'I get the joy you get from this.'"

Ollie stepped up beside him, leaning in so he could look Hank in the eye. "Sure you did." He grinned, but there wasn't anything happy in it. "You need to let me know if you have a problem with working with gay people. It seems shocking to me that it would come up now, but the only *other* reason I can figure for you behaving the way you are tonight is you're jealous." Ollie eyed him closer and Hank had to look away.

Hank laughed. "Yeah, right. Of what?"

"Okay, then. I think you and I need to have a little talk, but we'll save it for later. Right now, we have to make sure our guests have the pleasant meal we made for them. And drama, my dear, is not on the menu. So behave!" And Ollie smacked Hank's ass, hard.

Hank gasped and whirled around. He knew his face was turning scarlet from the fire he felt rising to his cheeks.

Ollie, he noticed, had reddened too. His mouth hung open. "I apologize. I shouldn't have done that." He leaned forward to glance out the kitchen window, peering up at the sky. "Is there a full moon out tonight? Seriously, Hank, I'm sorry."

"It's cool," Hank said, returning to his duties. And it really was, at least according to the little man in his pants, whose head had risen at the smack.

"No, it's not. Can we just forget I did that?"

"Sure." Hank could hear footsteps upstairs. "We better get everything together and ready to serve."

"Right."

The rest of the service passed uneventfully, and Hank managed to tamp down his anger, jealousy, whatever the hell it was, until they had their Mexican feast set out. It helped that Mike's sister, Ellen, a blousy woman with dyed-blond hair and an infectious laugh, had arrived. "Good Lord, Mike," she announced when she saw the steaming posole with its red broth, "if you could learn how to cook like this, maybe you'd have a man, and you wouldn't need to rope your poor sister into coming over for supper."

Mike had thrown an arm around Ellen and said, without a glimmer of a smile, "Ain't she cute?"

Once the meal was served and Mike and Ellen were oohing and aahing over the dishes Ollie and Hank had prepared, the two men slipped outside to give Mike and his sister some privacy while they ate. That was their usual modus operandi; they would come in and clean up after people were done.

Outside, the light was just beginning to wane, foretelling darkness. A cool breeze had blown up and Hank's anger deflated, replaced by a feeling of numbness that bordered on sorrow. He'd grown used to having Ollie all to himself these past few weeks, and living under the same roof and working so closely together, had, he now realized, caused his feelings of closeness to flourish even more quickly than they might have had they lived apart or worked separately.

Was this what falling in love felt like? Hank wondered. He knew he had never been in love before, so he had no benchmark by which to gauge his feelings. Seeing Ollie flirt with Mike, though, had confused him, and right now he wanted more than anything else just to be alone. He needed to calm the whirlwind of emotions inside him.

He lit up a cigarette, and Ollie frowned at him. "Come on, we're outside. And I need the break."

Ollie nodded but didn't say anything.

Hank took a long drag and then asked, "Hey, since you volunteered me to do all the clean-up on Friday, you think maybe you can handle it tonight?"

Ollie cocked his head, eyeing him, and it felt to Hank as though the man was trying to figure him out. "Yeah, but I'm the boss. I can do that."

Hank shook his head. "Okay. I'll stay."

"No, no, it's all right. You just gonna hoof it home?"

"If that means walk, then yes."

Ollie moved closer and reached up almost like he was about to touch Hank's face, but then thought better of it and dropped his hand. Hank wished he would have. "You okay?" Ollie asked. "Something's off."

"Yeah. Something is a little off. I just need a little time. I'll be fine by the time you get home." He was surprised at the hot pinprick of tears at the corners of his eyes and turned his head so Ollie wouldn't see.

"Okay. You know you can talk to me about anything."

Hank wasn't at all sure he could. Could he talk to him about canceling Friday's date, for example? He didn't think so.

He turned away and waved over his shoulder. "See you at home," he called out without looking back.

And he heard Ollie's voice come to him, dimly, an echo. "At home."

Hank moved forward into the rapidly encroaching night. He knew he needed to think, just not precisely about what.

Chapter
ELEVEN

OLLIE WONDERED where Hank was. He had been home now for a couple of hours and still, Hank had not shown up. Exhausted from the long day, Ollie told himself he should just crawl into bed with the book he was reading. He'd be asleep after fewer than a couple of pages.

But he felt like a worried parent—or lover. The house was quiet. Rose and Addison slumbered peacefully in their shared room. Ollie had looked in on them when he had gotten back from Mike's. He had crept into the room and stared down, smiling, at the little girl. She referred to herself sometimes, comically, as a "fierce bitch," and the fact was, even at four, she really was. But here, asleep with her thumb in her mouth and a purple teddy bear she called Violet tucked under her arm, there was no evidence of fierceness. There was only a sweetness and an innocence that brought out Ollie's protective side. He could see in the fat cheeks the baby she had so recently been, and his breath caught as he thought that somewhere her mother was without her. Could the woman, Hank's sister, bear being apart from her daughter? Hank had talked so little about his family, and Ollie had yet to press, but he wondered if Hank's odd mood tonight had something to do with the history he'd kept so quiet about.

Ollie's hand hovered above the little girl's sleeping form, and he wanted to gently touch her, to feel the baby soft skin beneath his hand. It sounded corny even just thinking it, but he thought that by doing so, it would put him closer to God. He also thought that if he touched her, he might wake her. Then the brown eyes would open and she would snap at him, asking him just what he thought he was doing. "I'm trying to sleep here!" she would bark. Ollie smiled.

He turned to Rose, who also slept, but not as peacefully as Addison. The young woman tossed and turned restlessly and, at one point, cried out. Ollie's heart clenched and he wondered what demons tormented her and if they were the very demons that kept her so quiet, so hidden in her shell.

He left the room silently, a whisper, a shadow, and crept back downstairs.

Now he peered out the window, hoping to see Hank's familiar form coming down the street. But all he saw was a group of kids gathered at the corner, illuminated by a streetlight. They were laughing loudly, raucous. Ollie wondered if anyone under his roof had ever felt that carefree—to laugh like the teenagers at the street corner.

He stepped out onto the porch and sat down on one of the three wide steps that led up to it, put his arms around his knees, and waited.

Surely, Hank would be home soon. It had been three hours since he had left Mike Sharpe's place. Maybe Ollie shouldn't have let him go off by himself. It was plain to see that Hank was upset. In fact, it wasn't hard to miss that something was eating him up inside.

Ollie mentally kicked himself for letting him go, for just standing there and watching Hank as he faded away into the distance. Hank's shoulders had been hunched, his hands stuffed into his pockets. His posture alone, Ollie thought, spoke volumes about the stress the young man must have been feeling.

But there was clean-up. And, Ollie had to admit to himself, he had wanted to see Mike again. Seeing Mike reminded him he had been living pretty much like a monk since starting his business, and he recalled fondly the hot morning he had spent with Mike. He also recalled thinking, at the time, that there would be more of the same. But when the days and weeks wore on with no e-mails or phone calls, either initiated or returned, Ollie was sure he had just been some easy sex for Mike, and like so many other sexual encounters in his life, their connection had meant little and was going nowhere.

He had been thrilled that Mike did indeed want to get together again, and he was excited to see what he thought of the meal he had prepared. He wished also that he might get a moment alone with Mike.

His wish came true as he finished washing up the dishes and packing everything away. Mike strolled into the kitchen, grinning. Ollie grinned back, not sure why, but he had to admit Mike's grin only made him look that much more fetching.

"What?" Ollie asked, thinking how the man brought out his most brilliant wit.

"I was just wondering if you accepted barter deals as tips."

Ollie's eyebrows had come together in confusion. He smiled weakly. "I'm not sure what you mean."

"I mean this." And Mike grabbed him and kissed him. This wasn't a little peck either. This was a passionate, full-on, deep tongue kiss that immediately aroused Ollie and had him grasping Mike for dear life. This was the kind of kiss that initiated nasty, mind-blowing, come-to-Jesus sex... and it took Ollie's breath away.

When he stepped away from Mike, whose grin had broadened into an out-and-out smile of the cat-who-ate-the-canary variety, he was left feeling almost disoriented. "Yeah," he gasped, trying to catch his breath and echoing a line from the movie *Babe*, "That'll do, pig."

Mike had laughed. "Oh man, I can't wait until Friday. Big fun is in store."

"Me neither." He turned back to his work, partly to hide the bright red he knew his face had turned and the obvious tent in his sweatpants farther south. But he also turned away because he felt confused. What should have been a happy, horny moment, a first step back on the road to dating, or at least sex, was also a moment that caused him to feel... what? Guilt?

What do I have to feel guilty about?

Now, as he sat here on the porch, warding off the evening chill by drawing his knees closer to his chest, he knew the reason.

It *had been* like cheating. Ollie was always a one-man kind of guy. Oh sure, he could look back on his days of serial dating and even serial hookups, but his attention never strayed further away than the guy he was with.

But cheating on Hank? That was crazy. There were so many good, solid, practical reasons for the two of them not to get romantically involved. For one, Hank was his employee. And, more importantly, Ollie didn't even think Hank was gay.

At least, he hadn't until tonight....

Ollie couldn't escape the idea that Hank's behavior had all the symptoms of jealousy. Hank had been fine, cheerful even, on the short drive over to Mike's house, chattering away about how good the posole he had prepared had come out. "Before you," Hank had said, looking at Ollie with what Ollie could not help but identify as fondness, "I didn't even know what posole was."

The happy demeanor had continued right up until they reached Mike's front door, when everything had gone to shit—at the exact moment when Mike and Ollie had locked provocative gazes with one another.

Coincidence? Ollie thought not. And the jealousy theory was further boosted by the fact that Hank's discomfort, maybe even rage, had grown proportionately right along with Mike and Ollie's shameless flirting.

But could it be? Ollie had never been one for labels. Gay men came in all different shapes, sizes, colors, and attitudes. The stereotype of the swishy, limp-wristed queen existed, to be sure, for a reason. But Ollie had found, in his years of being out, that guys like that were in the minority. What most people unacquainted with the gay community didn't know was that gay men were pretty much like every other man, except in where their attractions were focused.

So why was he now mentally berating himself for not picking up on any clues that Hank might be gay and might, if it wasn't too conceited of Ollie to think so, be attracted to him?

Had there been signs? Not of gayness, but of the fact that maybe Hank was a little drawn to him? Ollie wracked his brain trying to think of a time when Hank had perhaps met his eyes for a fraction of a second too long, when Hank's gaze might have been fraught with meaning. Ollie was well acquainted with the eloquent language gay men spoke to one another with their eyes, a language that had been forged long ago, back when any other sign of interest might have been greeted with a closed fist from the object of desire.

He couldn't think of one.

He also couldn't think of anything Ollie had said that might indicate Hank thought of Ollie as anything more than his employer or, during lighter moments, his friend. If there had been signs of affection, Ollie now realized he'd most likely attributed them to the fact that Ollie had been a kind of benefactor to Hank and Addison.

And what of Ollie's own feelings? Those were clearer and easier to put his sweaty finger on. Ollie knew he had been attracted to the young man from the very first time he had laid eyes on him, when he caught Hank in the act of trying to rob him. In spite of his anger and sense of violation, Ollie knew that beneath it all, his most basic self, his core, had thought Hank was hot. The bad-boy image Hank projected had only made it worse, or better, or whatever.

And why not? Hank was a few years younger, and he was certainly not the "type" Ollie had dated in the past. No, Ollie had always linked himself with other men like himself. They were usually older, professionals, college-educated, with comfortable incomes, nice homes, late-model cars, and designer clothes. They were the kind of men the term metrosexual had been invented for.

Hank was nothing like any of them. He was streetwise, brash. A tough guy. With his tattoos, red mohawk, grunge attire, and cigarettes, he was exactly the kind of guy Ollie would have said was exactly what he did *not* want.

Wasn't it funny how life continually surprised us, throwing curve balls our way? Maybe it was partly because Hank was so different that Ollie was drawn to him. Ollie couldn't deny that, when he was alone, he had thought of exploring Hank's naked body and finding tattoos he kept hidden. He also couldn't deny that, in weak moments, the young man was fodder for some of his filthiest fantasies.

He grinned. But the grin quickly turned to a frown as he looked up and down the now-empty late-night street and saw no sign of Hank. In the short time they had been together, an absence like this had never occurred.

They had always been together in the evenings.

Like a family.

"Hank, where are you?"

Only a breeze that rustled the leaves of the big maple tree across from the front porch answered.

Wearily, Ollie rose from the stoop and brushed off the back of his pants with his hands. He would go inside, climb the stairs, and crawl into bed.

He knew he wouldn't sleep. At least not until he heard the click and creak of the front door opening and closing and Hank's tread upon the stairs.

Chapter
TWELVE

HANK SAT alone in Volunteer Park. The park was officially closed, and he knew he could get in trouble if one of Seattle's finest were to come by, stealthily rolling on the broad roadway behind him. There would be a spotlight, a single whoop from a siren, and questions, lots of questions. For a former homeless boy with an arrest under his belt for possession, those questions could lead to big, jeopardizing trouble.

The smart thing to do, thought Hank, would be to take one of the shadowy sidewalks leading out of the park and find somewhere else to sit and ruminate. This part of Capitol Hill had many shady areas where he could certainly find an empty curb where he could sit and smoke, be alone with his thoughts.

But he liked it here, in front of the Asian Art Museum. Before him was a big sculpture that had a large center hole cut in it, perfectly framing the Space Needle, now lit up like a beacon against the black and starless night.

He wasn't thinking, at the moment, about Ollie and the night of drama they had had, although thoughts of that had tormented him early on. They were the reason he needed to be alone.

Now he was thinking of Lula. Theirs had always been a contentious relationship, yet somehow there had always been lots of love to go around between Lula, Hank, and his sister. There certainly wasn't much of anything else to go around, including sometimes food and clothing. But their poverty always, especially when Hank was growing up, made it seem like it was them against the world. And that feeling created a sense of closeness, one that might not be apparent to outsiders, who saw only a straggling white trash family with a mother far too young to have two kids.

Hank had never been one to put much stock in such things as psychic phenomena, dismissing them as the fancies of the rich, who populated their movies and TV shows with stories that could never happen.

Yet now Hank wasn't so sure.

He remembered lots about Lula. But at this very moment, he was thinking about their last time together.

In her last days, Lula had lain in a bed in a ward dedicated to "charity care" at Bay View Hospital in Seattle's First Hill neighborhood. All around her were others too poor to afford healthcare, but lucky enough to find mercy.

Hank sat next to the bed, as he had for the past several days, as Lula drifted in and out of consciousness, pressing the little button that would administer more morphine regularly when she did stir.

Although he never dared let himself consciously think it, there was a deep knowledge, a certainty within him, that told him these were his mother's last days. That's why he hardly ever left her side. Indeed, it was why he practically never let go of her hand, small as a child's.

He would think how fragile she looked propped up on the pillows, how the cancer had robbed her of the only currency she had ever been able to trade on: her looks. Now, she was a withered thing, a wraith. A shadow, as they say, of her former self.

On the last night of Lula Menninger's life, Hank felt he had connected with his mother in a way much deeper than the touch of their two hands. Hank had been about to doze off when he awakened to find Lula looking at him, her eyes bright and clear.

"My boy," she whispered.

The two of them had simply stared for the longest time, and Hank felt like there was an energy passing through their clenched hands. Lula's grip grew tighter than he had felt it in a long time, almost as if she feared letting go.

And in that quiet moment in the middle of the night, Hank had seen flickering images, like a montage from a movie, in his mind's eye. He saw things he couldn't have possibly known about.

There was a little girl Lula, looking only about Addison's age, on a sun-dappled street, riding a Big Wheel down its cracked cement surface, squealing. Her auburn hair was pulled up in pigtails, and she was laughing, being chased by an older man Hank knew, from pictures he had seen, was his grandfather. The man had left Lula and her mother behind not long after Lula had entered second grade.

And there she was, a young girl, maybe thirteen or so, at a kitchen table with a pile of books before her and a notebook open. Hank somehow knew Lula was supposed to have been doing homework and could practically hear in his own mind a younger version of his grandmother's voice telling Lula, "And you best not get up from that table until you get it all done, miss."

But Lula wasn't doing homework. On the blank sheet of notebook paper before her, she doodled hearts, dozens of hearts, all of them surrounding a boy's name—Kevin. Below the hearts Lula had written "Mrs. Kevin McElhaney" and "Lula McElhaney."

Hank didn't know who Kevin was, and he was fairly sure his mother had never mentioned a Kevin, even though there had been many men cycling in and out of her life over the years.

He saw Lula as a young woman, in her early twenties, on the back of a motorcycle, fiercely hugging the back of a dark-haired, bearded man wearing no helmet, aviator sunglasses, and a black Harley Davidson T-shirt that clung tightly to his physique, showing off the powerful musculature beneath.

Hank could see in Lula's eyes, beneath the wild mane of hair swirling about her gorgeous and unlined face… joy. Hank picked up on the sense that Lula felt invincible in this moment, young and alive, and that she wished this moment, this closeness, could continue forever. She even thought it would.

She was in love, and love guaranteed a life filled with happiness, with pleasure, with joy. From here on out, with this man, life would be perfect. Happy ever after.

In that moment Hank saw into Lula's imaginings, saw the children she would have with this man, the life they would build together, the home, the years growing old, the rockers on some front porch.

It was too perfect.

There was another memory, quick, a Christmas morning Hank remembered from his childhood. Lula watched, smiling, as Hank opened a box within which was Pepper, a black Cocker Spaniel and Poodle mix he and Stacy had gotten when they were only seven or eight. The puppy had leaped from the box and immediately begun licking Hank's face. They had all laughed, until he presented his next trick—turning in a circle and taking a runny shit on the living room rug.

Whatever happened to Pepper?

The memories suddenly came to darkness, and he looked over at Lula, whose eyes were shining. It looked like she was trying to say something, but her tongue confounded her.

Hank rose at once, taking his mother in his arms, feeling her bird bones fragile in his grip. "Mommy," he whispered, reverting back to a child. "What, Mommy?"

But Lula had only strength enough, he guessed, to do one thing. She could speak or she could cling to him tightly. She chose the latter. Hank held on, whispering in her ear, "I love you, Mommy. Love you, love you, love you, and I always will."

He continued the litany until she grew limp in his arms and he knew she was gone. He had waited, alone, with her until morning's light gradually gave form and definition to the room.

A nurse came in and gently pulled Hank away.

He got up and stood near the doorway as other medical professionals hurried in, but he already knew what they would confirm.

He turned to walk down the hallway, feeling more alone than he ever had in his life, and wondered if Lula had actually told him about her memories.

How else could he have experienced them?

Now, as he sat here in the dark that seemed to grow chillier by the minute, he knew that, in some way, his and Lula's minds, for the briefest moment, had become one.

It was that possibility that set him on his feet and made him begin the long walk home.

He now knew there was no reason to keep his feelings for Ollie a secret.

We all had so little time.

Chapter THIRTEEN

OLLIE WOKE to the sound of his bedroom door opening. Immediately, he was frightened, disoriented. He thought that there was no more terrifying sound than being alone in bed and suddenly realizing there was someone in the room with you.

Ollie liked it dark when he slept and had his blinds pulled tight against the feeble light of the moon and stars. He raised his head from his pillow, heart thudding, and peered intently into the pitch. He could make out a figure standing poised near the door, but it was nothing more than a dark shape.

He managed to find his voice. "Who's there?" he croaked out into the darkness, pulling the sheet up to his neck for the scant protection it would give.

"It's just me, Ollie."

The voice was familiar. Immediately, Ollie's respiration and heartbeat began to slow. "Hank? What are you doing?"

He heard a rustling sound as Hank moved closer to the bed, and in the dim light, he could just begin to make out Hank's features, shadowy and vague. "I'm sorry I woke you."

Ollie sat up a little straighter in the bed, his back against the headboard. "It's okay. Is everything all right?"

He could hear Hank breathing, quick, as though he was nervous. He could smell him too: a mixture of cigarettes and sweat that did not, surprisingly enough, conjure up anything other than a pleasurable association in Ollie's mind. Ollie repeated his question about things being all right.

In response, Hank moved closer, and Ollie felt the opposite side of the bed weighed down as Hank sat. Ollie had a quick thought that this was probably not the most appropriate employer/employee interaction, but that was quashed by the late-night hour. With the world turned down to silence all around them, somehow this closeness seemed right.

But what did Hank want?

"Ollie?"

"Yeah?"

"Everything *is* all right, you know."

"Good. I'm glad to hear it. I sat out on the porch for a long time, just waiting for you to come back. I was worried about you."

"Ah… in a weird way, that's nice, man." Hank went on. "I haven't had anyone worry about me, not for a long, long time."

"I'm sorry to hear that, Hank. Didn't your mom?" Ollie knew that Hank had recently lost his mother and knew too that she had raised him alone, though he didn't know much beyond these simple facts.

Ollie cocked his head as he heard a short hiccup of breath from Hank. "Sweetie, are you sure you're okay? It sounds like you're crying."

Hank didn't say anything for a long time, and when Ollie reached across him toward the little lamp he had on his nightstand, Hank said, "Don't. I like the dark. It makes it easier to talk."

"Okay." Ollie settled back against the pillows, the nearness of Hank at once comforting, worrisome, and arousing. He longed to reach out and touch him, to at least grasp his hand, but was afraid his actions would be misinterpreted, no matter how innocent, seeing how it was just the two of them alone in his bedroom.

Ollie felt Hank swing his legs up, and then Hank was next to him, also leaning against the headboard, his legs stretched out before him. Ollie could feel the length of his body against his own, just barely a whisper of a touch.

They said nothing for the longest time until Ollie asked, "Where did you go tonight?" He considered what he asked next very carefully, but he had to know. "Did you do something you regret?"

Hank laughed softly. "You mean like drugs?"

"I mean like drugs."

"Nah. I still dream about the shit I used to do, sometimes. I get it in my head that I want it again. I guess that will always be with me. But then I think about how corrosive that crap was, how it sapped my spirit and my body, and I know I don't ever want to go back to that again."

"That's good."

Hank stood. Ollie looked over and was able to discern that Hank was getting undressed. Ollie himself had slumbered naked beneath the sheets. "What are you doing?"

"Haven't your eyes adjusted enough to know?" Hank barked out a short laugh. Ollie listened as Hank's jeans fell to the floor, the chain he had attached to his wallet landing with a clunk on the hardwood.

Hank slid in next to him and pulled the sheet up over both of them. Ollie swallowed but found little spit in his mouth as he felt the long, naked length of Hank beside him once more.

Ollie moved away, confused. "I don't know what's going on here."

"Shhh." Hank planted a quick kiss on Ollie's cheek, then relaxed against the pillow. "You asked where I went tonight." He paused, as though he was considering it. "I went to see my mom, I guess you could say."

"I thought she was—"

"Dead?"

"Well, yeah."

"She is. But in a lot of ways, she's still with me. She'll always be with me. A weird thing happened between us the night she died." And Hank told Ollie all about how he had seen snippets of his mother's life just before she passed away, images that revealed precious moments of hope and joy. "For a long time, I thought she must have told me those things— you know, out loud—and somehow my brain screwed it all up."

Hank sighed. "But she was too weak to talk, too weak to do anything, really, other than summon up enough energy to make her way out of this world. I think, in those last moments, she shared with me some of the happiness of her life. Happy moments were all too few and far between, but I like to think these memories saw her off." Hank was quiet, and Ollie knew better than to interrupt with questions.

"Do you think I'm weird for believing that?"

"No, no, of course not. And I believe that could happen."

"Ollie? You know I think the world of you. You know you're a kind of hero to me."

"Ah, I just did what anyone would do."

"No, man, that's bullshit. What anyone would do, the night we met, was to toss my sorry ass to the cops. And that would have probably been the smart thing, the wise thing to do. Why didn't you?"

Ollie closed his eyes, reveling in the warmth of Hank beside him. He didn't know what any of this meant, but in spite of his bewilderment, he enjoyed it just the same. "I didn't because I went with my gut. I didn't see a criminal that night. I saw someone who was desperate and hungry." Ollie chuckled. "I can't help it. It's always been my 'thing' to feed people. I got that from my Italian family. My nana used to make us eat until we thought we'd burst when we went to her house. '*Mangia! Mangia!*' she'd say."

Ollie shifted in the bed and allowed himself to reach out and lay his hand on Hank's chest. When he didn't move, he stroked the smooth skin there lightly. "I think fate put us in each other's path. Do you believe in fate?"

"I do now."

They fell to silence once more. After a while, Ollie began to wonder if Hank's even breathing meant the younger man had drifted off, but then Hank said, "I don't want you to go out with that guy, that Mike, this Friday."

Ollie, stunned, sat up straighter in bed. "What?" A burst of laughter escaped him.

"I can't stand the thought of you with anyone else."

"Hank? What are you telling me?" Although getting naked and crawling into bed with another man was a pretty fair indicator of gayness, Ollie still hadn't quite wrapped his upper head around the idea. His lower head, however, was simply going with its instincts and had raised itself up to full mast, a fact Ollie was both afraid and hopeful Hank would soon discover. "You're gay?" Up until this very night, Ollie swore to himself, he'd had no idea.

Hank nudged him with his bare shoulder. "What gave you the first clue?" He laughed. "I don't know. I mean, yeah, hell yeah, I am. Never really thought about being anything else."

"Why didn't you ever tell me? You knew I was."

"I don't know why." Hank paused, then continued. "Or maybe I do. Being gay and sex and all that shit was so mixed up in my past." He sighed. "You don't want to hear this."

"I do, Hank, I do."

"You won't hate me?"

Ollie had always had ideas about Hank, about why he had ended up in such dire straits at such a young age, but he also knew he was a young guy trying so hard to make something of himself. He figured it was never worth it to press him on his past, so long as he worked hard and never gave him a reason to wonder. "Hank, I couldn't hate you. We all have pasts."

Hank snorted; there was bitterness in that simple sound. "Maybe you shouldn't answer so fast." Hank sat up, facing away from Ollie. In the dark, Ollie could trace the bumps along Hank's spine, and he had an almost irresistible urge to sit up and plant a kiss on each one.

"I'm just gonna spit this out. But you need to know who's under your roof. If you don't want me around after you hear this, I'll understand."

"Oh Hank, I could never—"

"Just shut up, okay? Listen." Hank's arms went up and he rubbed his head. "I was, I am, a crystal meth addict. I haven't done it for a long time, but like I said before, once you fall down that hole, it changes you. You never completely escape the want for it, even though you know it'll kill you eventually. Anyway, I used to do that shit—they call it Tina, you know. Cutesy name for poison. Once upon a time, I was big into it. It started out so simple. Some guy in a bar took me into the restroom and let me snort a little.

"Fuck. I still remember that night. I thought it was the best sex ever. That guy and me—we fucked all night long. Literally. That's what Tina does to you. That's how that bitch ropes you in.

"That little snort opened up this big yawning need inside me, man. A few snorts from a pen cap led to smoking the shit and finally slamming."

"Slamming?" Ollie didn't know, at first, what the term meant. In this moment, he suddenly felt that he was the younger of the men in the room. He had heard of guys doing meth, had even been offered it once or twice, but he had just never come into the drug's orbit much. It was something he never really thought about.

"Slamming. Injecting. The first time I did it, I felt like the whole world had turned golden. I was hornier than I had ever been and, at the same time, I was like this thing that could never be satisfied."

Ollie could see Hank slowly shaking his head. "Ah, you don't need to hear all the details. My habit went very fast from being a fun weekend kind of thing to a daily ritual of shooting up, whenever and wherever I could. I whored myself out for the drug. I'd find guys partying on Craigslist, at the bathhouses." Hank chanced a look over his shoulder at Ollie, and then turned away again. He said, very softly, "I'd have sex with anyone, and I do mean anyone, who could get me high. Fuck knows I couldn't afford to keep buying it. So I traded what I had.

"And then I got caught, smoking up with some dude in the wee hours of the morning in a fucking public park. The Tina was his, as was the pipe, but they still busted me for possession.

"Best thing that ever happened to me. Since I didn't have a record, and the amount we had was so small, I didn't have to do much time. But I learned that things would only get worse for me if I kept it up. Jail was what led me to Haven."

Hank bent over, placing his head in his hands. Ollie wasn't sure what to say. He really wasn't all that surprised. He was more surprised, he supposed, that Hank was gay, that he was next to him in bed. And what the hell was up with that?

"So you want me to get my shit together in the morning? Get the fuck out? You and Rose can manage." Hank stood up. Ollie could hear the break in his words and breath and knew he was close to, or was already, crying. "I don't blame you, man."

"Sit back down," Ollie said. "Don't be stupid."

Hank sat gingerly on the edge of the bed.

"Your past is your past. You can't change that. The only thing you can affect is the present and the future. And you're doing that, Hank. That's what I see. I'm glad you told me about your past. But all it does, really, is show me how far you've come."

"Really?"

"Yeah, sure." Ollie pulled Hank closer to him and was surprised that the feel of him, for the moment anyway, was not arousing lust. The moment was too fraught with unburdening, with meaning, to reduce it to sex.

At least for now.

"Why did you tell me all this, though?"

"Because you asked why I never told you I was gay."

Ollie shook his head. "I don't get it."

Hank blew out a sigh. "Sex, love, all that happy horseshit got so screwed up by Tina, I didn't know if I was capable of just having regular sex again, of ever having normal feelings for a guy. You know what? I haven't had sex without that shit coursing through my veins in years. I don't even know what it's like." This last, Hank spat out. "So I didn't really know what the fuck I was. Gay? Are you gay if you've kind of sworn off sex, if you can't have it without being high?"

"You can't?"

"I don't know."

"Wanna try?" Ollie laughed.

"What?"

"I'm fuckin' with you, man. Or I guess I should say I'm kidding. I think you're so hot, Hank, but if we ever head off in that direction, I know tonight is not the night. Even though we're here, together, naked."

"Yeah, we are. And I've got wood." Hank reached down between his thighs.

"I do too. But we both know this would not be a good first time, right?"

"You're so smart."

"Well, maybe I'll be thinking I'm so stupid in the morning for not pouncing on you."

"You can, you know. I want it." Hank brought his face close to Ollie's. "And that's a kind of first for me, man. I haven't wanted it without drugs in a long time."

"I know." Ollie hugged him, then flattened the sheet between them, cutting off the line of electricity where their skin met. "But it'll be better if we wait. Trust me."

"I know." Hank flopped back on the bed, his head near Ollie's shoulder. "When I saw you flirting with that guy tonight, Mike, it just made me so jealous. Furious!"

Ollie laughed.

"Don't laugh, man. It hurt!"

"Oh, I'm sorry."

"It made me realize that I cared about you. Don't go out with him, okay?"

Ollie didn't know what to say. After all Hank had told him tonight, he wasn't really sure what he thought about Mike anymore, although when he had left his place, he had been anticipating their date, and the sex that would follow for sure, with excitement.

Now Mike just seemed, well, trivial.

"I'll think about canceling."

"Okay," Hank said softly. He stood. "I should let you sleep."

"Like I'm going to sleep after this."

"You wanna go downstairs? Make some biscuits?" Hank asked.

"Oh, honey, you are a man after my own heart."

"I am, Ollie, I am. After it. In a big way." Hank pulled his jeans on and wandered out of the room. The electric blue light of dawn filled the room. Ollie could see Hank where he'd paused at the head of the stairs. "You coming, Ollie?"

"What a question. I'll be right there."

Chapter FOURTEEN

BAD ASS BROCCOLI SOUP

(Serves 4)

- 1 tablespoon butter
- 1 tablespoon olive oil
- 1 medium onion, diced
- 4 cloves garlic, minced
- 1 medium baking potato, peeled and diced
- 4 cups chopped broccoli
- 32 ounces chicken or vegetable stock
- 1/2 pint heavy cream
- Salt and pepper to taste
- Optional: Crushed red pepper flakes, shredded cheese (a cup or so)

Heat oil and butter until hot, add onions and garlic and sauté until soft, about five minutes. Add potato, stir to coat with butter/oil. Add broccoli and stock, bring to a boil and simmer for half an hour.

Puree in blender or food processor (or use an immersion blender if you have one), return to pan, stir in cream. Heat to just below boiling (do not boil).

HANK EYED the biscuits he had made, lined up on baking pans and ready to go into the oven. They would accompany the broccoli soup Ollie was busy preparing. The rhythmic thwack of Ollie's knife against the butcher's block as he diced potatoes was a comforting sound. It was nice, the two of them being alone in the kitchen, working as a team. It felt comfortable and harmonious.

He relished this time with Ollie without having to share him with Rose and Addison. It was all the more precious because he knew the two ladies of the house would be up and about soon, and everything would change.

He had told Ollie. *Everything.* All the bad stuff. All the good. He had revealed himself, laid himself open and vulnerable. Taken a chance. And Ollie had not judged him or seen him differently. It was a more powerful gift, Hank was sure, than Ollie even realized.

"I can put those in the oven for you if you want to go shower or something. I'll put coffee on too." Ollie smiled at him and Hank noted there was something delightfully shy in the smile, a different kind of warmth than had been there before they had had their little talk upstairs. Ollie's eyes met Hank's own, he thought, with a kind of hunger Hank found delightful.

"I'm not ready to shower yet, but I would like to, um…." He looked toward the back door.

"Go on. Indulge your filthy habit."

Hank was out the door quickly, thinking he now had another reason to say good-bye to cigarettes once and for all—Ollie. *Man, can you imagine the joy on his face when I tell him I've quit?*

For now, though, he brought the cigarette to his lips, lit it, and reveled in the calm that spread though his lungs along with the smoke. He sat down on the steps of their deck and looked out at a pale blue sky, tinged with gold. Along the sparse grass of their small backyard, tendrils of fog floated like ghosts, foretelling another sunny Seattle summer day.

It was summer when Hank had first come to Seattle. He was eighteen years old, fresh out of Summitville High School, and had taken a Greyhound bus across the country to get to this city surrounded by water and bordered by mountains. Hank had never been there, knew little about it beyond its reputation as the birthplace of grunge (Lula had been a Nirvana fan and had had a huge crush on Kurt Cobain; in retrospect, Hank knew he had too).

He chose the Emerald City for one simple reason: he looked at a map and saw it as one of the places farthest away from his hometown. In his eighteen-year-old mind, being far away meant reinvention and fresh starts. Innocently, he thought he could leave all of his problems behind. Begin anew. He was not mature enough to know yet that our demons follow us wherever we roam.

He plotted the move all of his senior year of high school, selling almost all of his meager belongings off one by one until he was left with almost nothing, save for the paltry funds that would purchase a cross-country bus ticket.

He had pored over pictures of Seattle at Summitville's Carnegie Library downtown and knew the first place he wanted to go was a park he saw in a Seattle guidebook: Kerry Park at the top of Queen Anne Hill.

That place was what he recalled when he remembered his first morning in Seattle. Although he arrived in town just about penniless, he was filled with hope. That hope was what gave him the energy to hike all the way from the bus station to the park he had read about, getting lost several times in the process, but finally making it to his destination very early in the morning.

The park, a small lookout really, was empty, and for the first time in his life, Hank's breath was literally taken away by a view. It was the stuff he had dreamed of. The pictures he had seen online on the library's computer could not begin to do the vista in front of him justice. With a panorama this gorgeous spread out before him, he felt like nothing could go wrong. Never mind that he didn't have enough money in his pockets now to buy even a decent breakfast, let alone provide a roof over his head.

But all of those concerns were trivial at this quiet moment, with the sun just risen.

Hank sat down on one of the benches and sighed, taking it all in. Spread out before him was the wonder of the downtown skyline and the blue waters of Elliott Bay. A green-trimmed white ferry cut through the serene and sparkling water, heading toward what Hank now knew was Bainbridge Island. He admired the Space Needle, which had been kind of like a beacon for him over the past year. It was an icon, something he'd think of in the worst moments of his last year in high school, knowing that the monument awaited him on the other coast.

But what really caught Hank's eye was the ethereal majesty of Mount Rainier, rising up seemingly out of a bank of clouds to the right of the city's skyline. The white-capped mountain didn't seem real, but some monumental force of nature conjured up by the most powerful of sorcerers. It appeared to float on clouds.

Now, Hank thought of how he needed to take Addison over to the park and share the view with her. It was a view that had given him hope and inspiration.

He leaned back on the deck, supporting himself with his outstretched arms, after taking a last drag off his cigarette and dropping the butt in a sand-filled diced tomato can Ollie had provided for him. The view of this backyard certainly wasn't as majestic, but it was home. And that, in and of itself, made the view here—some scraggly grass, a bank of blackberry vines climbing up a weathered fence, and a towering fir—all the more special.

It was something Hank had thought he'd never have.

When Lula was dying, she had gone from being the rough-edged woman Hank had learned to tolerate and sometimes love, to someone more philosophical, and right now, something she had said to him came back:

"I read in some magazine somewhere, or maybe I heard it on TV. Dr. Phil? Oprah? Whatever. The point is that we all come into this world filled with light and our job is to keep that light glowing. Because you know what happens if we let the light go out?"

Hank could see her, so frail, almost like a kid propped up against the starchy hospital pillows. "You don't have to pay the electric anymore?"

Lula's eyes narrowed and a little of the old, feisty mother he remembered came back for a second. "Don't be a smartass." She closed her eyes for a second. Then she grabbed his hand. "If you let your light go out, honey, it means you lost hope." She squeezed his hand. "Hope is what keeps us alive. Hope is what makes life worth living. Remember."

Hank stared down at the weathered wood of the deck between his bare feet, debated whether he should light up another smoke. He realized he now had more hope than he had ever had in his whole life. He had Addison. He had Rose. He even had Ollie, in a way, and hope was the thing that made it possible to dare believe love might bloom on the horizon.

He had more hope, more light, this very morning than he'd had that morning four years ago at Kerry Park, looking down on the city that would become his home.

He gave in and lit it up another smoke, remembering the times that had ensued after that morning when he first arrived. The years had certainly gotten off to a promising start. Within days, Hank had found work, helping a guy down in Burien build a house with a waterfront view. He had fallen into the job easily, following up on a lead another kid had given him about hanging out at the Home Depot on North Aurora Avenue, where people often sought cheap help for construction and home improvement projects.

He had worked with the guy for almost two years on his Burien house, but also on other houses the guy bought and then flipped or rented out. Hank made some decent money, all under the table, and had become his benefactor's right hand man. Until coming to the Pacific Northwest, Hank had no idea how handy he was.

He could have had a future in construction, even though that had never been his dream. But he ruined it all by fooling around in one of houses they were working on after hours with a guy who, like himself, had been picked up from Home Depot to work on fixing up yet another home renovation.

Hank smiled ruefully as he remembered Carlos and his gorgeous deep brown eyes, Mexican accent, and panther tattoo across his chest. Hank couldn't resist Carlos when he came on to him.

When Hank's employer found the two young men naked in an empty room just as twilight was changing the sky from purple to navy, with Hank clutching a sawhorse in his hands as Carlos pounded him relentlessly from behind, it was all over.

Both were fired on the spot.

But even that was okay, because Hank had saved up some money and was able to get himself couch space in an apartment with a bunch of other gay guys his own age on Bellevue Avenue in the Capitol Hill neighborhood.

He probably could have found another job easily, since he now had mad skills with a hammer and saw, but Tina found him first, in the restroom of a bar.

Everything went downhill fast after that.

Hank would have thought his light had been extinguished.

"What are you thinking about? I swear you look a million miles away."

Hank turned to see Ollie staring through the screen door at him. Hank stood up, brushing off the back of his jeans with his hands. "Sorry."

Ollie put up his hands. "No worries. We're at a good point in the prep work. Relax. You can even go back to bed for a couple hours if you want. We were up at the crack of dawn."

"We were up all night. Well, I was anyway." Hank came back into the kitchen—redolent with the yeasty smell of the biscuits, which Ollie had baked while Hank was outside. They now cooled on the countertop, their golden tops dusted with baking powder.

"That sounds like a good idea, man." Hank imagined a couple of more hours of slumber, dreaming of Ollie.

But why just dream?

Without stopping to give it much consideration, he grabbed one of Ollie's hands. "Come with me?"

"Where? Upstairs?" Ollie eyed him with an expression Hank could easily read. It said, "Are you sure?"

"Yeah. I kept you up. You could probably use some more sleep too, man." Hank's eyes rolled up to the ceiling. "I think our ladies will sleep a couple more hours, if I know them." Addison already had a teenager's propensity for sleeping in until noon.

Ollie chuckled as though he was laughing at a whispered dirty joke. "I don't know if we'll get all that much sleep."

"There's only one way to find out." Hank tugged at Ollie's hand.

But Ollie hung back. He cocked his head, eyeing Hank. "I thought we talked about this. About waiting. About taking our time." He reached out to ruffle the longer hair in the middle of Hank's head. "It makes good sense, Hank."

"Sure it does." He grinned. "I wasn't being sarcastic. It does make sense." He closed his eyes, considering his next words. He knew they could be thought of as words of seduction, but he also knew they were so much more: they were words that could be life changing. "Before you even say it, I know what you're thinking. We're moving too fast." He grabbed Ollie's other hand and squeezed both briefly, then continued to hang on. "And we are. Shit, yeah. Way too fast. All kinds of trouble could arise from the next steps we take. So we should sit down and consider very carefully what we're doing."

"Yeah, right," Ollie said softly. Was there disappointment in his voice?

"But Ollie, one thing I've learned in the fucked-up mess I've made of my life, a life you helped put back on track, is that *everything* moves fast. By its very nature, life moves fast. We can only hang on and hope for the best."

"Aren't you the wise one?" Ollie grinned.

"Me?" Hank laughed. "Not at all, man. But I do know that I didn't understand what love was until I met you. Speaking of too fast? I look back now and can see I fell in love with you the moment you set that plate of food in front of me. I was a no-good, thieving derelict, yet *you* moved fast. You took a chance. You fed me." Hank let go of one of Ollie's hands to swipe angrily at his eyes, where he could feel the hot pinprick of tears forming. He laughed, suddenly feeling self-conscious about his introspection. "It didn't hurt either that you were one hot man. I think, that night, it was more than the food that made my mouth water."

They both laughed, and Hank was thrilled to see a bloom of red rise to Ollie's cheeks.

Ollie then spoke so softly Hank had to strain to hear. "Wait a minute. You're in love with me?"

Hank shrugged and then nodded. "I would say that you should have seen it, but I don't think *I* even realized it until last night. I don't think I recognized it right away because I had never been in love before; I didn't know what it felt like." He kissed Ollie's lips lightly. "Now I do."

"This is too fast," Ollie repeated.

"Yup. No argument here. And if you want to wait, I can do that too. But listen—you moved fast when you brought me in and fed me; you moved fast when you rode me home with that big box of food for Addison and me, when you didn't even know if that little girl existed; you moved fast when you offered me a job." Hank moved toward the stairs, tugging Ollie along behind. "Life moves way faster than we can keep up. Crazy, crazy, crazy. But I believe in listening to whatever it is—instinct, a little voice inside, our *hearts*—because that, whatever you call it, is what tells the truth."

"So, for that reason, we should sleep together?"

Hank punched Ollie on the arm lightly. "Yeah… and because I love you and think you probably love me, a little bit anyway. But that'll change once I get you into bed. Then you'll be over the moon." Hank laughed. "And because you're super hot and I want to taste you all over. I want to feel you inside me and me inside you. I wanna make you sweat, buddy."

Ollie looked down pointedly at the front of his flannel sleep pants, which had tented out in front at Hank's words. He guffawed.

Hank hugged him, pressing up against Ollie's cock. "For that reason too."

"Ah, what the hell?" Ollie said, voice husky. "I'm no different than any other man on this planet."

"How's that?"

"I only have enough blood to think with one head at a time."

"Go upstairs?"

"Upstairs. Now," Ollie responded, and this time it was Ollie who tugged Hank toward the stairs.

Even though they took the stairs quickly, Hank felt like they were endless. Now that he had not only told Ollie about his past, but also confessed his love and attraction, it was as though a dam had burst. As they headed up the stairs, he felt like his feelings had been building up for a lot longer than he realized. They were aching for release.

And so was he.

In the bedroom, he turned to Ollie, suddenly shy. It had been so long since he had done this—had sex with a guy when he was fully in possession of his senses, when he was not listening to the racing course of a drug in his veins—that he was uncertain how to proceed.

Ollie moved toward him and placed a hand tentatively on Hank's chest, staring into his eyes. Hank covered Ollie's hand with his. "No words, okay?" He lifted the hand and kissed it. "We've talked enough."

"A man of action. I like that." Ollie grinned.

Hank put a finger to Ollie's lips to silence him, and then he replaced that finger with his lips. He kissed Ollie gently at first, delighting in the tickle of Ollie's dark, coarse beard against his skin. Feeling Ollie's body pressed against his own flipped a switch inside him, ramping up the hunger, the need that had lain dormant for a long time and was now suddenly ablaze, like a caged animal that had at last been set free.

Hank's kiss went from gentle to hard and hungry within seconds. Conscious thought went out the window, replaced by a desperate need, 100 percent physical. Hank's tongue pried Ollie's lips apart, invading the hot cave of his mouth. He pressed the full length of his body against Ollie's, lifting one leg a bit so he could grind against his crotch harder.

Hank was afraid he'd come in his pants, the sensations pulsing through him were so electric. And so sublime. His cock twitched in anticipation.

"Can we lie down before I shoot?" Hank asked.

Ollie's eyebrows came together. "Already?"

"Already. Man, it's been so fuckin' long," Hank said breathlessly, tugging at his clothes to get out of them as quickly as possible. They landed in a heap on the floor. He fell back onto the bed, his cock pointing up at his face, precome dribbling down the shaft.

Ollie eyed him. "I do believe that is one of the most beautiful sights I've ever seen." And he reached out to grab Hank's cock.

"Don't," Hank said, swallowing hard, squeezing his eyes together. *Wait. Wait. Not yet.* His breath came even quicker. "You so much as touch it and it's gonna blast. I swear."

"And that's a bad thing?"

Hank just shook his head, feeling for the first time in a long time that this drug he had done a deadly dance with, this Tina, was no match for the potent cocktail of love and pure, unadulterated lust. "I wanna see you get undressed, man. I wanna see you fuckin' naked."

Ollie grinned at him, never disengaging his gaze from Hank's. He stripped much slower than Hank did, teasing. Even though he had on only a pair of sleep pants, he took his time about taking them off, turning around to hide his dick as he lowered the pants.

Hank took it all in. Ollie may have thought he was hiding the prize, but Ollie's ass was certainly no runner-up. Firm, round, and creamy white, it was dusted in contrasting dark hair. When he bent over to remove his pants completely, Hank could see Ollie's ring of muscle, puckered, looking delicious.

And then Ollie turned around and Hank caught his breath. Ollie was all man—fur-covered, muscular, hard, with just the tiniest—and manliest—bit of a potbelly. His nipples were pink and stood out like pencil erasers, rimmed in the same dusky hair. Between his thighs rose one of the most perfect dicks Hank had even seen. It was thick, and its head was a deep purple almost like a plum, bulbous and leaking like Hank's own.

Hank dropped to his knees and crawled over to Ollie. "Remember, not a word." He began by kissing Ollie's feet, all over. He lifted one of Ollie's legs so he could take his toes one by one into his mouth.

Ollie groaned.

Hank moved upward, kissing the muscular calves, laving Ollie's inner thighs, until at last he arrived at Ollie's cock.

Ollie was not like so many other gay men, Hank thought, who shaved their balls and the area around their cocks. No, Ollie let what nature put there flourish, and the dark hair framed the straining cock perfectly.

Hank kissed the tip, scooping up some of Ollie's precome with his tongue. He wanted it to be slow. Everything inside told him he should take it slow, licking the shaft from the root to the tip of its weeping head, but Hank couldn't help himself. He swallowed Ollie's cock with one fluid motion, all the way down to the rough pubes. He wanted it so bad, he was in no danger of gagging. Mouth full of thick cock, he looked up at Ollie, whose head was thrown back in what Hank could only assume was ecstasy.

Hank moved his mouth up the shaft, swirling his tongue around it, letting his spit make Ollie's cock deliciously warm and wet. Then he went back down again, burying his face in Ollie crotch, breathing in his scent, his essence.

Hank's hand was not on his own cock, not at all. One hand gripped and tugged at Ollie's balls, while the other helped him keep his balance on the wooden floor. Yet in spite of the fact Hank was not touching himself, he looked down to see white arcs of come jet out of his cock to puddle on the floor, to at last run down his thighs.

He closed his eyes, surrendering to the tremors that coursed through him seismically. Then he looked up at Ollie, all contrition. "Sorry, man. I didn't mean to come so fast. But it's been so long. And you. Are. So. Fuckin'. Hot."

Ollie stroked his own cock, breathing fast and Hank thought he might come too, but what happened instead was he said, "I want to taste you." And he got down on his knees with Hank, bent over, and licked

Hank's come up from the floor. Some of the white stuff adhered to Ollie's lower lip as he leaned forward to hungrily kiss Hank.

Hank could taste his own come in and on Ollie's mouth, and the thrill of that made him get rock hard all over again. He reached down, squeezed his dick, pressing it downward and watching as it sprang back up, slapping against his belly.

They both laughed.

"Wanna fuck?" Hank asked.

"Who fucks who?" Ollie asked.

Hank didn't really care. It was all about the connection. All about having Ollie pressed close, their two bodies sharing this incendiary heat. But the moment demanded an answer, so Hank went with logic and fairness (in all his past experience, he had yet to come down on a definitive answer to the question: are you a top or a bottom?). "You've already got your dick wet. It's my turn."

Ollie stood and Hank followed. Ollie looked over his shoulder at him, eyes shining, color high. "How do you want me?"

"On your back." Hank gave him a shove, rough, and Ollie's smile told him he liked it.

Ollie tumbled back onto the bed, grabbing a pillow to position behind his head and one under his ass, then threw his legs in the air.

Hank grinned. "Your thighs look like tree trunks. Hair-covered tree trunks."

"I thought we weren't gonna talk," Ollie said. Hank could read the naked hunger in his eyes.

"Right." Hank positioned himself, kneeling, between Ollie's spread thighs. He leaned in and kissed the sweet pucker between Ollie's ass cheeks. He stuck his tongue inside, then a finger, and then stopped to lick the entire crack. He looked up at Ollie over Ollie's belly. "You taste good."

"Shut up," Ollie gasped.

Hank went back to his work, glad now he had come so quickly. Now he could take his time and revel in the taste of Ollie's ass, fingering and tonguing it until Ollie squirmed, moaning.

Hank pulled away from Ollie's ass and Ollie wriggled on the bed, moving his ass closer.

"You wanna get fucked?" Hank asked.

"Just shut up and do it. Stick your cock in me."

Hank pressed his shaft along the length of Ollie's crack and rubbed.

Ollie whispered, "Oh God, I just want you to slide it in. Just fuckin' use spit and precome as lube."

"Bad idea," Hank said.

"I know," Ollie agreed, the regret plain in his voice. "Condoms and lube are in the shoebox under the bed."

Hank wasted no time finding what he needed. He rolled the condom on first the wrong way, had to pull it off and start over. This was after he found it impossible to open the foil wrapper, finally being forced to hand it to Ollie for help. Ollie tore it open with his teeth.

At last, cock suitably, and safely, attired, Hank poised the tip at Ollie's asshole. "You ready?"

In response, Ollie wriggled his ass down on Hank's cock, swallowing the tip of it.

"I guess so," Hank said, laughing.

"All of it. Give me every inch, man."

And Hank did.

When it was over, and Hank lay in Ollie's arms, spent, sweaty, having not a little trouble breathing, he said, "You do know how to cook, don't you?"

Ollie reached over and slapped Hank's ass.

They kissed.

Hank felt himself drifting off to sleep and wondered, just before he fell into that warm, dark embrace, if he had been asleep all along. This had been so wonderful, he thought, it had to be a dream. He would wake to the sound of a garbage truck outside, Rose pounding on his door, telling him it was time to get up.

But the solidity of Ollie's chest, his heat, the coarseness of his hair, and his scent all told Hank this was real.

Chapter FIFTEEN

OLLIE FOLLOWED Hank down the stairs, uncertain that what just happened had indeed happened. When he had taken him in, he had no idea Hank was even gay, let alone that something could form between them. Something wondrous and real....

And yet here it was, like a gift. Life had the most surprising way of flinging curve balls at us. And speaking of balls.... Ollie had to shut his eyes for a moment with the thought of Hank's red-hair-covered ones, the perfect sac holding two delicate eggs. Ollie couldn't wait to taste them again.

Ollie took in Hank's broad shoulders, how the black cotton of his T-shirt clung to them. He loved the way that same broadness tapered down to a thin waist and an ass that rose and fell as though it were almost independent of Hank, the classic bubble butt. The faded denim covering it just made it all the more tantalizing. How would they ever get any *real* cooking done now? All Ollie wanted to do was grab Hank and haul him upstairs, fuck Hank just as he had fucked Ollie. Return the favor.

Over and over, never leaving the bedroom.

Ollie shook his head to dispel the porno movie starting up in his mind. Such thoughts would have to wait. He could hear two female voices in the kitchen, which made him freeze a little. He hoped that neither had heard his and Hank's coupling.

But when he entered the kitchen, just after Ollie, it was obvious they had not. Rose was at the counter, whisking a bowl of eggs, her head bent low to the task. Addison sat at the kitchen table, stirring Nestlé's Quik into a glass of milk. There was milk spilled on the table and a trail of brown powder all around the glass.

"Looks like you got more of that chocolate-milk stuff on the table than in your glass," Hank said.

Addison, grinning, shoved the glass toward her uncle. "Then you make it."

Ollie leaned against a wall and folded his arms across his chest, simply watching. This little scene touched him in ways he could not describe. Well, maybe he could. With the morning light filtering in and the people he had gathered around him busy with nothing more than the work of making the first meal of the day, Ollie could see before him a family. It wasn't a family he had ever thought would exist and, even as he was putting it together, he had never thought to think of the unit, the tribe, the foursome, by anything as weighted and wonderful as the term "family."

But that's the only word that came to mind as he watched Rose salt and pepper the eggs and Hank mop up the mess Addison had made, handing her at last her glass of chocolate milk. She guzzled it all down in one amazing gulp, belched, wiped her mouth with the back of her hand, and held out the empty for Hank. "Hit me again, Uncle."

Hank looked over at Ollie, smiling, and Ollie's heart swelled with love. "Do you believe this shit?"

"No swears!" Addison snapped.

Hank cleared his throat. "Do you believe this little imp?"

Ollie pulled out a chair and sat down at the table. He was about to say he didn't believe, that it was hard to believe what was forming under this roof was a family, but Addison interrupted.

"What's an imp, Ollie?"

"A demon, a troublemaker. You." He winked at her, and she grinned back at him, shyly. Ollie could see she took pleasure in the term.

Rose sat down at the table with them after she put the eggs in the skillet to begin their slow cooking. Ollie had shown her how to make perfect scrambled eggs, and she now knew to allow at least half an hour to get just the right delicate curds.

"How did you sleep, Rose?" Ollie wanted so much to reach out and touch her pale white hand, lying on the maple surface of the table like a lily, but knew better. Rose was not one for touching.

"Okay," she said softly. She lifted her head to peer up at him from behind a curtain of hair partially obscuring her eyes. "Better, actually. It keeps getting better."

It did Ollie's heart good to hear that. He thought maybe Rose was beginning to put some distance between herself and her demons now that she was settled, now that she had a purpose and a feeling, he hoped, of belonging.

The four of them, save for Rose, who didn't say much, chatted about what lay ahead for each of them that day. Addison was excited about going to the park a few blocks over that had a sprinkling fountain the kids could run through. Hank reminded Ollie of the big dinner they were doing that night—for a family of seven over on Mercer Island. They made a shopping list for Rose to take to the market that afternoon.

By the time all that was accomplished, the eggs were done and the kitchen was filled with their warm, comforting smell. Rose had wanted to serve, but Hank interceded. "Let me do it." Hank bustled about the kitchen, buttering toast, filling plates with scrambled eggs, and tuning the radio on the counter to King FM, so they could listen to a little Chopin and Vivaldi while they ate.

Before Ollie put the first bite in his mouth, he had a weird thought— the scene was almost too perfect. He wondered when the other shoe would drop. *Stop it now*, he mentally told himself. *It's not like you to think this way. Just enjoy what life has placed in your path.*

Yet he had barely swallowed when there came a knock at the front door. He shifted a mouthful of eggs to one side of his mouth and asked, "Who could that be?"

Rose, across the table, looked frightened. Anything out of the norm startled the young woman. She looked like she was ready to bolt from the table, gripping its edges with fingertips gone white.

"I'll go see!" Addison slipped from her chair and was running out of the kitchen before anyone could stop her.

The squeal and single word that issued forth from the little girl's mouth seconds later froze them all in their places for just a second.

"Mommy!"

Ollie looked across the table at Hank to watch as his expression crumbled, going from confused to terrified in an instant. Rose stared into her plate.

"What's going on?" Ollie asked.

"I sure as hell don't know." Hank threw his napkin down on the table and strode quickly from the room. Ollie could hear excited voices in the entryway. He debated whether he should intrude. If this was, indeed, Mommy, then that meant Hank's sister had returned. What was her name? Tracy? No, Stacy.

Ollie had always gotten the impression from Hank that she was in prison and wouldn't be around for a long, long time. Hank had always made it seem like Addison was with them for the long term.

The eggs churned in his gut. This surprise morning visit did not bode well. Why would the woman have traveled across the country and then not at least phoned first?

"What the hell are you doing here?" Hank's voice came into the kitchen from the entryway, causing Ollie to tense at the outrage he heard and Rose to cower, sinking lower in her seat as though she wanted to vanish.

Ollie slid his chair out from the table and went into the entryway.

They were like actors on a stage, frozen in position. Hank stood, staring defiantly, hands balled tight into fists at his sides, breathing hard. Addison had her face nestled into the neck of a young woman who knelt beside her on the floor.

Ollie was surprised at the appearance of Addison's mother and Hank's sister. He had expected someone a little wild, with tattoos and dyed red hair, like Hank, attired in shredded jeans, boots, an ironic T-shirt.

But if this woman had come to their door when Ollie was alone, he might have thought the Jehovah's Witnesses were paying a visit. Stacy's hair, a rich auburn shade that looked completely natural, was pulled away from her face and arranged in a neat little bun at the nape of her neck. Even on this hot summer morning and even though Ollie knew she was only twenty-two, she looked like she was ready to head downtown to work in some staid, uptight business, accounting maybe. She wore a deep maroon suit with a pinstriped maroon and white blouse underneath. Her only concession to adornment was a pink scarf around her neck, but even the shade of pink was subdued. On her feet was the classic definition of "sensible shoes." Low-heeled pumps in a deep shade of wine.

She wore no jewelry. And on her face, as far as Ollie could tell, was not a trace of make-up.

One thing Ollie could say, though, was that Stacy didn't need make-up. What was the expression his mother used to use? Painting the peacock? That fit Stacy. She didn't need make-up. He could see she was Hank's sister. She had the same full lips and button nose. But there was a radiance to her, a clarity to her skin and eyes that practically made her glow.

When she noticed Ollie standing near the doorway to the kitchen, she smiled. Her teeth were perfect, white, even, and her smile warmed him. Still, he felt confused. In the limited conversations he had had with Hank, he had always described his sister as a wild thing, always in trouble.

Could this woman who looked like a librarian be the same girl? And, if so, what happened to her? A case of multiple personality?

Addison wriggled to be let out of her mother's grasp, but Stacy held tightly. Addison wiggled harder. "Put me down, damn it!" Stacy did so, reluctantly, and stared at her daughter, open-mouthed. The blush that rose to Stacy's cheeks was immediate. "Addison! We do not talk that way." Stacy's voice had a lilt to it; it was lovely.

This was all wrong.

"I'll talk as I damn please," Addison glared at her mother and then moved over to Hank. She grabbed on to his leg and held on. Hank put a protective arm around her.

"What the fuck are you doing here, Stace? I thought you were in jail."

The angelic demeanor faded for just an instant as a look of fury creased Stacy's features, turning her ugly. But, like a mask being slid into place, the calm, serene exterior returned, and she moved her gaze away from Hank and her daughter and settled it on Ollie. "I don't think we've met. I'm Stacy Mellinger." She moved toward Ollie, hand outstretched. "I'm Addison's mother."

Ollie shook her hand, noting that, in spite of her put-together appearance, Stacy's palms were sweating. Profusely.

"Good to meet Hank's sister at last," Ollie said, smiling to hide the uncertainty he had about whether it truly was good. He would reserve judgment on that one. "I'm Ollie D'Angelo." He discreetly wiped his hand on his shorts. "You wanna come in the kitchen? Have a cup of coffee?"

"That would be lovely," Stacy said.

"That would be lovely," Hank mocked, his voice going high. "Who the hell *are* you?"

"Hank…." Ollie gave Hank a warning look.

Stacy followed Ollie into the kitchen. Ollie looked for Rose, but she had disappeared. She probably sensed the tension hanging in the air like static electricity and had withdrawn out to the deck in back.

They gathered around the kitchen table, curiously quiet. Ollie hurried to remove their plates from breakfast, piling them up in the sink. He put on a fresh pot of coffee and pulled out the Fiesta cream-and-sugar set from the cupboard above the sink.

While they waited for the coffee to brew, Ollie sat down at the table. It was then he noticed the black, faux-leather-bound book in front of Stacy. He could tell she caught his gaze. "It's the good book," she said, sliding it across the table toward Ollie. "I brought it as a gift."

Ollie picked up the bible and flipped through it as though it were the latest Stephen King. He had an absurd urge to giggle.

Hank said what Ollie was thinking. "Is that some kind of joke, Stacy?"

"What do you mean?"

"I mean the bible. Come on, girl, you and the bible on familiar terms?" He snorted. "I'm surprised the thing didn't burst into flames when you touched it."

If Stacy took offense at the comment, she didn't show it. Before she could answer, though, Addison surprised them all by hopping down from her chair. "I'm bored." She raced to the back door and threw it open. She looked back. "Can I go outside with Rose?"

"Sure you can, honey," Ollie responded.

"Stay close," Stacy said.

"I don't have to listen to you!" Addison screamed before running out the door, which brought a smile to Hank's face. He stared hard down at the table so his sister wouldn't see, Ollie guessed.

Stacy peered at the two of them. "Anyway, the good book and I have gotten on very familiar terms since the last time I saw you, Hank. I have been saved. Born again by the grace of Jesus Christ." She smiled and Ollie thought he saw something of the saint in her expression. Maybe a bit of the lunatic too.

What was she doing here? Ollie suspected he already knew the answer, but the dread in his gut told him he wasn't ready to face it just yet.

"What is this?" Hank asked, suspicious. A grin fluttered around his lips, like someone awaiting the punch line to a joke. "You're fuckin' with us, right?"

Stacy closed her eyes for a moment, obviously appalled. "No, I am not. And I would appreciate you keep from talking filth while in my presence."

Hank shook his head. "*You* taught *me* how to cuss. How to smoke too. And steal." Hank chuckled. "And french kiss a boy."

"I've changed, Hank, don't you get that? It turns out prison, for those few months, was the best thing that could ever have happened to me. It was there that I found Jesus. Or should I say He found me?"

"I think you should say insanity found you," Hank muttered.

"Hank, please," Ollie said softly. He got up to pour them all coffee. He had a curious sensation: like he was in a car with no brakes and his foot was stuck on the accelerator. He felt like they were just going faster and faster.

Eventually, they would crash into *something*.

"Anyway," Stacy continued, ignoring her brother. "That time not only helped me find the true path, it gave me lots of time to think." Stacy rose and went to stare through the screen outside. Ollie got up too to pour coffee, and he glanced over Stacy's shoulder. Rose was chasing Addison around the base of the fir tree back there, both giggling like crazy. Their laughter drifted in to them, tinkling. It was such a sweet sound. Ollie had to turn away from the scene. He set full coffee cups down on the table, and then added the creamer and sugar bowl. He sat down.

Both he and Hank stared at Stacy, who seemed lost in a world of her own as she watched Addison and Rose playing.

"Who's that girl out there?"

"That's the girl who's been taking care of your daughter. Along with Ollie and me here. You kind of abandoned her, you know? Abandoned Mom too. I was with her when she passed. Where were you?"

Stacy whirled on Hank, and Ollie could see the tears in her eyes. "I hadn't been released yet! You know that, Hank, because you tried to get in touch with me. I begged them to let me out to go see her, but they wouldn't." She pushed angrily at her eyes, wiping away tears. "Why do you have to be so mean? She was never mother of the year, that's for sure, but she was all we had." Stacy returned to the table and sat down, hard, at her place. Her lower lip was quivering and she was breathing fast, trying to rein in her emotions.

"I wanted to be there for her. I loved her," she said softly, looking at Hank.

Hank appeared to soften. His features took on a little less furious mien, and he reached out and touched his sister's hand. "She asked about you. She said she loved you too."

"Did she really?" Stacy's face lit up.

Hank nodded. "It was probably for the best you weren't around. It wasn't pretty. You can remember her as the party girl. She'd like that."

Stacy laughed.

The three grew quiet, the only sound in the kitchen the laughter and the yelling of the girls outside. Their innocence hurt Ollie deep inside.

Finally, it was Hank who had the courage to address the elephant in the room. "Are you here for the reason I think you are, Stacy?"

Ollie could see the fear in Hank's eyes, the despair. And—totally irrational—the hope.

Stacy sipped her coffee. When she began speaking, Ollie found himself unable to look at Hank. He couldn't bear it.

"Hank, I want to thank you for taking care of Addison during my troubles."

"But—" Hank started up, but Stacy silenced him by holding up her hand.

"Just let me finish. It means so much to me that you took her in and were a parent to her. I know you could barely take care of yourself, but you took on this little girl and somehow you managed. I am so proud of you, brother. I didn't know you had it in you. I look out there and see my little girl looking happy, healthy, well fed. She's as sassy as ever. That's all I need to see to know you loved her, that you saw to it she had a safe, happy life." Ollie looked up to see Stacy reach out to grab both of Hank's hands and squeeze. Hank yanked his hands away, settling them in his lap.

"I don't think I could ever repay you. By all rights, she should be in foster care or worse, I don't know."

"You think you're gonna take her back?" Hank's voice was one part defiance and one part sorrow.

"I don't *think* I'm gonna take her back, Hank. I am." She touched Hank's hand again, gently. "She's my little girl."

"A little girl you abandoned to run off with some druggie boyfriend. Some mother!"

Ollie wondered, suddenly, if he should leave the siblings alone. This conversation was so raw and obviously painful for the both of them. But he couldn't move. He stayed rooted to his seat at the table, watching the drama unfold with dread and horror, unable to look away.

Stacy didn't bristle at her brother's accusations. She gave him a sad smile and nodded. "You're right. I was terrible. Horrible. Selfish. A bitch. A whore." She shook her head. "Believe me, Hank, you can't call me anything I haven't already called myself a thousand times.

"But I'm changed." She smiled. "Saved."

Hank shook his head. "All that holy-roller crap is bullshit and you know it."

"Believe what you want, Hank. All I know is Jesus saved me when I was at my worst, and I intend to spend the rest of my life making up for the mistakes I made." She stood and moved toward the door again. "I want to see that Addison is brought up in a Christian home. She needs to know that Jesus loves her.

"I'm taking her back to Pennsylvania today, Hank. She needs her mama. I promise you I will make a good home for her. I will work hard and maybe, someday, if all goes well, there will be a daddy for her, too." She laughed. "But I'm in no hurry for that. Right now, all that matters is Addison—and giving her the kind of environment where she feels safe and loved."

"She has a home. Here." Hank stared down at the table and Ollie frowned as he saw a lone tear plop on its maple surface.

"I know you love her, Hank. And you can come back to Pennsylvania with us, be a part of her life and mine. Every day. That would be great." She moved to Hank, placed her hands on his shoulders, rubbed. Hank shrugged her hands away.

"I can't do that. I can't just up and take off."

Ollie couldn't help the sigh of relief that escaped him. He was afraid for a moment he would not only lose Addison, but Hank too. He realized the thought would more than break his heart; it would shatter it.

Stacy looked at Ollie. "Because of him?"

Ollie felt heat rise to his face. He wasn't sure why.

"Yeah, because of him," Hank said. "*He* gave me back *my* life when I was at my lowest. Him and not some pie-in-the-sky guy who hangs from a cross. A real flesh and blood man."

"You love him?" Stacy asked.

Hank looked at Ollie, smiling, and nodded.

"Then maybe he can help you. Ease the pain. Besides," Stacy said, moving back to the screen door, "I could never let Addison go on living in this environment." She shook her head. "It wouldn't be right."

Ollie could feel the anger rise up, hot, in his gut. Hank stood suddenly, his chair slamming against the wall behind him. His fists were clenched. "What do you mean, Sis?"

Stacy said, "God teaches us to hate the sin and love the sinner. And that's what I'm doing here. Your lifestyle is your choice, Hank. I respect that. But I don't want my daughter exposed to it. At least not to this degree. It's not right. It's not natural."

Ollie remembered making love with Hank only hours ago, but what now seemed like much longer ago, with Addison in the room next door. Had she heard? What would Stacy think if she knew?

Were they really and truly doomed? Was their little, and so new and so fragile, family about to burst apart at the seams?

Ollie knew it was, even if his brain and his heart had yet to catch up, had yet to accept the cold reality staring him in the face.

"Your daughter has been exposed only to love. Family. Food in her belly. A warm, safe place to live and to sleep. We gave her those things. The queers gave her those things," Hank said.

Stacy whined, "Hank, I said I appreciate what you did. And I won't ever keep you out of Addison's life. You and your friend will always be welcome to visit her." She cast a quick glance at Ollie, and he wondered what she saw. Perhaps a man frozen in pain? Someone waiting for the piano, hanging suspended by a rope above him, to drop on his head?

"You're clear across the country!" Hank shrieked, his voice filled with raw pain.

"No, you are," Stacy said softly.

"I won't let you take her."

Stacy laughed. "I'm her mother, Hank. You have no standing here."

"I won't let you take her," Hank repeated, moving toward the door. He called outside. "Rose! Rose! Take Addison. Run! Find someplace to hide. We'll catch up with you later."

Ollie moved to join the other two by the back door. Both Rose and Addison stood staring back, confused, silent.

"Didn't you hear me?" Hank cried, his voice an anguished wail.

Ollie moved behind him and wrapped his arms around him, holding Hank tight. "Don't," he whispered. "You can't win."

Hank whirled on him. "You're just gonna let this happen?"

"I don't want it to happen any more than you do!" Ollie cried, feeling the tears rise to his eyes. "I love that little girl too!"

They gripped each other, Hank sobbing in Ollie's chest. "We have to stop her," he kept saying, when he could find enough breath to put behind words.

"We can't. Not right now."

Stacy opened the door. "Addison," she called out. "Come on. Let's get your stuff together."

Ollie looked up to see the little girl standing with her arms folded across her chest. Defiant. "What for?"

"You're coming home with me, honey. Back to Summitville. I've got a new apartment," Stacy offered. "And you'll have your own room. We can paint it any color you like."

"No!" Addison screamed back. Rose stood by her side, motionless.

Stacy stepped out onto the deck. "Come on, honey, come with Mama. We belong together, sweetie," Stacy pleaded. "We're gonna take the train, honey. All the way across the country. You are going to see so much neat stuff!" Ollie almost felt sorry for her. Almost. His heart was too mauled, though, to muster up much sympathy for the woman who was about to break apart their family, so new Ollie hadn't gotten around to thinking of it as one until just this morning.

It was then that Addison made a run for it. She headed toward them, sobbing, then disappeared through the side yard. Stacy rushed after her, and in moments, came back with Addison in her arms, kicking, screaming, and sobbing.

Ollie wanted to cry just as hard. "I don't know if I can stand this."

"Go ahead, bail on me," Hank said tonelessly. "It's what everyone does eventually."

Ollie tried to engage Hank's eyes, but Hank wouldn't look at him. He stared, looking numb and devoid of emotion, as Stacy dragged Addison back inside. The little girl was putting up a pretty good fight too. There were scratches on Stacy's face, and Addison had managed to pull most of Stacy's hair from its uptight bun.

It won't do any good, Ollie thought. As Stacy had said, they had no standing.

Sure, they could get a lawyer, try to get custody. But Ollie knew, even as his optimistic heart envisioned it, it was an unwinnable case. Stacy was Addison's biological mother. She had found God. And it looked like she had managed to find a job and a home too. What court would take Addison away from that to place her with two unmarried gay men?

This morning, which had started off so bright, had turned into the blackest day in Ollie's life. He couldn't imagine the depth of Hank's pain.

Stacy didn't give up. She took Addison, still kicking and screaming, through the kitchen, into the entryway, and up the stairs.

"Can't you stop her?" Hank asked.

"What can I do?"

"You're useless. I hate you," Hank spat out. He turned and bolted out the door.

"Hank! Come back." Ollie called after him. "Please!"

Both Ollie and Rose watched as he took the same path as little Addison just had, but with much more success. In seconds, he was gone.

Ollie could hear the fight—one of epic proportions—going on upstairs. Screaming. Kicking. The sound of something shattering. He knew, though, that soon quiet would descend on the house. Too much quiet. The thought made him sick.

Quiet—it was the worst prospect he could imagine. He stepped backward until his knees connected with a chair. He slammed down in it, gasping for breath.

Rose came in, shaking. She put her hand on Ollie's shoulder and he grabbed it.

Chapter
SIXTEEN

IT WAS late afternoon when Ollie approached the King Street station, the historic, turn-of-the-century depot in Pioneer Square from which Amtrak trains arrived and departed. He stopped and eyed the building, its red bricks looking neat and orderly, its clock tower rising above, keeping track of the hours with precision.

The station's façade was very much at odds with what Ollie felt inside, which was turmoil and chaos. His stomach churned. He felt as though something had been amputated from him, leaving a gaping and painful hole in its place, tender. He didn't know what he'd do or say once he got inside. He prayed he wasn't too late.

He had to try. For Hank. For himself. For Rose. He needed to get the little girl back, somehow.

Ollie forced himself to move forward to the main doors of the station, trying to rein in the wild whirl of thoughts spinning in his head like some sort of mental tornado. He was trying to think of some compelling reasons why a mother, even one who had been as wild and unsettled as Stacy, should leave her daughter behind.

He forced down the guilt within him, the little voice that told him he was being selfish. *What are you doing, Ollie, thinking you might be able to get a mother to abandon her kid? What kind of victory would that be?* He thought of his own mother, Annette, who lived for Ollie and his dad, who would have been devastated, unable to live with herself, if she lost either of her men.

Notions like these were almost enough to make Ollie turn around and head back home.

But he couldn't bear the thought of coming back without Addison. He told himself, over and over, the little girl belonged with him and Hank. He questioned Stacy's sincerity. He knew about her promiscuity and her drug abuse. He told himself she had already abandoned the little girl once, to go off and chase after a man. Who was to say her conversion to Christianity wasn't a ruse, or an idea whose lifespan would be short? People who slutted around and used drugs couldn't be reliable parents, could they? She would revert, right? And then where would little Addison be?

These were the thoughts that kept him moving forward, through the doors and into the gorgeous station, restored to its original elegance only very recently. He shoved away the thoughts that Hank too had abused drugs, had the fingerprints of many men upon him. Hank was different.

Why? Why wouldn't Hank one day revert? Who was to say he wasn't, at this very moment, firing up a glass pipe full of crystal meth, hoping to obliterate his loss and pain in clouds of white smoke?

Ollie couldn't let himself think that way. He had to be the hero. It was his duty to restore his family, to make it whole again. *Think of how much Hank will love you if you bring Addison back! Think of that happy reunion. That's what you have to keep in mind. Keep the doubts at bay. The hell with Stacy—she left Addison once and she will do it again.*

Ollie consulted the boards listing arrivals and departures and saw that Stacy and Addison must be taking the "Empire Builder," the line that went all the way across the country to Chicago. What would they do when they got there? Take a bus? A different train? That was no way for a little girl to travel!

Addison needed him, Ollie told himself. She needed the both of them; they were her parents now.

His heart sunk. He knew he was wrong, knew deep within himself he had no business trying to pull Addison away from her mother, even if Addison herself would welcome his intervention, as Ollie knew she would.

He stood as crowds of people swirled around him, all hurrying to catch trains, to reunite with loved ones, and wasn't sure what he should do.

He closed his eyes and imagined Hank, picturing the tears in his eyes, the grateful smile as he gathered Addison into his arms. He imagined the two of them in the little garret where he had first found them, just the pair of them, struggling to eke out some sort of existence. He knew Hank needed Addison, needed her sass, her innocence, and her dependence for him to go on living.

What greater gift could he give to the man he suddenly found himself in love with?

He found the waiting area for the next Empire Builder, hoping that Stacy and Addison had not somehow managed to board an earlier train. Wouldn't that just be the way life goes? Ollie thought. *If they're already gone....*

But they weren't. Ollie spotted them sitting on a bench, Addison leaning against her mother, fast asleep, thumb in her mouth. Again, Ollie thought of turning around and going home. Then he told himself Addison's slumber was not from being at peace, but had its roots in exhaustion from emotional trauma.

Yes. That has to be it. He took a few steps forward. Stacy looked up and spotted him.

Ollie didn't miss how she moved her arm protectively over Addison's sleeping form. She cocked her head and her eyebrows came together in confusion or, perhaps, consternation. She frowned.

There was no going back now. Ollie approached the bench quietly, taking his time. He didn't want to wake Addison. He wanted the conversation he would have with Stacy to be levelheaded, reasonable.

Right. You're going to convince some right-wing Christian to not only give up her daughter, but to give her up to a couple of homos. Good luck with that.

The nausea increased in Ollie's gut with each step nearer he took. Gingerly, at last, he sat down close to Stacy, but not right next to her. At first, he didn't say anything.

It was she who broke the silence. "What do you want?" she whispered.

What he wanted to say was, "I want Addison back. Please, won't you reconsider? Please, please, please." He wanted to beg; he wanted to be like a spoiled child, and if only he pleaded hard enough, perhaps with tears, he would get his way.

But he knew that would be a very quick conversation. So instead he said, "I just wanna talk to you for a few minutes."

Stacy didn't say anything for a long while, as though she were considering. Finally, she said, "Okay. But keep your voice down. I don't want to wake her. She wore herself out with her screaming."

Ollie nodded. Where to begin?

Ollie stared at the other travelers, hurrying past, their minds elsewhere, and felt a stab of envy for them. Even though logic told him it wasn't true, he pictured their lives as ordered, with their loved ones all safely in place. No worries. He closed his eyes for a moment. Ollie had never been much for prayer, but he couldn't resist a quick petition to God, begging him for the wisdom to voice the right words. Words that, like magic, would change Stacy's mind, soften her hardened heart, and make her see that the loving thing to do, the selfless thing to do, was to give her daughter up to people who could love and care for her with all their hearts.

But isn't that really what Stacy wants to give to Addison too?

Ollie pushed this last thought away. No wise words came, and he knew his only hope was to take a leap and hope that the net would be there. Very softly, he began speaking.

"I know you're Addison's mom. And that's no small thing, sweetheart." He looked at Stacy to apprise how she had taken his term of endearment. Her face remained impassive, giving no clue.

At least she was listening.

"But Addison has been so happy with us. Just in a few months, I've watched her grow from a sullen, scared, and hungry little waif to a happy and well-adjusted little girl. I've seen your brother change so, so much too—and mainly because of the influence taking care of Addison has had on him. Addison's light has shone on all of us, Rose too, the young woman you saw at the house. In spite of her smart mouth, Addison has made us all better people." Ollie sighed, realizing the truth that lay in his words.

"And I like to think our light has changed Addison as well. Made her feel secure. Nurtured. A part of a family. I know I'm just talking here, but that word—*family*—means so much. More than words. It's emotion. It's love."

Ollie wished for more words, a torrent of them that would persuade and convince. But in the end, he realized he really had little else to tell Stacy.

Stacy didn't say anything for a long while. She sat quietly, examined her nails, and watched a group of kids hurry by, laughing. Finally, she got up and, holding on to Addison's sleeping form, she gently slid a sweater under her head. She moved away from her daughter and sat down on Ollie's other side.

She took a breath and then Ollie was surprised to feel himself drawn up in her embrace. She hugged him hard, and he could feel her breath on his neck. She didn't let go of him completely, but kept her head on his shoulder. She whispered into his ear. "Don't you think I know that? It's breaking my heart to tear Addison away from you guys, but she needs to be with her mama. I haven't been a good person for a long, long time, but I like to think I am now.

"And I know I love Addison. She belongs with me."

She sat up now and looked at Ollie. She looked composed, even though her eyes were a little red around the edges and watery. Ollie wanted so much to hate her. He wanted to draw on every horrible thing those fanatical right-wing Christians had ever said about gay people and cast her in the same mold. But all he saw sitting before him was a young woman who was struggling to put her life back together, seeking out help where she could find it, and desperate to make up for the mistakes she had made in her young life.

Stacy grabbed one of Ollie's hands and held it. "That book I left for you? That bible Hank made fun of? I read that every day when I was in jail, studied it. Do you know Philippians?"

Ollie nodded, knowing he had heard the name of that book of the bible, but recalling little else.

"There's a verse in it," Stacy said. "It says, 'And my God will supply every need of yours according to his riches in glory in Christ Jesus.' I remember that verse because it gives me strength. What it says to me is I have an ally in God, someone I can lean on." She chuckled. "I even had it made into a sampler. It's hanging on the wall back in my living room in Summitville. I think of that verse when I doubt myself, and I do doubt myself, and it helps me go on, helps me know that it's not all up to me."

With the force of her gaze, she compelled Ollie to look at her, deep in her own eyes. "I don't know what you believe, Ollie, but believe that God will supply your needs. You want a family? I could see you have one with my brother. You shouldn't be here. You should be back with him."

Ollie slumped back against his seat, the fight suddenly leaving him. The disappointment was almost debilitating as he finally accepted he would not be returning home a hero on a white stallion, bringing Hank the prize of a little girl both of them adored.

There would be only Ollie. And he had to hope that would be enough. He hoped that God would, for them, supply every need of theirs, which right now boiled down to one—that their love could survive what was happening. That this devastation, this loss, would bring them closer together and not tear them apart.

Ollie took a deep breath and said to Stacy, "Much as I hate to admit it, you're right. She's yours. We love her—oh yes, we do—but as you said, you're her mama. And nothing can ever replace that.

"I came here with different ideas and plans. I thought I could offer you money or a job or threaten you with a lawsuit…." Ollie's voice trailed off as he recognized the folly of his own misguided, well-intentioned selfishness.

He patted Stacy's hand. "You be a good mama. You treat her right. You love her. You feed her good food. You correct her smart mouth, but do it by example and with kindness. You call us whenever you need help." Ollie's voice began to break and he felt the first tears course down his cheeks as he felt his heart begin to let go, just a little bit. "And you let us talk to her when we call. Because we will need to hear her voice and keep a connection with her open." Ollie brushed away the tears and smiled. He could see Stacy was crying too.

"I wish it didn't have to be this way," she said softly.

"I know. Listen? Maybe for Thanksgiving, you come see us? I'll make a big dinner, turkey with all the trimmings, but with some Italian touches from my family: wedding soup to start, stuffed artichokes. We'll eat until we can't move, and then we'll fall asleep in front of the TV." Ollie was tearing up again, both at the scene his words were drawing in his mind, but also at the thought of how very long it was until Thanksgiving. How could he bear not to see Addison every day? "Doesn't that sound nice?" he asked.

"It does," Stacy nodded. "We'll see. It's expensive to come out here. I don't know if I can afford another trip so soon."

Soon? Ollie wondered. *Thanksgiving is, like, centuries away.* "We'll work something out. Don't worry about it."

Stacy nodded. She glanced down at her watch. "We need to be getting ready. They'll be boarding soon."

Ollie nodded. He looked over at Addison, slumbering. Her sweet face was innocent and, even though there was something demonic about her when she was up and running around, there was now the essence of an angel about her, in her creamy skin, fat, freckled cheeks, and amber curls.

"Can I say good-bye?" Ollie asked.

Stacy nodded. "Try not to wake her. This is hard for her."

Ollie got up and knelt down quietly beside the little girl and let his hand hover above her hair and her cheeks, close enough to feel her warmth, but not touching. Her simply stared at her, hoping there would be a future with her. At last, he dared to place a quick, soft kiss on her cheek. The taste of it would have to sustain him for a long time. "See you later, Addison," he whispered.

He got up quickly and hurried away. He didn't look back.

He couldn't.

Chapter SEVENTEEN

OLLIE RETURNED home to an empty house. Filled with a crazy kind of hope, he made a tour, opening and closing doors, praying he'd find Hank or Rose perhaps napping in one of the rooms. Logic told him with all the turmoil that had gone on that day, napping was unlikely, but still he wanted so much for them to be there that he didn't lose hope that they weren't there until he had looked in the very last room. He came away from the final room dejected.

He remembered, suddenly, that he and Hank had a dinner to cook and serve that night on Mercer Island. Oh God, there was no way.... Feeling fatigue like he'd never felt in his whole life, he trudged into the living room, where he had left his phone, and made a call, told his clients they would not be there, made up a quick story about a bad cold or the flu and not wanting to take the risk....

They understood, thank God.

He went outside and sat on the front porch. One of the things he loved about the house, along with the big, sunny, and cheerful kitchen, was that the wide front porch had a swing. When he and Hank had first come to view the place, the swing caught Ollie's eye immediately and stayed in his head, like some kind of infatuation, throughout the entire tour. It was the swing, he thought, that had prompted him to choose this place. It didn't matter what imperfections lay inside, Ollie was already sold as he imagined Hank and him sitting outside on a warm summer night, drinking wine or a beer, talking as the darkness deepened and the sounds of night surrounded them. He didn't even know then that he and Hank might one day wind up a couple, in fact the notion had been far from his mind, but it was this homey and comforting scene that he had focused on when he'd told the real estate agent, "We'll take it." He remembered now, he had said "we" not "I," and it had felt completely natural, even though it was Ollie who would be putting up the down payment and most likely paying all of the mortgage.

Now as he sat on the swing, it felt like just what it was: a creaky old thing with rust on its chains. Its white paint was chipped. Its promise reneged on. He pressed his feet to the floor to start a gentle rocking motion, but found no comfort in it.

Where was Hank?

Where was Rose?

He knew they, like he, were both traumatized and most likely were out there somewhere seeking to assuage their grief, to find a balm for their pain. He didn't know what form that balm would take for Rose because the young woman, in many ways, was such a mystery. The only thing he knew for sure about her was that she was damaged, but she had a core that was as sweet as honey.

But for Hank? Ollie knew about his addiction and worried that the loss of Addison might propel him back into Tina's arms. One could say a lot of bad things about the drug, up to and including the fact that it could eventually kill, but the one good thing it had going for it was that it brought oblivion.

The stress of the day, the loss, the upset.... Ollie could very well understand and even sympathize with Hank if he went down to Belltown or Pioneer Square or even the Hill and sought out an old connection. He could even feel in his own self how nice it would be just to forget.

But he hoped Hank knew what he knew—the drug was a false promise. Sure, it would wipe out whatever troubles you had for several hours, maybe even days, depending on your endurance, but in the end, you'd come home to the same problems even more unprepared to cope.

Ollie tried to let himself go numb, to just experience the setting sun and not think about things. But Hank's last words still rang in his ears, cutting like a razor-sharp blade, "I hate you."

There were few pains greater than hearing those words slip out of the mouth of one you love and one you hoped loved you back. The fact that Addison was most likely now on a train, headed eastward, and that the prospect of seeing her again was dim, could just be enough for Hank to truly hate Ollie, even though he had done all he could. Sometimes, hatred and rage was a substitute for pain, a way to circumvent its horrendous hurt.

Ollie didn't think he could bear Hank hating him. He also couldn't bear the very real possibility that Hank might never return. He had lived before on his own, toughing it out on the streets. He was a survivor. He didn't need Ollie. And the fact was that this house, and Ollie himself, might be too painful as reminders for him to return.

Ollie could understand that too. And he hated the thought.

The day wound down into dusk. Ollie thought, with a sad smile, that he wasn't hungry. This was so unlike him. But he hadn't given a single thought to what he would make for supper. The mere thought of food turned his stomach, a reality that, up until a few hours ago, he wouldn't have thought possible.

He thought he could sit on this porch all night, gently rocking. It seemed he had little energy to do anything else. He felt as though he could sit here forever, as long as there was hope he might look up and see Hank coming down the street.

Even though lots of people had passed the house while Ollie sat outside, and their passage barely registered, he spotted her right away, coming slowly down the street, almost dragging herself. In the dim light, he could see she carried something under her arm, but he wasn't sure what.

Rose. Her tentative walk gave her away.

Ollie found himself smiling as the young woman neared the house. Her features became more defined as she drew closer—the halo of curly hair, the downcast eyes, the baggy hoody and jeans hiding what Ollie knew was a terrific figure.

She stepped up onto the porch without a word. She crossed over to where Ollie was sitting and plopped down beside him, letting out a great sigh. She, too, stared off into the night.

Ollie leaned forward. "Whatcha got there?"

Rose lifted what she had clutched under her arm so Ollie could see.

Ollie's heart gave a little lurch, painful. He gasped. He bit his lower lip to hold in the cry he knew was just waiting to escape at the sight of the object.

It was Violet, Addison's purple teddy bear. She adored that thing and slept with it every night.

"Oh God, she must have forgotten it." Ollie felt, for a moment, more crushed about this stupid stuffed animal than he had about anything else. But the thought of Addison realizing it had gotten left behind truly broke his heart.

Rose's voice was husky when she at last spoke, and Ollie surmised it was because she had been sobbing. "I found it on our bedroom floor. I guess she meant to take it with her, but in the rush, it got dropped."

Ollie slowly shook his head. "Sad."

Rose nodded. "I picked it up and walked all the way down to the train station to try and find them so I could give it to her. I must have missed them because I couldn't find them anywhere."

Missed me too, Ollie thought.

Rose hugged the bear tight to her chest, and Ollie wondered if maybe there wasn't some divine providence at work here. Perhaps Violet was giving Rose the comfort she needed.

Ollie reached over and gently laid a hand on Rose's arm. She flinched, but she let his hand remain where it was. In fact, after a minute or two, she reached up with one of her own hands and covered Ollie's.

"We'll get it packed up and send it to her." Ollie very gently stroked Rose's skin with the tip of his finger.

"Sure."

Rose settled back, cradling the bear like a baby and allowed her head to settle on Ollie's shoulder.

They sat like that for a long time, swaying gently. Ollie thought they were both watching for Hank to appear in the street, heading home.

But he never came.

Chapter
EIGHTEEN

HANK STOOD outside, smoking. It was that weird hour of the day, not quite light, but darkness was rapidly losing its hold. There was a grayish quality to the light and an expectancy to the air. Hank sat down on one of the porch steps, almost expecting Ollie to rush outside and rag on him about the cigarette, but the house, like their street, was dead quiet at this wee hour of the morning.

He had walked. And walked. He felt like he had traversed all of Seattle from yesterday afternoon until now. He was sure there must be blisters on his feet, and once he could sleep and did sleep, he would waken with aching and stiff leg muscles. It just felt like if he kept moving, he could keep his thoughts and their turmoil, at bay.

It didn't work.

Now he leaned back against one of the porch posts, exhausted but unable to sleep, stomach rumbling but unable to eat. It felt like those simple and natural imperatives would remain foreign to him forever, or at least as long as Addison was gone.

He should go inside, find Ollie, and let him know he was okay. Or as okay as he could be after what had transpired yesterday. The ironic thing was that he hadn't even wanted Addison, had thought the little girl an insufferable brat the first time he met her and had actually fought with his mother so he wouldn't have to take her.

And now he would give anything to have her back.

She's not dead, Hank. You can still see her, even though she's far away. You can't pine for something you never really had to begin with. "Oh, but I can," Hank whispered to himself, shaking his head.

He finished his cigarette, getting up to extinguish it on the concrete walkway that led up to the house. Once he was sure it was no longer smoldering, he stuffed the butt in his pocket to throw out later. Ollie would kill him if he found any cigarette butts outside the house.

He sat back down and thought about all that had happened. A lot had taken place over the past several hours. So much, in fact, that it seemed much longer ago when Stacy arrived to interrupt their breakfast and turn their worlds upside down.

When he had first fled the house, he really did hate Ollie, much as it now pained him to think so. But it didn't take him long to realize that his hatred was a false thing, an emotional Band-Aid to cover up the wound of his pain. He looked up to Ollie, and part of him demanded protection, wanted Ollie to be the solver of all of his problems. But Stacy returning to claim her daughter, Hank realized, was not something Ollie could fix.

When he accepted that he didn't hate Ollie but in fact loved him, it didn't get any easier. What would he do with his pain? How could he bear it?

As he coursed the streets of Belltown, he found himself on Vine, in front of Jesse's house. Jesse was the one dealer he used the most. He paced in front of the old redbrick building with its green shutters and double-door entryway, still recalling the number to press on the intercom for Jesse's apartment (69) because the digits had once amused him. But it had been years since he had been here.

Most likely Jesse had moved on in one way or another, good or bad. Did he have the nerve to buzz him? To just show up unannounced? What would he say? Even if Jesse was still dealing, the balding, middle-aged man might still take offense at Hank showing up without calling first. Drug dealers were funny that way.

Hank remembered the last time he had been there; the two of them had smoked Tina through a special bong Jesse had procured, blowing great white clouds of toxic smoke into the air. There was hardcore porn on the TV (Jesse had a portable hard drive hooked up that had hundreds of bareback, hardcore titles on it) and the two of them had taken turns blowing and fucking the other, courtesy of Jesse's Viagra, because that bitch Tina had a nasty way of making one's dick limp as a noodle.

Jesse had wound up falling asleep face down on his bed. He had confessed earlier to Hank that he had been up for three days, so it was no surprise when sleep took him like an abductor.

Hank shook his head. The memory effectively wiped out any desire he had to try and see if Jesse was home. Even in the unlikely event that he was *and* holding *and* wanting to party, Hank realized, with a kind of relief, that *he* didn't want it. He didn't want the crushing crash that would follow. Sure, his problems could be wiped out for hours, for days maybe, if all went well (or badly), but those same problems would still be there, waiting. They would be uglier than before because, to add insult to injury, Hank knew how depleted and sick he would be after a binge with Tina.

He walked away, letting his feet and his heart take him in a completely different direction.

Before long, Hank found himself pacing outside another building. This one, though, was the opposite in so many ways of the last place he'd been. This simple, industrial, cinder-block structure represented hope, recovery, self-reliance, a future.

He stood in front of Haven. Even though only good had come from his residency there, Hank was uncertain about going inside. He was no longer part of the folks who called Haven home, so down on their luck they had no place else to go and considered themselves lucky to have found the meager shelter and nourishment that Haven provided.

Curiously, he didn't feel a part of this scene any longer either. He knew he could slip inside and probably find E.J. in the kitchen, steam dampening her ebony brow as she stood at the stove, stirring something in an industrial-sized pot. He could unload his woes and she would listen; she always did.

But that wasn't her role anymore. He had someone else for that.

And now Hank stood up and headed toward his own front door. He fitted his key into the lock and slipped inside, feeling like a thief. Even after months of living in the house, it still felt odd to Hank to think of it as his own, to realize the key in his hand was really his—it was a kind of magic. A gift. Something he had never expected to have.

The interior of the house was quiet. Hank moved to the living room on his right. They were so busy, they hardly ever got a chance to use this room. Now it was flooded with morning sun from the big bay window and the scattered Persian rugs, leather furniture, and mission-style oak furniture looked revitalized and clean in the morning light. He sat down sideways on the couch, throwing his legs up and letting his head rest on its quilted arm. Opposite him was the fireplace they had yet to use, fashioned from gray fieldstone, with a big black mantel. It made Hank sad to look at it, because it brought on memories of his imaginings of what it would look like in winter, on a dreary, rain-soaked day, with all of them gathered around a roaring blaze, together. The images came back, full force, and caused an ache to rise up in Hank that could only be described as a hole, an empty abyss, yawning.

For the briefest of seconds, he had an image of Addison sitting on a little stool by the fire, the light from the flames dancing across her face, looking rapt and happy.

The image took his breath away, and he had to bite his lower lip to prevent a sob from escaping.

He didn't even want to think about Christmas and stockings hung from the mantle.

He rolled over on the couch so that he faced its back.

He had almost drifted off into a troubled, restless sleep when he heard a footstep, whisper-soft, on the hardwood.

He sat up suddenly, as though he had been caught doing something he shouldn't.

Rose cowered near the entryway to the living room, pressed up against the wooden arch.

"You came back."

Hank rubbed his eyes, which were burning. "Yeah. Of course, where else would I go?"

Rose moved closer and stood near the couch, with a finger at her lips.

"You wanna sit down?" Hank asked.

She hurried to do so. "Where did you go?" she asked.

"Around. Just walked. I honestly didn't know what to do with myself, so I just took off, trying not to think, trying not to feel." He gave Rose what he knew was a sad smile. "Didn't have much luck with that."

Rose scooted a little closer and regarded him out of the corner of her eye. "We were worried about you."

"I'm sorry. I just needed time."

Rose nodded, staring ahead. Hank noticed how the sun hit her face, the pale freckles he had never noticed. In this light, her irises looked pale green, almost a jade color.

Rose was beautiful.

"I understand." She turned her head to look outside the room at the staircase. "Ollie was afraid you wouldn't come back. It would have broken his heart."

"Oh, he shouldn't have thought that! I really didn't mean to worry him—or you." Hank thought, *What else was Ollie to think? You rushed out of here and the last words out of your mouth were that you hated him.*

They didn't say anything for a long time. So long, in fact, that Hank was about ready to say he should go upstairs and reassure Ollie that he was home. But Rose, surprisingly, began talking. The woman who rarely said more than a sentence at a time suddenly had something to get off her chest, it appeared.

"I know I never say much. It's like I want to hide. And I do." Rose took a breath and Hank wondered if she was drawing on some inner reserve of courage. There was something determined in the set of her features.

"I don't talk about myself because I don't want to think about myself. I don't want to think about what happened to me before I came to Haven." She looked quickly at Hank, then away again, staring straight ahead. "I don't want you to tell any of this to Ollie."

"Okay," Hank said.

"When I was a little girl, a man took me."

"What do you mean? Like, kidnapped?"

Rose nodded. "Just like that. From a mall in Portland. I was five years old. I don't remember the family I had, where I lived, who my mom was, who my dad was. Little snatches will come to me in dreams, a yellow house with white shutters, a woman with red hair, pulled back into a ponytail. I don't know if these are memories or if they're something I just made up because I wanted so much for them to be true.

"Anyway, this man took me. He put me in a van and shoved a smelly rag over my face. When I woke up, I was in a house somewhere, probably in a basement room, because there weren't any windows.

"No one looked for me. Or at least that's what I thought because no one ever came to save me. The man told me my folks were dead, car accident or something. Sometimes, he would get confused and tell me my parents didn't want me and would tell me that my dad sold me to him for fifty dollars and some cocaine.

"I don't know what the truth was. I don't know if I ever will.

"Anyway, he kept me in this room, pretty much a prisoner. He took care of me, though. He kept me clean; he fed me. If I got sick, he brought me medicine and watched over me until I got better." Rose smiled, a million miles away. "Sometimes, if I was very good, he'd bring me upstairs to the house proper. He'd let me sit on the couch and we'd watch TV… always nature specials. He had a little dog, a black-and-tan mutt named Josie, and she would curl up beside me." Rose's eyes got shiny. "I liked that. I loved that little dog.

"But what I didn't like was that the man made me do things to him and he did stuff to me. Stuff that hurt. And he brought other men by who would do the same thing. They would take pictures and stuff.

"They were always so, so quiet when they were hurting me, except maybe for some grunts and groans. I could barely stand it, but I learned to go someplace else in my head." Rose smiled and her eyes took on a faraway cast. "There was this place I imagined, very green, in a forest. You'd follow this long path, winding, and finally you'd get to this little clearing where there was a pond with lily pads. Trees overhung the water. It was nice there, cool but not cold. You could sit in the grass and listen to the birds sing, dip your toes in the water. It was my place. No one else in the world knew about it.

"That's where I would go when the men were on top of me, when they did what they needed to do."

Rose quickly peered at Hank for a moment, as though gauging his reaction.

"This went on for years. Until one day, I woke up and the house was quiet. My door was open and I walked out."

"Just like that?"

"Just like that."

Rose gave him a sad smile. "I guess I was too old. He didn't want me anymore. I left because he was gone, and so was the little dog, Josie.

"I wandered the streets for a long time, until I collapsed. I was so hungry, but I had no idea how to get food. I didn't even know how to talk to people!"

Hank wanted so badly to hug Rose, to stroke her hair, to deliver her from the pain of these memories. But he had seen how she would shrink from the slightest touch and knew the best thing he could do was listen, even though this tale was breaking his heart.

She shrugged. "Long story short: I was malnourished, almost starving, and I barely knew how to speak, even though I was, like, sixteen. They took me to a hospital. Then all these social workers got together and tried to decide what to do with me."

"Did they ever find your mom and dad?" Hank asked. He couldn't help himself.

Rose shook her head. "No. Never. They looked, but there was no record of my even disappearing, which makes me wonder if that story about me being sold wasn't true."

"Oh, Rose."

"Don't be sad. The people who found me took good care of me. They got me healthy again. And they taught me how to read, got me into that vocational school in White Center. A nice family eventually took me in, and even though I was so scared of them I could barely talk, they treated me nice, even when I would hide under the bed and wouldn't come out." She laughed at this last part, and that made Hank's heart hurt.

"You know the rest. I found my way to Haven after school and they helped me get even better at cooking."

Tentatively, she reached out a hand and touched Hank's cheek, then drew it away fast, as though the touch burned. "And then you and Ollie found me." She stared at the floor and whispered, "I'm a very lucky girl."

Hank wanted to burst into tears. How she could say she was lucky after all she had been through astounded him and touched a place inside him that was very tender. Again, he resisted the urge to hug her, to smother her with kisses. All he did was say, "Oh, Rose."

"See, here, with you guys, I have a family."

"Yes, yes, you do. We love you, Rose."

She looked at him then, her green eyes wide and staring. "You do?"

"Of course."

"Then don't leave again."

"I won't."

"And don't tell Ollie what I told you. He doesn't need to know."

Hank thought eventually Ollie should know, but he would respect Rose's wishes. "Why did you tell me?"

"Because I knew you'd understand. Because I wanted you to know that we're a family, even if Addison isn't with us anymore."

Hank thought about that. "I need to go talk to Ollie."

Rose nodded. "You do."

"Will you be okay down here?"

"Sure. This is my home."

Hank thought about that too. How much that must mean to her. And to him.

"We'll be down in a little bit," Hank said.

"Okay," Rose smiled. "I'll put the coffee on."

"And Ollie and I will make you pancakes."

"With chocolate chips?"

"You bet."

And Hank got up from the couch and headed upstairs, feeling shaken to the core.

Chapter
NINETEEN

OLLIE HADN'T slept. He knew that sometimes when we were gripped in the clutches of that restless demon known as insomnia, we did, in fact, actually sleep for stretches; it just didn't seem like it. But that wasn't the case this time. Ollie knew he had lain awake the entire night. They had a grandfather's clock downstairs in the entryway that chimed the hour, and Ollie had heard each and every one. It had taken forever to get through each hour and hear the next series of chimes.

He had lain awake in a state of restless waiting. Waiting for the creak of the door opening downstairs. Waiting for the somewhat heavy tread of a step on the stairs. Waiting for his bedroom door to open and Hank to appear in the darkness once more.

A state of fear gripped him. He was afraid he would never hear those familiar sounds again. It made his stomach ache to think that not only was Addison gone, but Hank was too. Ollie wondered what he could have done that might have changed things. His only cold comfort was that, in the end, he knew there was nothing.

He had done his best.

And he knew, painful as it was to think about, that the change in their very new and very small family would be okay. He didn't believe Stacy was without a heart. Ollie had a feeling she saw that she would do Addison no favors by preventing her from seeing Hank and Ollie (and Rose). At least he hoped so. Ollie had to cling to the hope that there would be visits, phone calls, birthday cards, and presents. Addison would be secure in the knowledge that she had two uncles who adored her. And, by the grace of God, who saw her, at least on holidays. It wasn't ideal, but what in life was? Ollie hoped only that Stacy's determination to be a good mother and to be there at last for her daughter was genuine.

But none of that could happen unless Hank returned.

He threw the sheet off and went to his bedroom door and opened it. He heard murmuring voices below.

Relief so strong it left him weak in the knees and clinging to his bedroom door gripped him as he recognized Hank's voice. *Hank. Home.*

But Hank wasn't doing most of the talking, which was surprising. The soft voice he heard more of was Rose's. Ollie crept halfway down the stairs, sat slowly on one of the steps so it wouldn't creak, and listened.

He closed his eyes, and his mind and ears honed in on what Rose was saying. He thought he should be shocked, but he'd known from the moment he met the painfully shy young woman that something awful had happened to her, some kind of abuse. He had no idea the depth of the horror she had endured, but he knew it was something terrible. She was like a whipped dog.

He did catch, too, that she didn't want him to know her tale, and he would respect that, but he couldn't help but wonder why. Perhaps it had something to do with the fact that she and Hank were closer in age and had the bond of the streets.

Or maybe it was because of what she said: that they were a family now, and families shared their heartaches as well as their joy.

He didn't want them to know he'd been listening, so he crept back up the stairs when he could hear them finishing their conversation, to lie back in bed, to wait some more.

He didn't have to wait very long.

There Hank stood in the doorway, outlined by the morning sun. A potent mixture of fatigue and deep melancholy marred his features. Ollie knew there were no words that could relieve the hurt, so he simply held out his arms.

Hank hesitated for a moment and then rushed to the bed. In seconds, he was under the sheet with Ollie and Ollie was holding him as he cried. Ollie ran one hand over Hank's head, whispering, "Shhh," while his other hand gripped Hank tightly, pulling him close into Ollie's own warmth.

They were like that for a long time, neither of them saying anything. Neither of them, Ollie thought, needed to put their emotions into words. There was pain. And there was comfort. And that was all.

At last, Hank sought out Ollie with his mouth. His kiss was hungry, not only lustful, but a desperate need for connection. They melded into one another, shedding their clothes quickly. There was no thought of penetration or sucking, this was all about succor and oblivion. Their bodies, slick with sweat, simply rubbed together, their joined mouths never parting, until each spurted his seed on the other's stomach.

They lay back, Hank's head on Ollie chest, breathing hard and still not speaking.

Sleep overtook them at the exact same instant, as though drawing a warm comforter over them both.

When Ollie awakened later, it was to the slant of late-morning sun and Hank staring at him from the pillow beside him.

"I'm glad we could sleep," Hank said. "I'm sorry I worried you."

"I *was* worried, but I understand." Ollie sat up a little straighter. "I have to ask, but know that whatever your answer is, I won't judge. Were you… um, good?"

"You mean did I use?"

Ollie nodded.

Hank shook his head. "No. I'd be lying if I said I wasn't tempted, but no. In the end, I knew Tina would just trick me again. Yeah, it may have taken away the hurt for a while, but then that same hurt would be back with a vengeance, compounded by the shit I put into myself. I knew better." He looked at Ollie and smiled. "I guess I'm growing up a little bit."

Ollie hugged him.

"Did you really think I'd use?"

"Yeah." Ollie shrugged. "I wouldn't have blamed you. But I think, even if you had, you would have come to the same conclusion. I think it would have been what they call an isolated incident. I believe that." Ollie sighed. "I was more worried that you would never come back." Ollie caught his breath as he made the admission and felt the hot burn of tears gathering in his eyes.

"Really?"

"You said you hated me."

"I could never hate you."

"But I wasn't able to stop her from taking Addison away. I tried." And Ollie told Hank all about seeing them in the train station and the tacks he had taken to get Stacy to change her mind.

"You did that for me?" Hank asked in wonderment.

"Of course. I did it for us."

Hank rested against the headboard for a long while, again saying nothing. At last, he said, "I love you."

"And I love you, Hank. I know all of this is fast, but we fit together like puzzle pieces, and I think when the heart knows, it knows."

Hank laughed. "You old softie."

"That's me. But I'm also a tough taskmaster when it comes to *our* business, and we have a dinner to make for tonight."

"I know. I know! But just let me say one more thing to you."

"Okay."

"I came back to this house, this *home*, because I chose to. Even with Addison someplace else, I realized we were starting to make a family here. No, we *are* a family. And I realized that happiness is a choice. I can choose it or let it go."

He grabbed Ollie, pulled him tight into his arms, and whispered feverishly into his ear. "I choose you. I choose happiness. I choose love." He pulled away slightly so he could stare into Ollie's eyes. "You can pine for what you don't have, or you can choose to love what you do."

Ollie nodded and kissed Hank lightly. "I do. I love you."

"Okay, let's go downstairs and start cooking."

Epilogue

STUFFED ARTICHOKES

(This is more of a technique than a recipe. Here's how you make one; simply multiply the directions below by the number of artichokes you have.)

- 1 globe artichoke, with stem trimmed off so it sits level.
- A good handful of finely ground breadcrumbs (store-bought, or better, make them yourself), seasoned with dashes of dried basil, oregano, parsley, and salt and pepper.
- A good handful of grated good-variety Romano or Parmesan cheese
- Olive oil

Pull the toughest outer leaves off your artichoke, then trim the tops of the remaining leaves so they're square and even. Spread the artichoke leaves out with your hand (like opening a flower). They will open just a little bit. Mix together your cheese and bread crumbs and sprinkle the mixture down into the leaves, trying to make sure each leaf gets a little of the mixture. Drizzle a bit of extra-virgin olive oil over the artichoke.

Place in a pan of water where the water comes about 1/4 of the way up the choke. In the water, throw a bay leaf, a couple of cloves of garlic, and a few lemon slices. Cover and steam artichokes for approximately 30-45 minutes. Check to see if you need to add more water occasionally. You'll know they're done when the outer leaves come away easily.

Is THERE anything more wonderful than the smell of a roasting turkey in the oven on Thanksgiving Day? Ollie bustled around the kitchen, taking in its oak pedestal table practically overflowing with the weight of the preparations for their feast. There was way too much food, but wasn't that the point on Thanksgiving? It was the one day out of the year when Americans celebrated their love for food as much as giving thanks. Not to overeat would be, well, un-American.

But Ollie tried to keep himself equally focused on gratitude. It wasn't hard. This year, he had a lot to be thankful for. He paused for a moment, staring down at the foodstuffs laid out before him, wondering where it would be best to start. The bird was already in the oven, after having been brined overnight. He would work on the stuffing first. He was one of those people who thought putting the stuffing in the cavity of the bird was gross. He had a nice ceramic casserole dish—huge—pushed to one side, ready to accept the stuffing after he assembled it on the stovetop.

First, he pulled a loaf of sourdough bread out of its brown paper bag. He had bought it a couple of days ago from a local bakery in Wallingford. The fact that it was a couple of days old would only make for better stuffing. Then he grabbed the handful of fresh sage leaves he had laid out, celery, a large Vidalia onion, his homemade chicken stock, and a bowl of bulk Italian sausage, mild. He made short work of finely chopping the onions, celery, and sage, and then set it aside to put the sausage on in his big All-Clad skillet. While it sizzled in olive oil and butter, he began cubing the bread.

"Oh my God, that smells like heaven."

Ollie turned. Hank stood in the kitchen doorway, clad only in the special boxer shorts Ollie had bought for him on impulse at Target the other day. They were navy flannel with a pattern of bright orange turkeys. They were ridiculous! Hank looked sexy as hell in them.

"Would you go at least put a T-shirt on? You standing there like that is going to ruin my concentration and make me burn something for sure."

"Really? You're telling me to put clothes *on*? Seems like all you have been doing the past few months is trying to get me out of them." Hank laughed.

"Exactly." Ollie turned to the stove, so he wouldn't have to look at Hank. The sight of him half-naked was already making him hard. Three more glances and he would be leading Hank back up the stairs and ripping those preposterous holiday boxers right off him so he could get to the *real* Thanksgiving feast in a hurry. "It's not much of a leap to picture you completely naked, which is what I am trying to avoid. I have a lot of work to do here!" Ollie began breaking up and turning the browning sausage with a wooden spoon.

He could sense Hank moving up behind him. Suddenly, he was in the grip of Hank's wiry arms and could feel the pillar of Hank's erection pressed up against the crack of his ass. "Get away!" Ollie yelled, laughing. He bumped Hank's front hard with his ass and Hank grabbed his hips and mock thrust.

"Oh Jesus Christ, please, Hank. Before this turns into a porno movie."

Hank showed him some mercy, stepping away and planting a quick, very chaste kiss on the nape of Ollie's neck. He whispered in Ollie's ear. "Later. You can be my turkey and I'll be the sausage stuffing."

Ollie snorted. "Lord."

Hank left the room, calling out over his shoulder. "I'll go put something decent on—"

Ollie interrupted him, "Much to my regret!"

"And get back down here to help you out."

"Take your time, I've got it all under control."

"Do you? Smells like the sausage is burning."

"Shit." Hank turned back to see perfectly caramelized sausage in the pan. He shook his head and made a "tsk" sound. "What are you talking about? Nothing's burning."

"Except you. For me."

"Oh, go get dressed."

Ollie watched as Hank continued to the stairs, thinking Hank was what he had to be most grateful for this year. He was thankful Hank had stayed, thankful he had finally quit smoking, thankful he was a partner in a business that had been a pipe dream but was now a big success with half a dozen people on the payroll.

But most of all, he was thankful for the love he and Hank shared. That was what made all the other stuff so wonderful, the supporting foundation that held their lives aloft. Ollie had been in love before, but it had never been like this. He now understood what people meant when they said they had found their soul mate. Once upon a time, Ollie thought the very idea was merely a fanciful concept, the stuff of romance novels.

But now he knew it was real. And the big irony of it was that Hank was not at all the person he would have imagined spending the rest of his life with.

But yet, there he was. And here Ollie was.

And there were still surprises in store. Ollie grinned.

He turned back to his work, emptying the sausage into the casserole dish, being careful not to get too much grease mixed in. He spooned some, but not all, of the rendered fat from the sausage out of the pan, threw in another big pat of butter, let it melt, and then tossed in his onions and celery. He salted the veggies, and gave them a couple of quick tosses.

He turned to begin cubing the loaf of sourdough.

"How can I help?"

Ollie looked up as Rose entered the kitchen. He smiled. Since she had told them the dreadful story of her past, it was like she had released something inside. The darkness that had been there before was filled with golden light—and it showed.

Gone were the baggy clothes for one thing. Along with casting off the horror of her past, she had cast off the shame about her body. This morning, Rose was a knockout in a tight black Rat City Rollergirls T-shirt and a pair of shorts that showed off her long, coltish legs to good advantage. Her auburn hair hung loose around her face. Ollie noticed she had painted her toenails a shocking shade of crimson, something the old Rose would *never* have done.

But it wasn't her hair or her clothes that underscored her beauty; it was her demeanor. In just a few weeks, she had become more confident and less shy. Now there was the air about her of joy, infectious. She couldn't help but radiate it.

Some of it had to do with her setting free her demons at last, but Ollie knew there was more.

Rose had found love too.

"I got it under control."

"You always say that, even when there are a million things to do." Rose sauntered over to the coffee maker and poured herself a mug. "The house could be burning down around you, and you'd say 'I've got it under control.'" She sat down with her coffee at the table and began picking at the cubes of sourdough.

"Hands off! That's for the stuffing," Ollie warned.

Rose tossed a piece of the bread at Ollie. "What's a poor girl to eat?"

Ollie rolled his eyes. "Like there aren't a million things you can choose from, my dear! Look in the fridge; look in the pantry! Must you eat the bread for the stuffing?"

Rose sipped her coffee.

Ollie looked over at her. "Really, have some toast. There's that peach jam I made still in there."

"Don't worry about me. I won't go hungry."

"I'll make sure of that." Ollie turned at the sound of the other voice, sultry. Standing in the kitchen archway was Sophie Lombardozzi. The young woman was clad only in a pair of very brief pink pajamas Ollie remembered his mother calling "baby dolls." Every time Ollie saw Sophie, he was taken aback by her beauty. She had long black hair, eyes so dark the pupils disappeared within the irises, olive skin, and the kind of lips that the term "cupid's bow" had been invented for. And she was all Rose's. The two had met at Haven on one of the Thursday afternoon lunches Dinner at Home donated each week to the facility. That had been Hank's idea too—it was a wonderful way to give back.

"Sophie! Good morning. I didn't know you were here."

"Get used to it, handsome." Sophie crossed the kitchen and poured herself a coffee. Unlike Rose, she did not take hers black; she added a healthy dollop of cream and three heaping teaspoons of sugar.

She sat down at the table with Rose and gave her a long, lingering kiss. "*Sei bella,*" she whispered.

Ollie rolled his eyes, mumbling to himself, "I should have let Hank stay down here. We could have a big old gay orgy in the kitchen." He poured the bread cubes in with the simmering, fragrant vegetables and stirred them to make sure they were coated with the butter and rendered fat. He did a few twists of the pepper mill above the mixture.

"What was that, Ollie?" Rose asked from the table, once she could pull her lips away from Sophie's hungry mouth.

"Nothing. Why don't you girls take your coffee back to bed? After I get the stuffing in the oven, I'll call you. We can have a proper breakfast."

Ollie added a few ladles of hot chicken stock to the stuffing mixture, then poured it all in the casserole dish to combine with the sausage. He sprinkled the chopped sage in, added more salt and pepper, dashes of dried thyme, rosemary, and garlic powder, then stirred everything together, moistening it with another big ladle of stock. "Perfect."

The girls giggled. Sophie was behind Rose and she pushed her out of the kitchen. Ollie thought he heard one of them say something about "sausage in the oven" that sent them off on even more gales of laughter.

OLLIE WAS proud of the table he had set. He had grown up in a household where holiday meals were something his mother worked on for days beforehand. So he knew what constituted a good family meal.

This *is a good family meal,* he thought as he lighted the taper candles in their sterling silver holders. The table practically groaned from the weight of the food. Hank had wanted to help with setting the table and putting out the serving dishes, but Ollie had shooed him away, saying, "This year, this year only, I want to do it. For my family. Please let me."

Hank had reluctantly joined Rose, Sophie, and their other guests in the living room and told him, "Okay, but Christmas is my turn."

"Christmas is your turn. As long as you let me make the *pizzelles* and *giugiuleni,*" Ollie said, referring to his favorite boyhood Italian cookies. He had jumped the gun and already made platters of the cookies for dessert tonight. They waited on the already crowded kitchen counter, along with the pumpkin soufflé Rose had made and a bottle of *vin santo.*

Now laughter bubbled out from the living room, along with the chatter of excited voices. Ollie paused to listen. There was music playing too: Duke Ellington's "Take the A Train," part of one of Ollie's jazz playlists. But the real music lay in the happy voices of the people he loved, talking over one another, bursting out in laughter.

Ollie was glad he'd given himself this moment alone to simply listen… and savor. *Speaking of savoring, Mr. Sentimental, you need to finish getting dinner on the table!* Ollie turned back to retrieve the last plate, a platter of stuffed artichokes just like his mother used to make, and set it among the other dishes on the Venetian lace tablecloth that also reminded him of home back in Illinois.

He stood back and admired. The turkey had a gorgeous sheen, thanks to his brushing it with a mixture of orange juice and honey just before taking it out of the oven. He had adorned the turkey platter with fresh cranberries and a mixture of sprigs of fresh rosemary and flat-leaf parsley. The mashed potatoes were fluffy, with a huge dollop of butter melting in the middle; the gravy boats were full; there were caramelized brussels sprouts with pancetta and lemon, a kale, apple, and red onion salad, fresh-baked popovers, and, of course, the steamed artichokes, stuffed with breadcrumbs, herbs, and grated *Parmigiano-Reggiano*. When he was growing up, the thistles had been a holiday staple at every Thanksgiving and Christmas.

"You guys. Supper!" he called out.

The voices came to an abrupt halt. Ollie waited, standing near the kitchen doorway, to watch them come in. He wanted to witness their faces as they took in the feast laid out before them. And, again, he simply wanted the time to savor each of these people who had come into his life and who had enriched it beyond his wildest imaginings.

Hank came in first. He had let the Mohawk grow out and now his hair was one even, buzzed length, a rich auburn color. The new cut showed off the sharp planes of his face and his large eyes even better. He winked at Ollie, and Ollie could see the happiness on his face. He was practically glowing. Hank had been through so much this past year, and it touched Ollie's heart to know how he had contributed to turning Hank's life around. Yet he knew Hank could not have done it without his own internal reserves of strength and smarts. Hank wasn't much of one for dressing up, but Ollie was glad to see he had tried. His jeans were clean, dark, the cuffs rolled, and above them was a crisp white Oxford-cloth button-down shirt.

He looked gorgeous. And, as much as Ollie couldn't wait for everyone to enjoy the feast he had prepared, he couldn't wait to be alone with Hank.

Hank pulled out chairs from the table. Rose and Sophie came in next, each in velvet dresses, Rose's a deep, emerald green and Sophie's a fiery red. "I wonder how we can work these calories off," Sophie blurted, giving Rose a significant glance and a raise of her eyebrows.

Rose cocked her head and shook her finger at Sophie. "Watch your mouth. We have a child here."

And Ollie's breath caught as Addison entered the dining room, followed by Stacy. The pair had come into town the night before as a surprise for Hank. Ollie had bought airline tickets for them about a week after they had left the summer before, and it had taken all of his will not to blurt out the news that they would be here in Seattle for the long holiday weekend.

Addison wore brown corduroy pants, a harvest gold blouse, and a little vest with autumn leaf appliques. She looked adorable, even though Stacy had confided she had bought Addison a ruffled pink dress to wear for the occasion. But Addison had folded her arms across her chest, saying, "I ain't havin' nothin' to do with that. You like it? You wear it."

Addison and Ollie's eyes met, and he smiled. For once, the little girl was quiet, but her bright eyes were eloquent as she took in the food and the image of Ollie, standing near the table, waiting. They seemed to be saying "thank you."

"I can't resist." Ollie crossed the room and gathered Addison up in his arms. He hugged her tight and gave her a peck on the cheek. "We have missed you so much, little girl!"

The adults laughed, but Addison only wriggled. "Put me down, damn it! I'm hungry!"

Ollie set her down in the chair fitted out with a booster, clucking his tongue and moaning about how some things never changed.

"Thank God for that," Hank said, stepping up next to Ollie. He turned Ollie's head toward his and gave him a kiss.

"Are we gonna eat or stand around all day kissing?" Addison asked.

"We're going to eat," Hank said.

They all sat down. Ollie said, "I know it's corny, but before we get started, can we go around the table and say what we're thankful for?"

Addison rolled her eyes. "Everything's gonna be cold by the time we get through all this."

Stacy said, "Hush, honey. This is nice. Why don't you go first?"

Addison joined hands with Stacy at her right and Hank at her left and closed her eyes. "Jesus, I'm just glad you could get me and my mom back here for Thanksgiving with the boys." She opened her eyes and grinned at Rose and Sophie across the table, then closed them again. "And the girls.

Thank you for letting us all be together today. Thank you for this great food! It looks so good, except for the green stuff. Amen!"

Hank said, "Thanks, God, for putting Ollie into my life and showing me how the two most important things in life are food and love."

The others went around the table, all giving thanks, really, for the same things—each other and the feast set out before them, steaming and intoxicating them all with the rich blend of aromas rising up.

Ollie had a whole speech prepared, but Addison's very common sense alert that the food was getting cold caused him to cut it short.

They dug in. For a while, Ollie was thrilled that the only sound in the dining room was the clink of flatware on china and appreciative noises about the repast.

They had saved the artichokes for last. Ollie explained that was how they had always done it at the holiday meals he had experienced growing up. "I think it's because it's a food you can just pick at while you talk and let the rest of the meal settle." He plucked a few leaves from one of the artichokes and moved to lean over Addison. He set the leaves on her empty plate and couldn't help but notice how suspiciously she eyed them.

Ollie squatted down beside her. "Let me show you how you eat these."

"I need a lesson too," Rose said.

Stacy and Hank said the same thing.

Ollie smiled. "Okay, what you do is you sort of flip the leaf upside down, then you scrape the filling and the pulp off with your lower teeth. Like this...." And he picked up one of the leaves and acted out what he had just described. "Mmmm." He handed a leaf to Addison. "You try."

"You're crazy if you think I'm putting that in my mouth!"

Stacy said, "Come on, honey, Ollie made these just for us. We can at least have the courtesy to try them."

Ollie eyed her gratefully, but could see she wasn't so sure about the artichokes herself. He went back to his seat.

"Y'all do what you want, but I am having an artichoke." With his bare hands, he lifted one off the platter and set it on his plate. He made short work of several outer leaves. "Delicious! Really. When I was a kid, my mom used to scold me because I would just eat the stuffing. Addison, the stuffing is just bread and herbs and lots and lots of cheese."

"Cheese?" Addison cautiously picked one up and put it in her mouth. "Not bad," she pronounced.

The others followed suit. Ollie was glad to see their trepidation about the artichokes quickly turned to bliss as they got the hang of skimming the savory pulp from the leaves. The rich stuffing didn't dampen their enthusiasm either. Sophie was the only one who didn't hesitate, which wasn't surprising because she was a fellow Italian, a *paesana*.

"You know," Ollie said as his artichoke grew smaller and smaller on his plate while the pile of discarded leaves grew progressively larger, "the leaves get more and more tender the farther down you go. By the time you get near the heart, you almost can chew the leaves whole." He lifted his to show the others. He peeled away the last of the leaves, and then pulled off the purplish green top of very tender leaves. He lifted what was left—an avocado green lump. "Ta-da! The heart. It takes some work to get here, you have to get through all those tough, thorny outer layers, but trust me, this is the best part. The sweetest and most tender. It's worth all the trouble you take to get to it." His gaze met Hank's across the table and they smiled.

"You guys are so corny," Addison whispered.

EVERYONE WAS asleep, save for Ollie and Hank. They too were tired, with full bellies and other appetites sated in their damnably creaking bed. But it had become their habit, back when Hank still smoked, to crawl out onto the roof covering their porch outside their bedroom window to admire the night.

Now they sat next to one another, Hank in sweats and an old T-shirt and Ollie in flannel pajamas, a quilt wrapped around the both of them to ward off the damp chill hanging in the November air. Ollie's grandmother, his *nona*, had made the quilt long ago, fashioning it from old dresses she had worn as a girl in Sicily. The quilt was faded, ragged, and a tumble through a modern-day washing machine would probably obliterate it, but Ollie treasured it for its humble warmth and the memories stored in its soft, soft cloth.

Below them, a mist, seemingly almost possessing a life of its own, shape-shifted on the ground, coiling and uncoiling into various phantasmagorical shapes. Hank swore that, at one point, the fog had taken on the form of Sophie Lombardozzi, a voluptuous reclining nude. Ollie responded that Rose would approve and wished that he had a camera to capture the image for her.

They cuddled, each relying on the other for warmth. Ollie ran his hand over Hank's head, reveling in how it felt beneath his fingers and the very idea that it was all his to savor. Hank kissed Ollie, rubbing his smooth face into Ollie's bearded one.

They laughed.

Above them, the sky was clear, a deep midnight blue. For once, the ambient light of downtown Seattle did not compete with the stars, and the twinkling sky jewels stood out in resplendent contrast to the darkness.

Ollie stared at the stars, not thinking, just taking in their distant beauty, glad all of them were gathered under their diamond-like beauty. He wondered if Hank was thinking the same thing. Ollie could make out the shape of the Big Dipper and outlined it with his finger for Hank.

"I'm getting sleepy," Hank said into Ollie's shoulder. "I wanna get under that down comforter, feel those flannel sheets." He kissed Ollie's neck and whispered in his ear, "But most of all, I want to get wrapped up in my big, furry man blanket."

Ollie kissed the top of Hank's head. "Just a couple more minutes? It's so beautiful tonight. And so quiet, for a change." And the neighborhood was, for once, silent. Tonight, no one was out marauding in a car with a bad muffler; there were no sirens in the distance; no loud conversations as people, in clusters, passed their house.

"Okay."

"Things went well today, didn't they?"

"Yeah. I can't thank you enough for the surprise. Having Addison here made this a day I'll never forget." Hank thought for a moment, then said, "Stacy too."

"All of us. All of us." Ollie looked quickly at Hank, then back at the stars. "You told me once that you realized we should love the things we have. And I do, baby, oh so much. You know what? If some genie flew up to this roof right now and offered me a wish or three, I wouldn't know what to say, because right now, I feel like I have everything I ever wanted."

Hank kissed the side of Ollie's mouth. "That's sweet."

"I mean it. Just a few months ago, I thought my life was ruined. I lost my boyfriend and my job. Some lowlife tried to rob me." Ollie chuckled. "And look! Now I have work that means something to me, that I can take pride in because I feed people. And I have a family, not your typical unit, but a family that's mine and that I treasure with all my heart."

"Me too, sweet man, me too."

"I'm so glad you're like me, Hank."

"What do you mean?"

"That you like to cook. That you like to feed people. You nourish them and at the same time, nourish your own soul. I think that, more than anything else, is what really drew us together."

"You mean more than my big dick?" Hank snickered.

"Well, there's that. But I'm serious. We're both about feeding people and showing love through what we put on the table. Feeding them is loving them, and I don't think there's a better or more basic way of letting someone know you love them than by giving them something wonderful to eat and filling up their bellies."

"You've had too much wine," Hank said. "But you are a dream come true for me, man. And I am right there with you—I have everything I could dream of. Right here. Right now."

Ollie reached into the pocket of his pajamas, where he had managed to stuff a small velvet bag. He pulled it out so Hank could see.

"What the hell's that? A Crown Royal mini? Haven't we had enough tonight?"

Ollie tugged on the bag's drawstring and brought out one of the sesame seed cookies he had made for dessert, one of the *giugiuleni*. He turned it in front of Hank like it was some kind of wonderful prize, chuckling.

"Oh God, Ollie, I'm so stuffed. I couldn't."

"Just a little bite, for me. I made this one special." He nudged the cookie toward Hank's mouth. "Please."

"No, man, I'm stuffed. Come on, it's getting cold out here. Let's get in bed and snuggle. I'll give you a taste of my *giugiuleni*." Hank wiggled his eyebrows.

"Just one bite."

"Oh for Christ's sake." Hank snatched the cookie from him. "Just to get you to shut up...."

"Careful," Ollie warned as Hank bit down on the sesame-seed cookie.

"Ow! What the fuck?" Hank pulled the cookie away from his mouth. "I could have chipped a tooth, or choked. What the fuck is this?" Hank held the ring up to the sky, where it became a silhouette in the starlight. He gasped when he saw what it was.

"It's a ring, sweetie. A simple platinum band. I hope it'll be a wedding band one day, but for now, you can consider it an engagement ring. That is, if you'll have me."

Hank turned to Ollie. Hank's mouth was open. Ollie felt a momentary flash of panic. "You want to, don't you?"

Hank grabbed him and pulled him close. "Of course I do. Of course. Yes, yes, yes."

They kissed and Ollie slipped the ring onto Hank's finger. They sat for a long time, contented, staring out at the stars.

Finally, Ollie said, "I was thinking we could serve Italian food at our reception, start off with my mom's wedding soup, with escarole and egg and little, tiny meatballs."

"Do the two of you never stop thinking about food?"

Hank and Ollie turned as one to see Addison backlit by the hall light, standing at the window, hands on her hips.

"Get in here and come to bed before I come out there and slap you both silly." Addison turned and walked away.

"She's right."

Ollie grabbed Hank's hand, pulling him up to head inside to bed, to *home*.

Glossary of Recipes

SINFULLY SOFT SCRAMBLED EGGS

(Serves 2)
- 1 tablespoon of olive oil and 1 tablespoon of butter
- 6 eggs
- Splash of half-and-half or, if you're feeling really decadent, cream
- 4 scallions, sliced thin, very top of the green reserved for garnish
- 1/2 to 3/4 cup shredded Beecher's Flagship or other mild, flavorful cheese
- 1/4 pound pancetta, cubed

Melt butter with olive oil in a skillet over medium heat. Whisk eggs and half-and-half together. When the butter's froth just begins to dissipate, add the pancetta and cook until lightly browned. Pour off some of the fat, return pan to stove and lower heat. Add scallions and sauté until just fragrant. Add beaten eggs and give a quick stir to distribute scallions. Add about half of the shredded cheese. Now, let the eggs cook on low heat. It may seem like nothing is happening, but after ten minutes or so, gently push the eggs with a spoon. Soft curds should begin to form. This is what you want—gentle curds. Continue to gently push the eggs, forming more and more curds. When the eggs are still a bit wet, but mostly curds, add the rest of the cheese, turn off the heat, and cover. Let sit for 2-3 minutes. Serve.

Comfortably Curried Carrots and Lentils

(Serves 4)

- 2 cups green lentils
- 2 carrots, peeled and diced
- 3-1/2 cups chicken stock
- 2 tablespoons grated ginger
- 1 small red onion, chopped
- 2 tablespoons curry powder
- 3 tablespoons tomato paste
- 1 cup coconut milk
- 1 teaspoon salt
- 1 teaspoon cumin
- 1/2 teaspoon coriander
- 1/2 teaspoon cinnamon
- 2 cups baby spinach
- Garnishes: Greek yogurt, chopped parsley, sliced jalapeños

Use a 4-quart slow cooker. Rinse lentils and pick through for any stones. Combine all ingredients, except for baby spinach, and set cooker to low for six hours or until lentils are tender. Add baby spinach at the very end, replace cover, and let wilt. Serve with optional garnishes. Can also serve over rice or couscous.

Mom's Spaghetti Sauce and Meatballs

(Serves 4-6)

- 1 29 ounce can tomato puree
- 1 12 ounce can tomato paste
- 1-1/2 teaspoons salt
- 1-1/2 teaspoons pepper
- 1-1/2 teaspoons sugar

- Pinch of baking soda
- 1-1/2 teaspoons garlic powder
- 1 teaspoon each oregano, basil, and onion powder
- 2 handfuls grated Romano or Parmesan cheese (approx. half a cup)
- 7 cups water or 1-2 cups red wine with the remainder water (I usually use the wine)

Note: Most all of the above ingredients can just be eyeballed. Mix everything in a big pot, add meatballs and pork and simmer for at least four hours. Highly recommended: brown some pork (ribs, chops, whatever's cheap), a little less than a pound, in the pan you're going to cook the sauce in. Just caramelize it. Once it's done, pull out, deglaze with a splash of red wine, and begin making your sauce.

Meatballs
- 1 pound ground beef (or beef and pork, or turkey)
- 1 egg
- 1 slice bread
- 1/4 cup milk
- Salt, pepper, garlic powder, parsley, onion powder, basil, oregano (just eyeball all of this)

Take a slice of bread, wet with milk, crumble into meat, and add seasonings and egg. Mix with hands, form into balls, brown in hot fry pan on stove in a little olive oil, and drop into the sauce.

LUSCIOUS TURKEY MEAT LOAF

(Serves 4-6)
- 1/2 pound button mushrooms, finely chopped
- 1 cup finely chopped onion
- 1 cup chopped bell pepper (a mix of red and green is nice)
- 2 cloves garlic, minced
- 1 tablespoon olive oil

- 1 teaspoon kosher salt
- 1/2 teaspoon ground black pepper
- 1 tablespoon Worcestershire sauce
- 7 tablespoons ketchup, divided
- 1 tablespoon brown sugar
- 1 teaspoon apple cider vinegar
- 1 cup panko bread crumbs
- 1/3 cup milk
- 2 large eggs, lightly beaten
- 1 1/4 pound ground turkey

Heat oven to 400° F.

Line a baking sheet with aluminum foil then lightly oil the bottom. Chop vegetables (mushrooms and onion should be very finely chopped, garlic minced, and the peppers diced).

Heat onions and peppers in oil over medium heat until soft 3-4 minutes, add garlic and cook for one more minute.

Add chopped mushrooms with a 1/2 teaspoon of salt and a 1/4 teaspoon of pepper. Cook, stirring occasionally 8-10 minutes.

Dump cooked vegetables into a large bowl, add 3 tablespoons ketchup and 1 tablespoon of Worcestershire sauce. Cool for a few minutes.

While those are cooling, stir the breadcrumbs and milk together and let stand for a few minutes.

Add breadcrumbs and beaten eggs to onions and mushrooms, then mix well. Next, add turkey along with remaining 1/2 teaspoon of salt and 1/4 teaspoon of pepper. Mix well with clean hands. (It will be wet!).

Shape mixture into a loaf in the middle of prepared baking sheet.

Then combine remaining ketchup with brown sugar and apple cider vinegar. With the back of a spoon or a spatula, spread on top of meat loaf. Bake for 50 minutes or until an instant read thermometer reads 170° when inserted into the thickest part of the loaf.

Satisfying Banana Ginger Caramel Pudding

(Serves 8-10 or one very hungry little girl)

- 3/4 cup sugar
- 2 tablespoons cornstarch
- 3 cups milk
- 4 egg yolks
- 1 teaspoon vanilla extract
- 1/2 stick butter
- 3 medium ripe bananas, sliced
- 1 small box Ginger Snaps (you'll need about 12-16)
- 2 tablespoons caramel topping of your choice

Mix together sugar and cornstarch and add milk. Cook in the top of a double boiler or over low heat, stirring constantly until it thickens—don't leave it alone! Beat egg yolks and temper with a little of the hot custard; stir. Add egg mixture to custard pot and cook 2 more minutes. Take off heat and add vanilla and butter. Let cool. In a 9x9 inch ovenproof baking dish, alternate pudding, bananas, and ginger snaps, beginning with pudding and ending with pudding. Drizzle caramel over the top.

Slow-Cooker Posole

(Serves 4)
- 2 cloves garlic, minced
- 1 medium onion, chopped
- 1 poblano pepper, diced
- 2 stalks celery, sliced
- 4 tomatillos, peeled and quartered
- 1 pound boneless, skinless organic chicken thighs
- 2 cups chicken stock
- 14-1/2 ounce can hominy (I prefer gold, but white is fine too)

- 14-1/2 ounce can diced fire-roasted tomatoes (with chiles or other Mexican seasoning)
- 4 ounce can sliced jalapeños, with juice
- 2 tablespoons ground cumin
- 1 tablespoon dried oregano
- 1 teaspoon red pepper flakes or more to taste
- Salt and pepper to taste

Sauté garlic, onion, pepper, celery in pan for 5 minutes, add tomatillos and sauté for two more minutes.

Combine the above with remaining ingredients in the slow cooker and cook on low for 7-8 hours (or high 4 hours).

At end of cooking time, pull out thighs and shred with two forks, return to pot. Test seasonings, adding more salt and/or pepper if necessary. Garnish with chopped cilantro, sliced radishes, cubed avocado, and lime juice.

BAD ASS BROCCOLI SOUP

(Serves 4)
- 1 tablespoon butter
- 1 tablespoon olive oil
- 1 medium onion, diced
- 4 cloves garlic, minced
- 1 medium baking potato, peeled and diced
- 4 cups chopped broccoli
- 32 ounces chicken or vegetable stock
- 1/2 pint heavy cream
- Salt and pepper to taste
- Optional: Crushed red pepper flakes, shredded cheese (a cup or so)

Heat oil and butter until hot, add onions and garlic and sauté until soft, about five minutes. Add potato, stir to coat with butter/oil. Add broccoli and stock, bring to a boil and simmer for half an hour.

Puree in blender or food processor (or use an immersion blender if you have one), return to pan, stir in cream. Heat to just below boiling (do not boil).

STUFFED ARTICHOKES

(This is more of a technique than a recipe. Here's how you make one; simply multiply the directions below by the number of artichokes you have.)

- 1 globe artichoke, with stem trimmed off so it sits level.
- A good handful of finely ground breadcrumbs (store-bought, or better, make them yourself), seasoned with dashes of dried basil, oregano, parsley, and salt and pepper.
- A good handful of grated good-variety Romano or Parmesan cheese
- Olive oil

Pull the toughest outer leaves off your artichoke, then trim the tops of the remaining leaves so they're square and even. Spread the artichoke leaves out with your hand (like opening a flower). They will open just a little bit. Mix together your cheese and bread crumbs and sprinkle the mixture down into the leaves, trying to make sure each leaf gets a little of the mixture. Drizzle a bit of extra-virgin olive oil over the artichoke.

Place in a pan of water where the water comes about 1/4 of the way up the choke. In the water, throw a bay leaf, a couple of cloves of garlic, and a few lemon slices. Cover and steam artichokes for approximately 30-45 minutes. Check to see if you need to add more water occasionally. You'll know they're done when the outer leaves come away easily.

RICK R. REED is all about exploring the romantic entanglements of gay men in contemporary, realistic settings. While his stories often contain elements of suspense, mystery, and the paranormal, his focus ultimately returns to the power of love. He is the author of dozens of published novels, novellas, and short stories. He is a three-time EPIC eBook Award winner (for *Caregiver*, *Orientation*, and *The Blue Moon Cafe*). Lambda Literary Review has called him, "a writer that doesn't disappoint." In his spare time, Rick is an avid runner, loves to cook, and reads voraciously. Rick lives in Seattle with his husband and a very spoiled Boston terrier. He is forever "at work on another novel."

Visit Rick's website at http://www.rickrreed.com or follow his blog at http://rickrreedreality.blogspot.com/. You can also like Rick on Facebook at https://www.facebook.com/rickrreedbooks or on Twitter at https://www.twitter.com/rickrreed. Rick always enjoys hearing from readers and answers all e-mails personally. Send him a message at jimmyfels@gmail.com.

Photo copyright 2013 Madison Parker.

Also from RICK R. REED

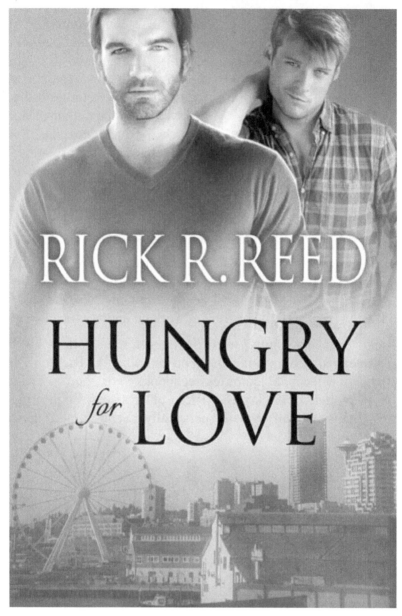

RICK R. REED

HUNGRY
for LOVE

http://www.dreamspinnerpress.com

Also from RICK R. REED

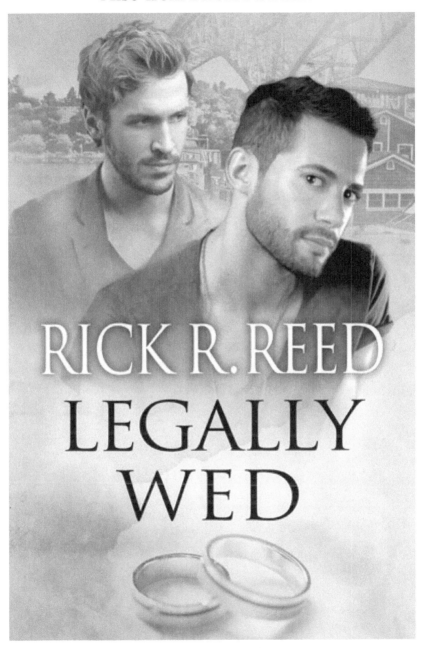

http://www.dreamspinnerpress.com

Also from RICK R. REED

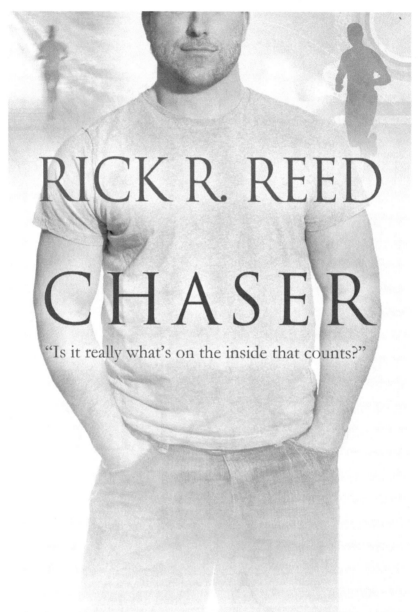

RICK R. REED

CHASER

"Is it really what's on the inside that counts?"

http://www.dreamspinnerpress.com

Also from RICK R. REED

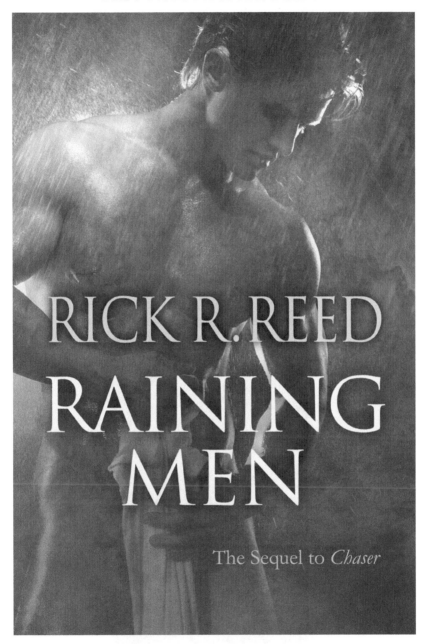

http://www.dreamspinnerpress.com

Also from RICK R. REED

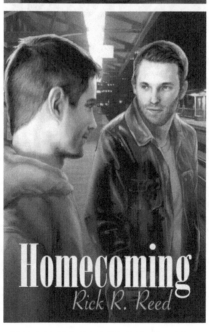

http://www.dreamspinnerpress.com

Also from RICK R. REED

http://www.dreamspinnerpress.com

For more of the
best M/M romance,
visit

Dreamspinner Press

www.dreamspinnerpress.com

CPSIA information can be obtained at www.ICGtesting.com
Printed in the USA
LVOW01s0705040514

384313LV00003B/68/P

9 781627 988353